UNFINISHED BUSINESS

A MUNCH MANCINI CRIME NOVEL

BARBARA SERANELLA

POCKET STAR BOOKS

New York   London   Toronto   Sydney   Singapore

This book is a work of fiction. Names, characters, places and incidents are products of the author's imagination or are used fictitiously. Any resemblance to actual events or locales or persons, living or dead, is entirely coincidental.

 A Pocket Star Book published by
POCKET BOOKS, a division of Simon & Schuster, Inc.
1230 Avenue of the Americas, New York, NY 10020

Copyright © 2001 by Barbara Seranella

Originally published in hardcover in 2001 by Scribner

All rights reserved, including the right to reproduce this book or portions thereof in any form whatsoever. For information address Scribner, 1230 Avenue of the Americas, New York, NY 10020

ISBN: 0-7434-2209-0

First Pocket Books printing April 2002

10 9 8 7 6 5 4 3 2 1

POCKET STAR BOOKS and colophon are registered trademarks of Simon & Schuster, Inc.

For information regarding special discounts for bulk purchases, please contact Simon & Schuster Special Sales at 1-800-456-6798 or business@simonandschuster.com

Printed in the U.S.A.

Books by Barbara Seranella

No Human Involved
No Offense Intended
Unwanted Company
Unfinished Business

For Ron, of course

Stockholm syndrome *n.* The tendency of a hostage, under certain circumstances, to try to cooperate and occasionally even to aid his captors. [Referring to the cooperative behavior of hostages held in a bank robbery in Stockholm (1973).]

—*Reader's Digest*
Illustrated Encyclopedic Dictionary

CHAPTER 1

FRIDAY

Munch scooted down in the front seat of the big, silver limousine and fought back a yawn. She was tempted to climb in the back and see if there was anything good on TV. Three things stopped her: one was the obvious oxymoron—good TV; the second was that she didn't want to run the car's battery down; and last, knowing her luck, as soon as she got settled in the passenger cabin, someone would come out of the big house in need of her services. It wouldn't look very professional if she were stretched out on the blue velour–covered bench seat watching Tom Selleck cruise the mean streets of Hawaii in his borrowed Ferrari.

The limo was parked near the four-car garage on one end of a large circular driveway in Pacific Palisades. Rolls-Royces, Mercedes, Lincolns, and

Cadillacs lined the curbs. There was also an assortment of economically correct smaller vehicles. Ever since the last so-called gas crisis a few years back in '81, the market had been flooded with four-cylinder vehicles—many of them coming out of Detroit, though the Japanese still had it all over America's big three when it came to making a smooth-running smaller engine. The four-bangers made in America—the Vegas, the Pintos, even Lee Iacocca's K-cars—all had rocky idles and usually stalled when their owners put on their air-conditioning. All Munch's cars had V-8's under the hood. She'd take power above fuel efficiency any day of the week.

She sat up and stretched, then pulled down the visor and flipped open the center panel. In the reflection of the soft amber vanity mirror light, her hair looked more brown than blond. She brushed it back, wiped away a smudge of mascara with her gloved hand, and yawned until her eyes watered.

Tonight's gig was an expression of gratitude from Diane Bergman and the board of the Bergman Cancer Center. Munch had donated three hours of limo time to the nonprofit organization, to be auctioned off at next month's fund-raiser; but for tonight's black-tie gala, she was being paid full wage. She got there early enough to watch the caterers carry the food up the walkway of the split-level home, past the discreet blue-and-white placards proclaiming: REAGAN.

Diane had taken her for a quick tour, explaining that the house belonged to a Beverly Hills plastic surgeon who had been kind enough to loan it out for the evening. The house, she was told, was a Norman Foster design. Munch acted suitably impressed, not recognizing the name, but picking up the reverence in the hostess's tone. Munch had spent the greater part of the seventies, her teenage years, riding with outlaw motorcycle gangs. Knowledge of contemporary architects had not been a prerequisite for sitting on the back of a Harley and looking cool. The house was awesome though, the way it seemed to spring out of the rocky bluffs. Wide balconies skirted the home's ocean-facing side. Forty-foot floor-to-ceiling windows showed off an uninterrupted view of Catalina Island, the deep blue Pacific Ocean, and when weather and smog permitted, spectacular sunsets.

For tonight's two-hundred-and-fifty-dollar-a-plate dinner, the fund-raising committee had also hired security in the form of three big-gutted guys in cheap black suits who stood out like crows in a float of swans. Munch had pegged them for off-duty cops.

Now, the sounds of the band filtered through the limo's closed windows as Munch's boss for the evening, Diane Bergman, emerged from the house.

A man behind Diane, his face obscured by shadows, put a hand on her elbow, but she wrenched away with more force than necessary, almost losing her balance. A folded section of newspaper fluttered to the ground. Was Diane drunk or just angry? Munch couldn't tell, but something alerted her to pay close attention. The man towered over Diane, who backed away from him, a hand half-raised to her face in defense.

Munch opened the car door and yelled out, "Everything all right?"

Though she was very strong for a woman who stood a little over five feet tall and weighed in at one hundred and five pounds, she was still a "munchkin" and would hardly be anyone's first choice as bodyguard. She looked around for one of the security guys, but, of course, they weren't anywhere in sight now that they were needed.

The man bothering Diane waved a dismissive hand at Munch. It was the sort of signal you might use with a dog when you wanted it to stay.

Munch knew the best way to deal with an opponent who outweighed her was to gang up on him, preferably by ambush. Like that time years ago with Terrible Tom. Second choice, when the element of surprise was unavailable, was to employ an equalizer. She reached behind the seat and grabbed a long-handled black flashlight. The cops called them "five from the sky," and she aimed to show this bully why. The adrenaline rushed through her veins in anticipation as somewhere in the back of her mind the theme music to *Mighty Mouse* played.

Diane regained her balance and stood straight. She half-turned to Munch. "Really, it's all right."

Munch hesitated. The head of the flashlight rested on her shoulder. Both hands gripped the handle. "You're sure?"

The man turned toward Munch. His face was obscured by shadows, but his body language had the feel of one big sneer. Munch lifted her makeshift club so that there would be no doubt of her intentions. The guy made a derisive snort, but he turned around and went back into the house. Diane walked over to the limo.

"What's his problem?" Munch asked, suddenly feeling embarrassed about the quasi-weapon she held. This was Pacific Palisades, after all. When people here got angry, they dueled with checkbooks, not clubs.

"It's a long story."

Munch nodded. She knew the shorthand for "none of your business." She had enough "long stories" of her own, some of which would take years to tell, depending on statute of limitations laws. Besides, she was there to provide a service, not to pry where she wasn't wanted.

"Do you have a cigarette?" Diane asked. Trembling hands picked at the gold cuffs of her maroon jacket. She was a well-preserved fifty, with only the first hint of a double chin. Even now, her hair and nails were salon-perfect.

Munch wondered how much time it took to achieve those kinds of cosmetic results. "Won't they shoot you if you smoke?" she asked.

Diane laughed. "They might at that."

The evening's event was a cancer research fundraiser, the proceeds to go directly to the new Bergman Cancer Center. Diane was not only the event coordinator and president of the board, but a recent nicotine widow. Sam Bergman had smoked three packs a day before his death from cancer last spring. Munch knew both Bergmans from the Texaco station where she worked as a mechanic on their cars.

"I might have a pack in the trunk," she told Diane now, slipping the flashlight back behind the seat and pushing the yellow button inside the glove box to open the trunk.

Diane followed her to the back of the big car and waited while Munch searched through her boxes of supplies for an open pack of Marlboros. "I can't testify to their freshness."

Diane inhaled while Munch held a lit match to the cigarette's end. Diane didn't speak again until she'd taken a long drag.

"Thanks. I hope you're not bored out here. God, you must be exhausted." She twisted one of the solitaire diamonds weighting down her earlobe. Munch was glad to see that her shaking had ceased.

"Nah, I'm all right," Munch assured her.

"But you worked all day at the station and now this."

"I'll sit in any driveway you want for forty-six bucks an hour." The truth was, this was one of her sweetest gigs in a while: waiting for someone to get drunk enough to need a ride home. And being paid full rate to wait. It was as good as any wedding charter. Ten times better than a high school prom.

Diane took another hit on her cigarette and looked at the house. "How old are you?"

Munch had to think a minute. "Twenty-eight."

"And your daughter?"

Munch didn't hesitate. She knew every detail, and cherished every moment of her adopted daughter's life. Asia had been six months old when Munch met her. She was the orphaned daughter of an old lover, and destined perhaps for a much different life if Munch hadn't taken her as her own and given her the best home she could. Fortunately the child welfare services had agreed when Munch finally got around to telling them earlier this year.

"Asia is seven and very proud, the little pumpkin head. She lost her second front tooth yesterday."

"What's she doing tonight?"

"She had a sleepover, so this job worked out great."

"And how does your boyfriend feel about giving you up on a Friday night?"

Munch grinned with a lasciviousness she didn't really feel. "I'll make it up to him." Then, remembering Diane's still recent widowhood, she felt like a jerk.

But Diane only smiled. "What's his name?"

"Garret. Garret Dimond."

"How did you meet?"

"At a class I took at Santa Monica College this summer. He works at a Chevy dealership downtown." Garret also didn't drink or smoke, and was crazy about her. Tall, dark, and predictable. Garret was the kind of guy who, when he went out for a quart of milk, always came back. A healthy, well-adjusted woman would appreciate that kind of thing, she often reminded herself.

On top of that, he worked. Five points for that. Derek, her previous boyfriend, had been a dud work-wise, and she wasn't going to make that mistake again. She already had one kid. Seven-year-old children have a right to be dependent. Thirty-seven-year-old men should stand firmly on their own two feet.

"And it's going well?" Diane asked.

"Actually, we've gotten to the third stage."

"What's that?"

"You know. First comes excitement. That's when everything is new. Then you get to know each other, and you're both trying real hard to be your most likable. That's two."

"But that only lasts so long."

"Exactly. Then you have stage three when you wonder if the guy's worth the effort."

"What's stage four?" Diane asked.

"I don't know. I've never made it that far yet."

Diane patted her arm in a sisterly gesture. "Are you hungry? Would you like some shrimp?"

"No thanks."

"Is there anything I can get you?"

Munch looked at the line of luxury vehicles, maybe thirty in all, and thought of all the potential clients they represented. "How about a copy of the guest list?"

Diane laughed good-naturedly, stubbed out her cigarette, and accepted a breath mint. "I'll see what I can do," she said, disappearing back into the house.

Munch leaned against the car, thinking back to the night justice had been dealt to Terrible Tom in the parking lot of the Venture Inn. It was years ago, when she was still drinking and hanging with a loose-knit group of bikers who jokingly referred to themselves as the "Road Buzzards." They'd spend most evenings cruising the local Venice Beach bars, drinking and carousing, or as she and her friends put it: "causing fun."

Terrible Tom had ridden with the gang occasionally, but he was never completely accepted as one of them. His Harley was too stock; his long black hair and beard always looked too neatly trimmed. Munch suspected he had named himself, too.

One of the group's common hangouts was Hinano's on Lincoln Boulevard, a beer bar with sawdust on the floor and pool tables. Melissa, a mellow hippie chick with long, straight brown hair and wire-rimmed glasses, served pitchers on tap. Melissa showed no interest in hanging out with the Road Buzzards after hours, but she was always friendly and cool. Hinano's was a good warm-up bar; however, for serious drinking Munch preferred the Venture Inn or Sundowners, where they sold generous shots of Jack Daniel's in bucket glasses.

So there they all were this one night at the Venture Inn when the rumor floats down that Terrible Tom had been at Hinano's and for no good reason he picked up a pool ball and hit Melissa square in the face. That was Tom's first mistake of the evening. His second was showing up at the Venture Inn.

Munch gathered the other biker chicks around her, forming a huddle of five with herself as quarterback. One of the women was new to the group so she got the bait assignment.

"Promise him anything," Munch said. "We'll do the rest."

One by one, the women filtered outside. Munch had her friend Roxanne wait by the doorway. Tom was lured outside; Roxanne dropped behind his legs and then Munch charged into him, causing him to trip. When he was on the ground, Munch and her cohorts kicked him until he curled into a ball and begged them to stop.

"And don't ever come back, woman-beating punk," Munch told him, and then, giggling with excitement, the women returned triumphantly to the bar and were treated to a round by the management. Although in retrospect the free drinks were probably more of a thank-you for taking it outside than a reward for delivering justice.

Munch shivered as a damp, cold wind blew in off the ocean. She got back in the car, settled down in the cushioned seat of her Caddy, and also remembered being outraged at how quickly the truth of that night had been corrupted. In the version being told the very next day it was the *guys* who had made Tom lie down and *let* all the women kick him. She had made the decision then to let the exact facts of the matter go. Where was the sense in taking credit if it meant it might make you a target later on?

CHAPTER 2

On Saturday night, the ever-popular seven-year-old Asia Mancini had yet another sleepover. Munch gave her a gift-wrapped chemistry set for the birthday girl, and reminded Asia how much she loved her as she took her to her little friend's door. Garret had plans for dinner at a just-opened but already trendy restaurant in Santa Monica. He enjoyed those kinds of places with their overpriced but artfully designed cuisine. But, hey, the guy was a gainfully employed normy. ("Normy" as in *not* an alcoholic, sober or otherwise.) Who was she to criticize how he liked to spend his money?

The restaurant was housed inside a blue three-story Victorian mansion. Munch wished she had known that ahead of time as she wobbled up the two flights of stairs toward their table. Garret steadied her elbow as her foot twisted beneath her. "Are you all right?" he asked.

"Yeah, sure. I'm just not used to climbing in these shoes."

They were seated at a small round table with a white tablecloth and matching napkins, surrounded by a decor of parchment-colored wallpaper and portraits of old guys. She kicked off her heels and wiggled her toes in relief.

A waiter arrived and asked what they'd have to drink.

"I'm okay with water," Munch said.

Garret started to reach for the wine list and then pulled back.

"Go ahead," Munch said. "I don't mind." In fact there was nothing like abstaining at a social function to reinforce her commitment to sobriety. She derived no small degree of satisfaction in watching people grow stupider and louder with each round. When she'd first started the limo business she had picked up two couples in Thousand Oaks and taken them to a fancy dinner at the Biltmore in downtown L.A. By the end of the evening, the ladies' makeup had melted, their hats had wilted, and both couples had gotten into big arguments. It hadn't mattered that the booze that undid the evening had been poured from crystal decanters.

Garret perused the thick, leather-bound wine menu and made a selection. The waiter nodded his approval and Garret seemed proud of himself. He then ordered the oyster appetizer, which Munch also let him enjoy all by himself.

"How was the run last night?" he asked.

"Great. A cancer shindig in the Palisades. I only had to take one guy home and he tipped me twenty bucks."

"Must have been some party."

"Yeah, they even had fireworks."

He reached across the table and took her hand. "I missed you."

The waiter returned, saving her from responding, and recited the specials. She couldn't help but make a face when he described the bone marrow served on Parmesan crisps. Garret went with the duck in orange sauce. She ordered the safest-looking and least expensive item on the menu. It had a fancy name, but basically it was skinny spaghetti with chopped tomatoes, garlic, and a little olive oil.

They swapped a few work stories while waiting for their food. Munch had the feeling that there was something on Garret's mind.

Fortunately, the service was quick—even overly persistent—and there wasn't a lot of time for awkward silences.

"How is it?" Garret asked after she took a bite of her pasta.

"It's all right," she said.

"Good, good," he said, biting into his duck.

He spent the rest of the meal commenting on every aspect of the room's decoration. He talked so much she wondered what he wasn't saying.

It was almost ten when they got to Munch's two-bedroom rented house in West Los Angeles. She was exhausted. As they started to undress in silence, she remembered not so long ago when the undressing had been a big part of the act itself. The first time they ever made love had been on a lazy Sunday. Asia was at a friend's house. Munch brought Garret home with the express purpose of seducing him. He had been surprised, he told her later, that she had wanted to go all the way on their first actual date.

She pointed out that they had been seeing each other every Monday night at the college so it wasn't as if they were strangers off the street. She didn't add that she hadn't done the cute-hitchhiker-hit-and-run thing since her first lonely year of sobriety, and certainly never since Asia had come into her life.

The automotive air-conditioning class where she met Garret had fifteen other attendees. Fifteen guys who were either married, or too old, too goofy, or too stupid to be interesting. Week after week Garret proved he could hold a conversation, had a sense of humor, and could grasp the concepts of conductive heat exchange and pressure differentials. He was also employed, single, and not a doper.

In fact, it was surprising how slim the pickings were considering all the functions she went to where she was the only woman. Automotive seminars, NIASE exams, even the punishment class she had to attend for eight hours once when she wrongly issued a smog certificate to a car from the Bureau of Automotive Repair's undercover unit. The fuel evaporative canister had been removed and she hadn't noticed. They fined her and Lou one hundred and fifty dollars each. She got a black mark on her record and had to spend a Saturday being lectured to on smog control.

Even on that day, surrounded by thirty men, the only guy who was worth a second look turned out to be married. He revealed his marital status over lunch at a nearby Mexican restaurant, for which he paid anyway. They exchanged business cards and tips on spotting future undercover BAR cars over enchiladas.

On their first, off-class date she and Garret went to a car exhibit at the Convention Center. Driving home, she had ventured a kiss or two. He had received them with reluctance. This had been new to her. This reticence. She had felt even more attracted to him, though now she wondered if maybe it had been the added challenge she enjoyed. By the time they got back to her house, he was offering no more resistance.

She looked at him now, sitting on the edge of her bed unbuttoning his shirt with the absentminded nonchalance of habit. She missed the anticipation of a new lover—the excitement of discovery—the first-time jitters. Not that she wanted to risk all that went with the unknown. There were nasty diseases out there. Diseases with no cures. Herpes was bad enough. Somehow she had managed to dodge that bullet. But now there was this AIDS shit.

"What's the matter?" he asked.

"Nothing."

"You have a weird look on your face."

"Just thinking."

"About what?"

"How lucky I am."

He draped his shirt over the chair and kicked off his loafers. "Lucky in what way?"

"To be alive. To be sober. To have Asia. Not to have to worry where my next dime is coming from."

"Oh," he said, looking dejected, "I thought you meant about us."

"I've been thinking about that," she said.

"Me, too." He undid his belt buckle and the top button of his pants, but then stopped undressing and sat down next to her on the bed. He took her hand in his.

"Maybe I should go first," she said.

"All right." He waited, his puppy dog eyes fixed on her.

"I was thinking maybe we should back off a little," she said. "You know, take some time apart."

He blinked.

"What were you going to say?" she asked.

"I was thinking we should move in together." He laughed. "Boy, talk about mixed signals."

She smiled back at him, glad to see he was taking this so well. They might even still make love, which was never a bad thing between them.

"I just think we've reached the point where—" she began.

"Say no more," he said. "I know exactly what you mean. We need to grow or go. This is why I think it's time to take the next step." He hunched his shoulders forward and scooted closer to her. "Think about it a minute. What do we have together? Just this one-night-a-week thing. I don't even keep a toothbrush here. This place is nice, but there's only room enough here for you and Asia. Of course you feel like you need space. But it's not space away from me. At least I don't think it is. What our relationship needs, what you need, is more commitment, not less. I need a place with a garage. There's a house up the street with three bedrooms, two baths, a two-car garage, and a laundry room. There's even an RV pad for the limo and a fenced backyard. We could have a dog."

She listened to his pitch. The bit about the dog was a good closer. Asia wanted a puppy in the worst way.

"Between the two of us," he said, "we could swing it."

"And this house is available now?"

"Almost. I'll show it to you next weekend."

He kissed her then. His mouth tasted sweet with wine. With his lips still on hers, he unzipped her dress, and worked her breasts out of her bra. She succumbed to the sensations, groaning as he took one of her nipples in his mouth, a shiver shooting through her body. They giggled through the awkward process of untangling panty hose and briefs. When they were both naked, they joined.

For long minutes, they coupled with a slow, delicious rhythm that had them both making small moans of pleasure. Then gradually the tempo increased. With only half an ear, she heard the bed frame pound the wall. She arched her back and cried out in orgasm, expecting him to follow. Instead, he flipped her over and dragged her to the edge of the bed, somehow finding the strength to stand there. Their bodies slapped together wetly, and still he wasn't finished. She grabbed fists of sheet, trembling with exhaustion.

"I can't take any more," she gasped finally.

He released, thrusting one last time and then collapsing on top of her. They lay panting for a long minute, and he rolled off her, letting out a long "Whew."

"Man," she said, "what got into you?"

He laughed. "How could you even think about breaking up when we've got this going for us?"

She didn't answer. She drew her knees to her chest, and bunched the pillow to her cheek. Maybe this was going to work out. She'd just have to learn to be quieter when Asia was in the next room.

Please, God, she prayed, *make my life easy. Let me fall in love with him.* As she dropped off to sleep, her last nagging thought was that he was a good guy. He deserved better than a grudging compromise.

CHAPTER 3

SUNDAY

He fingered the button lightly, realized he was holding his breath, and forced himself to exhale and inhale several times before he proceeded. This was not the last act of the plan, but certainly the most final one.

He wondered again if he'd missed anything. The house, he knew, was clean. He'd even mailed her mail and brought in the Saturday paper.

He looked at her lying there and thought she had never looked so beautiful. He was tempted to stroke her face. One last time. It would make no difference if he did. There was no turning back now. He wrapped the duct tape around her head, covering her eyes. It was true, he acknowledged in some detached part of his brain, what the cops always said. That when the murder victim's face was covered it meant that he or she was known to his or her murderer. He could only pray he wasn't giving himself away in any other small way.

The bitch had brought him to this juncture, he reminded himself. He wasn't going down for her. Why should he?

He inserted the 220 plug into the special circular wall socket and twisted it into the locked position. His hands were awkward in the thick rubber mitts. The four-foot hank of cable and plug had once been attached to an industrial dryer. Earlier he had separated the three wires inside the cable and soldered copper spikes on the ends of the two hot leads. He capped each sharp point with cork, taking care they wouldn't touch inappropriately. Contacting only one lead at a time was safe enough. But to connect with both simultaneously could prove fatal.

He used extreme caution as he scooted the insulation off the end of each of the rods and poised them at opposite ends of her body. He knew that there was no point in delaying, yet still he hesitated. A drop of sweat tickled as it rolled down his chest. He wiped his sleeve across his brow and with that gesture pushed away remaining doubts. Grunting slightly, he brought the tips of the rods down until they connected with her white, white skin.

The world around them exploded in a bright, paralyzing flash of light followed instantaneously by a sharp crack. Her body arched, lifting off the floor. Muscles contracted, veins darkened. The skin over her chest bubbled and turned to chalky ash as the current arced across, singed, and then penetrated the resisting layers of epidermis and subcutaneous fat tissue. The charge soared through her body, muscles contracted in one last violent spasm. The smell of burnt flesh filled the room, bearing a curious resemblance to roast lamb.

He stepped back, holding one of the two smoking rods high over his head. With his free hand he twisted the bulky 220 plug away from the outlet.

"Well," he said, after a moment, still feeling awed at the force of the current. "That's that."

Then he got busy. The night's work was far from over.

CHAPTER 4

TUESDAY MORNING

Munch was the first to see the blonde in her hot pink dress park her little three-series BMW near the hibiscus hedge at the far end of the lot. The BMW's door opened, and a long shapely leg wearing a red stiletto-heeled shoe emerged.

Munch edged into a position where she could watch the show. Because the shop was in Brentwood, they catered to a variety of professional athletes, movie stars, and millionaires. There was also an excess of beautiful women. Actresses, models, trophy wives and their trophy daughters. The gas station's south driveway poured into a small cul-de-sac of merchants. Parking for those businesses was limited. The gas pump attendants weren't supposed to let non-customers park in the station's lot, but they were known to make exceptions. Lou, the owner, looked the other way in the interest of morale.

Another long leg swung out the door of the BMW and then the woman stood. Her dress was tight for all the right reasons, as Lou would say. This was going to be interesting.

Munch always got a kick out of how these women would come to the station in sexy outfits and make their voices go all high and helpless. Didn't the guys realize there was no way these women were going to put out for a tune-up?

Even Lou would tell them right to their faces, "I can't take it to the bank, honey." Two years ago Lou might have acted differently. He had been a much happier man then, working on cars instead of owning his own business. She looked at him now through the office window, bent over the morning's books. Business had been slow all month and nobody was happy about it. The mechanics worked strictly on commission, getting paid half of what the shop collected on labor, and nothing on parts except for tires and batteries, for which they received five bucks per unit. When there wasn't enough work to go around, it brought out the worst in everybody. Lou's face reminded her of one of those depression-era farmers in those old photos, looking out the window of a rusty pickup truck, a litter of kids in the back, the dust bowl in their wake.

The blonde was halfway across the property now, acting oblivious to the rubbernecking of every man on the lot, from customer to pump jockey.

Munch laughed out loud when one of the guys interrupted his windshield washing to gawk and dribbled soapy water on the crotch of his pants.

She turned to go back into the lube room but stopped when she saw Mace St. John's department-issued Buick pulling into the driveway.

Her heart did one of those fluttery things it had been doing lately at the sight of him. In the old days, the sight of a cop had always been enough to release spiders in her stomach. Not that she had anything to fear now. But it was interesting what close cousins fear and excitement were, how the physical manifestations were identical. The dry mouth, the increased pulse. As with everything else, it was all a matter of how you interpreted your perceptions.

Mace St. John was an LAPD homicide cop. Seven and a half years ago, February 1977, when they had first crossed paths, she had been a prime suspect in one of his murder cases. She'd been twenty-one and floundering. He'd been floundering, too. Each had saved the other: he, by giving her a chance; she, by showing him that not all offenders were necessarily lifetime assholes. That people could change. Seven years had passed before they met again, when different murders had brought them together. And through her help, the killer had been stopped, and a new phase of their friendship had begun.

The sex dreams starring the detective had started only recently. In the dreams, they were more than just lovers, they were married. She always woke up just about the time she thought to ask, "Hey, what happened to Caroline?"

When he called yesterday and said he would be stopping by, she figured it had something to do with his never-ending restoration work on the Bella Donna, his 1927 Pullman train car. St. John had bought the Santa Fe–designed green-and-gold business car twelve years earlier, in 1972, and had been working on it ever since, proving once again what willing slaves men were to their passions.

If anybody noticed that Munch had worn a little makeup to work, mascara and blush, no one had said anything. Not that she was being obvious. And not that she ever in a million years would act on her private fantasy. She'd been through this situation before and knew that the solution to an inappropriate infatuation was just to wait it out silently.

She figured this latest crush was some kind of phenomenon like the Stockholm Syndrome. Spend enough time with a pistol-packing guy who doesn't hurt or kill you and you start to wonder if he's "the one."

The detective parked his car in front of the office.

"Hey," she said, tucking in her uniform shirt and smiling. "You just missed seeing Asia off to school."

"Yeah, I got a little delayed this morning." He brushed what looked like dog hair off his navy blue sports coat and grinned back. Mace St. John had one of those craggy faces that work so well on some men. He was a shade under six feet, with a boxer's trim physique. A touch of gray had crept into his temples and a thick gold wedding band shone at her from the ring finger on his left hand. She wanted to touch it.

"You got a minute?" he asked.

"Maybe even five if you're lucky."

Her ex-boyfriend Derek had once said to her, "You think you can have any man you want." She didn't remember what the argument had been about, only the exasperation in his tone, and her answer.

"Yes," she had said, "I do." It wasn't that she thought she was so earth-shatteringly beautiful, but she knew she was cute. That her body was well proportioned. And when she took her shoulder-length hair out of its severe braid and applied a little makeup, she garnered a few second looks of her own. But all that aside, she also knew that all it really took was letting a guy know you were his for the asking. The art was in how you let him know. Men were always watching for the signs, and women learned from an early age how to exploit that. Another lesson courtesy of her late father, the unlamented Flower George, who had also taught her that exploitation was a two-way street.

Behind St. John, the panting face of a mutt appeared in his driver's-side window. It was an appealing face, brown with white markings, ears

fringed in black. The dog grinned at her with a look
that seemed to say, "I'm lucky and I know it."

"Who's this?" Munch asked.

"I don't know. I found her on the freeway."

Munch reached her hand in the semiopened
window and ruffled the pooch's shaggy ears. She
didn't see a collar. There was an empty hamburger
wrapper from Jack in the Box on the floor of the
backseat. The dog's breath smelled of secret sauce.

"What do you need?" she asked St. John, but she
accompanied the question with no sly smile.

"I wanted to borrow your air-conditioning
tools," he said, gracing her with one of those grins
that transformed his deeply lined face into a thing
of beauty. That little cigar clamped in his teeth
seemed appealing and manly, even sexy.

"Is this for the Bella Donna?" she asked.

"I'm ready to add Freon."

"Let me help you," she said. "I can swing by after
I pick up Asia from school. How's five sound?"

"Tonight?"

"Is that a problem?"

"How long will it take, you think?"

She shrugged. "Hour, maybe."

"Okay, let's do it. I've got a case I'm working,
but an hour won't make or break it."

"Hey, that reminds me," she said. "What was
that all about yesterday morning?"

"All what?"

"By the Sunset off-ramp. Major cop activity. I
saw the coroner's wagon, too. What I didn't see

was a fire engine or a tow truck or any kind of wreckage."

"So you were just wondering," he said.

"Can you tell me anything?"

"Not much to tell, yet." Behind them, the dog barked once sharply as if to remind them not to ignore her. St. John stuck his hand in the window and stroked the animal's head. The dog closed her eyes and soaked in the attention.

"All the radio said was that a body had been found," Munch persisted, "that the police hadn't ruled out foul play. Is that your case?"

"We're still working on identifying the deceased." St. John reached into his suit pocket with his free hand. He removed a Polaroid photograph but didn't show it to her immediately. "You always say it feels like the whole world passes through here."

That was true. The office wall was filled with signed celebrity photographs, everyone from James Garner to Betty White. DeLorean stopped in for a fuse once in the middle of his trial. Munch had felt so sorry for him—how the cops had entrapped him—that she hadn't charged. O.J. Simpson and Magic Johnson regularly had their Ferraris waxed by Pauley, the detail guy. Even presidential motorcades passed by occasionally.

Munch held out her hand.

He handed her the picture. "Did you know her?"

Munch studied the photograph, feeling an odd dropping sensation in her stomach, knowing she was experiencing one of those moments that would always be etched in her memory. This was the way it always was when she learned that someone she knew and liked was dead.

St. John watched her closely.

"Yes," she said, staring in surprise at the lifeless face. "It's Mrs. Bergman. Diane. Diane Bergman."

"Was she a friend?" His thin cigar had gone out. He tossed the butt in one of the shop's fifty-gallon-drum trash cans.

"She's a customer. I mean, I liked her. But I knew her from work. In fact, I worked for her the other night. My limo was on standby for this party she gave in the Palisades."

"When was this?"

"Last Friday. She was perfectly fine then." *Oh that was brilliant,* she thought. *How many people got sick before they were murdered?*

"Does she live nearby?" he asked.

"On Chenault."

"With her husband?"

"No, she was widowed about six months ago, around the middle of April. They both used to come in here. Then he got sick and stopped going out. I read about his death in the paper and sent a note." *Why was that important to say?* she asked herself. *So you can impress him with what a good person you are?* She tried to do three good deeds a day, but not tell anyone. It was a character-building exercise. Getting credit negated the whole point.

"Can you get me the address?" he asked.

"I'll have to look it up."

She looked at the picture again, still wondering how such a vibrant woman could become a police statistic. "What's that black stuff on her face?"

"I can't comment."

"She was murdered?"

"I really can't say."

Can't or won't? she wondered. As if his being there with a dead woman's photograph and being cagey with information didn't already tell her that foul play was involved. "I'll go get that address."

She went into the office, leafed through Lou's Rolodex, and removed the Bergman card for St. John. There was no point in hanging on to it now, but she felt a guilty twinge. Deleting a human being from your life shouldn't be this easy.

"What's going on?" Lou asked.

"Remember Diane Bergman? Honda Prelude?"

"The one who just lost her husband?"

"Yeah, now she's dead, too."

"How?"

"I don't know. That was her body they found yesterday morning on the freeway. She must not have had any ID on her."

Lou spun around in his chair. "What do they think happened?"

Munch shrugged helplessly. "I don't know. I just know she's dead."

"Wasn't she always doing all that charity work?"

"Yeah, she was very active. And really a nice woman, too. Not stuck up at all."

"It's a goddamn shame," he said, going back to his accounting.

"Yeah, it really is." She waited a moment, but he said nothing more. What did she expect? Tears? Why wasn't she crying?

St. John was studying her diplomas on the wall when she returned to the service desk. She had three certifications from NIASE, the National Institute for Automotive Service Excellence, her smog license, and, most recently, the letter of completion from Bosch for the fuel injection course she'd taken.

"Impressive," he said.

"Yeah, I figured it would be reassuring to the customers." She straightened one of the frames. "How's Caroline, by the way?" It would be weird if she didn't ask. She loved Caroline, too. Caroline St. John, formerly known to her as Miss Rhinehart, was Munch's onetime probation officer. Now Caroline and Mace were godparents to Asia, and everything was just as neat as could be.

"We're good," he said. "When are *you* going to get married?"

All the good ones are taken, she thought. She didn't dare say it. *This too shall pass,* she told herself.

He took the Rolodex card from her and squeezed her shoulder. "Thanks."

"There's something else," she said. "About Diane. This guy was hassling her at the party Friday. I don't know who he was, but I saw them arguing about something."

"But you didn't recognize the guy?"

"No, I never really saw his face. I was in the car and he and Diane were up at the house. He was just your average middle-aged white guy. White hair, stocky build, three-piece suit."

"What do you consider middle-aged?" St. John asked with a smile.

"Fifties," she said. "Much older than you."

"Not that much." He rolled his head from shoulder to shoulder, his eyes never shutting. "Call me if you think of anything else. Otherwise, I'll see you tonight."

Munch watched him drive away, then went back outside to finish removing the radiator from a Ford Torino. It took a half an hour to drain the coolant, then disconnect the hoses and transmission lines and finally the bolts that attached the radiator to the Torino's frame. But even after all that activity, her shoulder still felt warm where St. John had rested his hand.

Inappropriate infatuations. That was the crux of it. Wanting what you couldn't have and having what you couldn't bring yourself to want. Such was the ongoing condition of her love life.

She stripped the radiator of fittings and shroud clips and called the radiator shop to pick it up.

Midday, Lou emerged from his office.

"Lover boy is here," he said, his lean face expressing his displeasure.

CHAPTER 5

As soon as Munch had given St. John the deceased woman's name and address, he had gone to the house on Chenault, made a cursory search, and posted patrol officers who barricaded the premises with yellow tape. He also arranged for a block on the phone. This would garner him a listing of all calls placed to and from the house starting from today and going back as far as he deemed pertinent. More than twenty-four hours had gone by since the murder, and it was the first twenty-four hours that were so critical in a homicide investigation.

Two boys looking for aluminum cans on the side of the freeway had discovered the nightgown-clothed body on Monday morning around 7 A.M. Neither of the boys would ever forget such an image. That first real-life glimpse of a fresh murder was like that. The dead woman's legs were spread open, her heels separated by a distance of more than four feet. There were scorch marks along the torso and her eyes had been taped shut with silver duct tape. Pictures had been snapped before and after the tape was removed. It was a later photograph that St. John had shown Munch.

The coroner sent the victim's fingerprints to the police database when they received the body on Monday. A match was always a long shot. Some day fingerprints might all be put on a computer database, but for now law enforcement personnel mostly had to rely on some poor schmuck sitting in a room with a magnifying glass. His only job all day was to compare ridges and whorls. And St. John thought *he* had problems. The coroner's primary function was to determine cause and mechanism of death. The duties of the office also included identifying the deceased, protecting that deceased's property, and making arrangements for disposal of the body.

St. John knew the coroner's office was overworked and perhaps not moved by the same sense of urgency that drove him. And beyond that, nameless toe tags haunted him, especially when attached to women who had been brutalized.

He had been all set to run the dead woman's picture in Wednesday's *Los Angeles Times*. He hated soliciting an ID that way. The woman had been wearing a wedding ring. Hell of a way to find out your wife had been murdered—to see her lifeless face on page three of the Metro section. Although, the husband usually already knew, especially when no missing persons report had been filed. One out of three female murder victims is killed by her husband or boyfriend.

Diane Bergman had been a widow, so there would be no bereaved husband to console and investigate. St. John's next task was to contact the victim's relatives. Actually, this was also the domain of the coroner, but in cases of violent and wrongful death, St. John knew he needed to be there when the news was delivered. It was important to clock the reactions when the loved ones heard about the death.

The Scientific Investigation Division criminalists arrived at the Bergman house at nine-thirty. While waiting for them, St. John contacted the coroner's office and let them know the probable identity of the deceased. They would call Sacramento and request a copy of her driver's license photograph. More scientific methods of identification would be used in the coming days: comparisons of ante- and postmortem X rays, dental records, fingerprints. The autopsy, the coroner's office told him, was scheduled for the following morning. Deputy Coroner Frank Shue had been assigned to the field investigative portion of the case and met St. John at the address on Chenault. Even if the house turned out not to be the murder scene, it could very well hold clues that would assist both men in their jobs. St. John always arranged to meet the coroner's office personnel at the scene. The last thing he wanted was to be stuck in a car all day with one of those guys.

The detective had worked with Frank Shue on at least a dozen occasions. No matter what hour of the day, the man always looked as if he were emerging from a three-day binge. Today was no exception. Shue's upper torso was clothed in the incongruous mix of a tweed jacket and a plaid flannel shirt. He had also managed to find a color of slacks that didn't match or complement a single hue in either shirt or coat. His two-tone saddle shoes hardly pulled the outfit together.

The two men had spent the remainder of the morning at the Bergman house. It was a modest home for the area, which put it in the $900,000 price range. There was no sign of forced entry. The double garage had one car parked inside, a Mercedes. The Sunday paper lay on the driveway.

"This is the biggest goddamn kitchen I've ever seen," St. John told Shue as he stood at one end and looked across the expanse of endless counters and brand-new appliances.

"My wife would love this," Shue said, scratching his two-day growth of beard. "And technically what you got here is two rooms. This part here with the table and atrium is a breakfast nook."

"You've got a wife?" St. John asked.

"Yeah, why?"

"She lets you leave the house dressed like that?"

"Like what?"

"Never mind." St. John opened a shuttered door that still smelled of fresh paint. He'd been expecting to find a pantry or a laundry room. Instead, he discovered a desk and hutch. "Here we go," he said. Her checkbook rested atop a stack of bills. The most recent postmark was October 5, 1984. The envelopes had been opened and the invoices spread flat. The body had been found Monday morning, the eighth, so this mail must have arrived on Saturday. It had most certainly been the last bit of mail she'd ever picked up.

He also found her appointment calendar, an address book, and a stack of credit card receipts. He collected the trash from the wastebasket under her desk, knowing how critical those miscellaneous scraps could be, especially when attempting to re-create the last few days of a person's life. Among the trash was an unopened announcement of a sweepstakes winning and an advertisement from a dating service called Great Expectations. Must be nice, he thought, not to be in search of love or money.

He filled a cardboard box with all the various paperwork and had the photographers chronicle the unmade bed in the master bedroom. A lot of people who lived alone didn't bother to make their beds, but considering the immaculate condition of the rest of the house, and the fact that the vic was wearing only a nightgown when her body was discovered, the bed might be important. He also ordered fingerprints collected off all amenable surfaces.

Photographs in expensive frames crowded small, circular antique-looking wooden tables in the living room. Several of the pictures showed the victim coupled with an elderly man, his arm draped over Diane Bergman's shoulder in a proprietary manner. The man seemed to be doing all the smiling.

While St. John searched inside the house, three two-man teams of uniformed cops and two pairs of major crime detectives from the West Los Angeles station knocked on the neighbors' doors, asking if anyone had heard or seen anything suspicious in the last couple of nights.

Not only had the neighbors noticed nothing suspicious, the investigators reported, no one could even remember setting eyes on Diane before Wednesday.

"That's a big help," St. John said, dissatisfied. "I need to know what happened after Friday night."

The cops looked down at their notebooks but could add nothing more. St. John understood the problem. The driveway was shrouded by drooping eucalyptus trees that provided the ultimate in privacy.

At eleven-fifteen, St. John sealed the front door and made certain that the officer guarding the entrance would let no one inside without St. John's authorization.

"I need to check back at work and then we'll notify next of kin," St. John told Shue.

"Sounds good to me," Shue said, tucking in only half his shirt. "I'll follow you."

The drive back to the windowless two-story bunker that the West Los Angeles PD called home took fifteen minutes. St. John found several messages in his box. He had put out a Crime Alert bulletin to other homicide departments yesterday, describing the corpse with its odd burn marks on the ankles, abdomen, and breasts. He also described the negligee she had been wearing, and that her eyes had been bound shut. He withheld only that duct tape had been used. The first call he decided to return was to the major crimes target team of the Rampart Division.

"Investigations," a man's voice answered.

"Yeah, I'm looking for Rosales."

"You got him."

"Mace St. John, West L.A. Homicide. You rang?"

"Yeah, I got your twenty-four-hour Crime Alert report today. You got a DB in a nightgown?" DB being cop speak for Dead Body. "Scorch marks on the torso?"

"That's right. Sound familiar?"

"We've got a case that might interest you. A rape call, two months ago. White female dumped on the shoulder of the freeway. Wearing only a 'baby doll' style nightgown. Vic's name was Veronica Parker. She dances at a titty bar out by the airport under the name Ginger Root. Place called Century Entertainment. That's where the suspect, ah, abducted her."

"Did your vic give you a description?"

"No, the suspect taped her eyes shut."

"Duct tape?"

"You got it. The suspect provided the nightgown and used a condom. Was your victim electrocuted?"

"I don't have the post in yet. Why?"

"Our guy used some kind of modified stun gun to control his victim. He also told her he could do worse. Who's the ME?"

"Sugarman probably."

"Tell him to look for boiled blood."

St. John made a note on his desk blotter. "What else?"

"He disguised his voice with an electrolarynx, one of those speech aids that people who don't have vocal cords use. We took a ride out to the club, but didn't get much help from the other employees or management. Shit, the manager didn't even want to give up his name. Had to damn near beat it out of him."

St. John didn't ask if the guy was speaking figuratively. "What was it?"

"Joey Polk."

"Joey Polk?"

"Yeah, you know him?"

"Yeah, he has a long pedigree around these parts. I busted the father a few times." The realization that he was on the second generation of yet another family of bad guys made St. John feel old. He didn't need to count his years on the job. Every cop he knew kept a running tally, happy to boast on a moment's notice the number of days until retirement.

St. John didn't consider himself decrepit, but he wasn't the same young buck who had left the army in '64 and gone straight into the academy. Twenty years had gone by fast. Although he still felt too young to have been doing the same job for two decades. Perhaps the fact that he'd worked in different locations helped. He sure didn't regret his most recent transfer from Parker Center's Robbery/Homicide to the West Los Angeles Division. That long drive downtown every day to Parker Center had added stress to an already pressure-filled existence—what with the 3 A.M. calls to murder scenes, and the twenty-three-minute code sevens that allowed only enough time to choke down a Big Mac and fries before hitting the streets again. Add to that the drinking that so often seemed necessary just to wind down at night. At forty-two, he was just eight years shy of middle age, according to Munch. He couldn't remember when he hadn't answered to a chain of command.

Oh fuck it, he thought. The next thing he knew he'd be having an irresistible urge to buy a Porsche or start dyeing his hair or some crazy shit like that. He turned his attention back to the matter at hand.

"I might run over there and see what I can find out," he told the Rampart dick.

"Let me know what happens," Rosales said. The voice sounded young and enthusiastic. "I'd love to catch this guy."

They hung up after promising to share all pertinent information.

St. John pulled out the murder book he had started the day before. He made a note, "Boiled blood," and laughed that one-note expression of amusement and disbelief men use to save their sanity in morbid situations. He studied photographs of the body and dump site. Photographs he had taken himself while waiting for the coroner's wagon to arrive.

The position of the body had seem staged, with one leg pointing north, the other pointing west. The killer would most probably have driven to the site, as it was a freeway underpass. No tire tracks were distinguishable on the asphalt, but there was an inch-deep layer of run-off soil where the body had been dropped. Dropped and positioned, not dragged. He made another note to himself and then put the pencil between his teeth and bit down. Absently, he checked his shirt pocket for a box of Tiparillos, forgetting he was out.

The shoe prints were all around the freeway side of the body. The muck lining the road was equal parts road oil and dirt with a high clay composite. It should have recorded excellent impressions, and yet the shoeprints weren't that distinctive. The dental-plaster casts he had made of those smeared shoeprints had picked up some blue fibers. There was something else about those shoeprints as he studied them now, something strangely familiar about their fuzzy edges.

CHAPTER 6

Munch didn't have to turn around to know who Lou had sarcastically referred to as "lover boy." D.W. Sanders had arrived. She heard the creak of his van door opening.

D.W. called himself a contractor, which basically meant that he owned a set of carpentry tools and did odd jobs around the neighborhood. He also delivered Meals-On-Wheels every Tuesday. She had met him when his van was towed in a month earlier needing a fuel pump.

D.W. was Lou's height, about two inches shy of six feet, and closer to forty than thirty. He had a receding hairline and grew the remaining strands of his black hair long enough to tie back into a ponytail. Not a bad-looking guy, but he would look better if he lost some of the stoop in his shoulders.

He made it a habit to stop in most mornings, always bringing her coffee fixed just the way she liked it. He'd claim to be on his way to a job. The way he told it he had quite a business. The big time, he hinted, was right around the corner. He referred to his customers as "clients" and his helpers as his "crew." In fact, he had said last week, the way things were going, pretty soon he was going to need help with the bookkeeping and scheduling. He wanted to hire somebody who was handicapped to run his office. From her own experience with the small-business circuit, Munch knew D.W. had far too much free time to be able to afford office help.

He always dressed in standard contractor garb: jeans, long-sleeved cotton shirts, and work boots, which he never tied until after his first cup of coffee. The untied shoes reminded her of her daughter, Asia, who also liked to leave her laces dangling. When Munch pointed it out the other morning, Asia had archly informed her that "None of the second graders tie their shoes."

"Well, then," Munch had replied, swallowing a smile.

The week after D.W.'s fuel pump went out, he came in needing rear brakes. Rather than have one of his "crew" pick him up, he stayed at the shop and watched her work. He was standing behind her when she removed his tires. The brakes were a mess. Both drums were scored too deeply to salvage, the retaining springs were ruined, and the wheel cylinders needed rebuilding.

New brake drums cost a hundred dollars each. The whole bill came to just under four hundred.

When she delivered the news, D.W. cried. Not big heaving sobs or anything, but tears had definitely filled his eyes. She looked away until he composed himself. She knew it was a fair amount of change, but c'mon, this was business, and he should have heard the grinding metal noise every time he stepped on the brakes. Had he caught it in time, he would have saved himself the expense of the extra hardware.

Munch and her fellow mechanics, Carlos and Stefano, always put their initials on the work orders so that the correct monies would be credited to their pay. They also made a game out of each other's monograms. Munch's M.M. became "Motor Maid." Carlos's initials were C.K., so he was rightly dubbed the "Comeback King." Stefano was S.B., "Show Boat," although there were times she wanted to insert an O in the middle and let him figure it out. It was only natural to come up with alternatives for D.W. After the brake-and-tear incident she had begun to think of him as "Darth Whiner."

His reaction had also served to kill any spark of romantic attraction she might have felt for the guy. Not that she was actively looking. She already had the thing going with Garret.

She also knew better than to get involved with any guy around the workplace. Especially knowing how guys will talk. She'd worked too hard to match her reputation to her license plate: LDY MECH. She had already perfected the slightly offended look when a stranger cursed in front of her. And if one of the guys at the shop started to tell a dirty joke, she walked away before he finished, shaking her head after the first line was uttered. The old Munch would have stayed tuned until the punch line and laughed the hardest. The old Munch had done a lot of stupid things. She was working her way up to the moment when she could slap the face of a man getting "fresh." Like they did in those old black-and-white movies when the ladies used to wear white gloves and all the men wore hats.

Other than Lou, none of the guys she worked with now knew anything about the wild part of her life. Most of them didn't even know about her not drinking or getting high. And even fewer knew that the qualifier "anymore" belonged in that statement of fact. They knew her as hardworking. Money hungry, some of them said, but that was just jealousy talking. They all worked on commission and if she could do more jobs faster she made more. Didn't take Einstein to figure that out. Besides, she had a kid to support. A little girl with a bright future that would never include her debasing herself. Not while Munch was alive to prevent it. A lot of things were going to be different for Asia.

She looked at her visitor now and sighed. D.W. was nice enough, although too sensitive for her tastes. She liked her men a little more in touch with their masculine side, maybe to counter some of her own rough edges.

Sometimes D.W. showed up midday and ate his lunch while he watched her work. It looked as if today was going to be one of those days.

"Want an apple?" he asked.

She noticed the Meals-On-Wheels placard on his dashboard. "Thanks," she said, taking the fruit, and hoping he hadn't ransacked anybody's box lunch to get it.

"I can't stay," he said. "I've got three more deliveries to make."

"It's really nice of you to do this," she said.

"Yeah," he said, "I figure it's so little effort on my part for the help I give to those less fortunate."

Cue the halo, Munch thought. "How long does your route take?"

"Only about an hour and a half. All my shut-ins are in the same general area. It's hard to just leave the food and split though. With a lot of these people you're the only human contact they have in a day. They want you to stay and talk. Sometimes they need you to help them do something around the house. Some of them can't even get out of their chairs."

"So are they all old?" she asked.

"Not all. They just have to be housebound and alone. In fact, one lady I deliver to in Barrington Plaza Gardens is closer to our age."

"What's her name?" Munch asked.

"Robin Davies."

"Robin Davies?"

"You know her?"

"Sure. Toyota Celica." She realized Robin hadn't been around in at least a month. "She volunteers at Asia's school, mentoring drama students. Apparently she has a lot of theater experience. She helped choreograph the school's summer drama production. We did *Pinocchio*. Robin was really good to Asia—to all the kids. I should go see her or something. I didn't realize she was sick."

"As I understand it, she was in the hospital for two weeks. When she was discharged it came out that she had no family nearby to help her. They signed her up before she left the hospital to receive meals as part of her aftercare."

Munch looked back over the mostly vacant shop. Carlos and Stefano were sitting on the workbench, watching the driveways for work to roll in. They reminded her of that cartoon of two vultures sitting on a tree limb. One is turned to the other and saying, *Patience, my ass. Let's go out and kill something.*

She turned back to D.W. "Can I tag along?"

"You want to come with me?" he asked, brightening. "You mean like right now? Today?"

"Yeah, I can take a lunch break for once."

"Give me a second," he said. He slid open the back door and shoved back a stack of two-by-fours. Then he lifted a milk crate full of power tools from the floorboard of the front seat and jammed it into the clearance he'd created. His movements were jerky, hurried. Twice she saw him catch his fingers in between the crate and the building materials.

Lou stood in the office doorway and watched with an amused expression.

"I'll be back in a little while," she told him.

D.W. had a whisk broom now and was briskly attacking sawdust clinging to the upholstery of the passenger seat.

"Really," she said. "It's all right." He stepped aside and she climbed in.

The van smelled like fried chicken. She didn't fasten her seat belt. Their destination was only a couple blocks away. But it wouldn't have made a difference even if it had been miles. She hated the feel of restraints. She didn't buckle up unless Asia was with her. D.W. looked as if he was going to say something as he fastened his own, but then apparently changed his mind.

The Barrington Plaza Gardens was an upscale housing development complete with spa, fitness center, and lots of Mercedes in the individual carports. It was also surrounded by a twelve-foot block wall. They entered the complex through the security gate off Barrington Way. The gate guard walked out with his clipboard. D.W. pointed to the placard on his dash and was waved through. Robin's apartment was toward the rear of the complex. They drove around the complex's large central fountain. The roads were well maintained and bordered by flower beds full of roses.

Robin's Celica was in her carport. A fine layer of the heavier particles of Los Angeles's atmosphere covered the car. This was odd in itself. Robin was meticulous about how she kept her vehicle. She had it hand-washed once a week, waxed at least once a month by the detail business that operated out of the gas station. She was one of those customers who seemed almost disappointed when you couldn't find anything that needed fixing or servicing.

D.W. parked in a space marked LOADING ZONE.

Munch waited while he got his blue plastic grocer's basket ready. In the back of the van he had three large square quilted bags. Each was stamped SANTA MONICA HOSPITAL. When he unzipped the first bag she saw it was lined with silver insulation fabric. He removed a rectangular aluminum box and put it in the basket. Definitely chicken. The second quilted bag contained a cold meal and from the third carrier he pulled two small cartons of milk and one of orange juice. He placed all of these in the basket, started to loop the wire handles over his arm, seemed to think twice about that, and then grasped them in his hand as if he were carrying a briefcase.

"This way," he said, as he headed down a concrete path. She followed.

The morning's newspaper was on the mat. D.W. picked it up and added it to his care basket. To the right of the door was a potted geranium; the foliage was wilted and the soil dry. Behind the dehydrated plant was a spigot and hose.

D.W. knocked on the door. Munch turned the faucet, found it fully functional, and gave the plant a good drink.

"Yes?" a voice called suspiciously from behind the door. "Who is it? What do you want?"

"Meals-On-Wheels," D.W. said. "Robin, it's me. I brought Munch. You know, the lady mechanic from the gas station."

Moments passed. D.W. didn't seem unduly alarmed or impatient. Munch tried not to tap her foot. Then came the sound of a dead bolt lock being snapped open. D.W. put his hand on the knob, waited another ten seconds, and opened the door. "We're in," he said.

He ushered Munch inside. The house was dark and smelled strongly of cigarette smoke. She heard D.W. locking the door behind them and turned sharply, the skin prickling on the back of her neck.

"What are you doing?" she asked.

"Kind of a routine we got going," he said. "Robin doesn't like leaving the door unlocked."

The foyer where they stood looked over a sunken living room. There was a piano made of dark wood. A large yellow swag lamp with fringe hung over the piano. It was on but didn't provide much light.

"Robin?" D.W. called out. "I'm going to put the food in the kitchen." He stepped down the two marble stairs leading away from the entry hall. Munch kicked off her greasy shoes before following D.W. across the thick carpet.

Robin emerged from the back hallway. She was dressed in a bulky white bathrobe. When she saw Munch, she blinked and gave a small nod of acknowledgment.

"Hi," Munch said, feeling as if she were intruding. "We've missed you at the station."

D.W. set down his basket on the kitchen counter. The woman startled at the noise then cleared her throat. "Sorry," she said. "I didn't get much sleep last night." She pushed back her hair with a skeletal hand.

Munch decided that it would have taken more than one sleepless night to account for the dark circles under Robin's eyes.

D.W. opened Robin's refrigerator. It was full of boxes similar to the one he now put there. The door of the fridge was lined with small cartons of milk and juice. D.W. sneaked a look at Munch, making sure she registered the implications of all the uneaten food. Robin lit a cigarette.

Her jumpiness was contagious, the silence only serving to amplify the tension in the air. "So, how's it been going?" Munch blurted out, instantly regretting the question.

The gaunt woman laughed and waved her hand in the air as if to encompass the house. A thin trail of smoke followed the movement. "I haven't been out much lately."

Munch shook off the goose bumps dancing up her spine with a quick hunching and jerk of her shoulders.

"Have you seen Robin's work?" D.W. said. He flicked on the light. Robin recoiled slightly. Munch saw neatly bundled bags of trash lined up next to the sink and the blinking light of the answering machine on the counter. The message counter showed ten messages. There was a calendar on the wall that was still turned to last month, September.

"She was on the cover of *Omni*," he said, pointing to a framed photograph on the living room wall.

"Do you mind if I look?" Munch asked her, gesturing to the living room, knowing instinctively that in Robin Davies's present fragile state it would be disastrous to make any sudden moves around her.

"Go ahead."

Munch studied Robin's trophy wall. The *Omni* cover was framed. It showed Robin gazing into a crystal orb. Blue bolts of electricity radiated from the sphere. Robin was dressed in an ethereal gauzy white gown. Her hair fanned up and out from her head as if suspended in a weightless atmosphere. In addition to the cover portrait, there were studio head shots, movie stills showing Robin in various costumes, and cosmetics ads. Robin was beautiful in all of them. An auburn brunette with green eyes. Eyes that once had been capable of a mischievous glint but now darted side to side, making Munch think of a dog who had been beaten and expected more of the same.

"Is there anything I can do for you?" Munch asked.

Robin looked at the pictures. She didn't speak for a long time. Munch glanced back at her and saw that the ash had grown long on her cigarette.

Munch prayed for guidance before she spoke. "What happened?" she asked softly.

She saw D.W.'s reflection in the glass of one of the picture frames. He stood very still, a light sheen of sweat on his forehead. Robin took quick breaths; soon her shoulders were heaving. A high whimper escaped her throat. Three times she made attempts to speak before she finally said, "I was . . . he . . . a man . . ." She stopped, swallowed, seemed to dig deeply for a last reserve of strength. "I was raped. Raped and tortured. Sometimes I think I was killed."

Tears of empathy filled Munch's eyes and closed her throat.

Robin dropped her voice to a whisper.

"You'll have to go now," she said. "I still get tired so easily."

D.W. picked up the bags of trash. "I'll see you next week."

Munch didn't want to leave her. She seemed so damaged and alone. Surely there was something more she could offer this woman, some way she could intervene with the tragedy playing out. No doubt Robin had been made aware of all the counseling services available to her.

Munch flashed back to her own experiences in the Emergency Room all those years ago. They'd all been very nice to her, even though they surely knew who and what she was then. The cop who had driven her there had waited in the hallway. The nurse had held her hand while the doctor did that whole rape kit number. And later, there had been a kind-faced woman who had offered her card and her ear if Munch needed to talk. But Munch had just walked away on her own two feet, wanting to put the whole ordeal behind her. At the time, the only counseling she turned to came in the form of liquid or powder. She had even managed to turn the incident into a joke with a few select drinking buddies, laughing and saying, "Next," as if it were no big deal, as if nothing could touch her.

"I'm going to give you my home phone number," she told Robin now, finding a pad of paper in the kitchen.

D.W. headed for the door. Munch scribbled a note beside her phone number. *Call me, please. We can talk or we can do more than talk. Whatever it is you need.*

When D.W. and Munch were back in the van and heading for the gas station, D.W. spoke. "She'll never be the same."

"Probably not," Munch said.

"Fucking guy," he said with vehemence.

Munch couldn't help but wonder if D.W.'s emotion was a little put on. Maybe he pegged her as some sort of raging feminist and thought this attitude would appeal to her.

"He promised her he would come back."

"The cops didn't catch the guy?"

He looked back at the house. "They didn't have enough to go on."

CHAPTER 7

Lou was standing outside by the gas pumps when Munch and D.W. returned. "Radiator shop called," he said, looking annoyed. "They said you're looking at a recore."

"You get a price?" she asked.

"Yeah, the numbers are on the desk."

"I'm going to take off," D.W. said.

Lou nodded as if he thought that was a good idea, then went back to the office.

"See ya later," Munch said, her mind already turning to the next hurdle, the Ford owner's reaction to the cost of a new radiator.

The detail guy, Pauley, was bent over a red Ferrari using a soft chamois on one of the front wheels. Pauley ran his detail business out of the station. The tip of a bluish tattoo peeked out the sleeve of the black T-shirt as he worked the chrome. He always wore black: black Levi's, black tennis shoes, black jackets. Carlos called him Johnny Cash behind his back. Pauley's hair was cut very short. So short that several healed-over scalp wounds showed through, the largest of which was a horseshoe-shaped scar above his left ear.

"You going to start going out with this guy?" he asked as D.W.'s van pulled away.

"This was about something else," she said.

"It's obvious he's got a thing for you."

"Yeah, he's a nice guy."

"But?"

She put a hand on Pauley's muscular shoulder and picked which truth to tell him. What she said was, "I'm already seeing somebody." What she thought was, *I already have a fixer-upper house and car. One fixer-upper boyfriend in a lifetime is enough.*

Pauley answered as if she'd spoken her thoughts. "Yeah," he said. "You can do better." She wondered if she was that transparent.

He straightened and held out his hand. "Give me your keys," he said. "I'll wash your car."

She dug them out of her pocket and handed them over. They bartered wax jobs for repair work, and he still owed her for the water pump she had replaced on his van the week before.

"I've got to deliver this one," he said, indicating the Ferrari, "but I'll get to yours before you leave."

"You know Diane Bergman? Honda Prelude? Lived on Chenault?"

Pauley found a spot on the hood of the Ferrari

and bent over it, his chamois working to blend in the blemish. "What about her?"

"She's dead."

"Yeah?" He still didn't look up. His cheek hovered above the red glossy paint, checking for imperfections only he could see. "I didn't know her that well."

Fair enough, she thought. At least Pauley wasn't one of those types of people who claimed instant kinship with someone newly dead, thereby diverting sympathy and attention to himself.

She called the owner of the Ford and got an authorization to do the work. While waiting for the radiator shop to deliver her parts, she couldn't get Diane Bergman or Robin Davies out of her mind. Maybe Brentwood wasn't the safe haven people thought.

In the world she grew up in, sexual assaults were inevitable, like black eyes, and motorcycle injuries. You learned quickly never to get drunk around strange bikers. Or put yourself in a position where you were alone in a room with three or more of those guys. And when it did happen, it did. She had always viewed rape as an occupational hazard, given bikers' predilection toward it and the fact that sex was a commodity that she had often bartered. Everybody she knew got ripped off at one time or another.

And then there was that time with Culley. She had been sixteen, almost seventeen, and had temporarily left her father's little slice of hell for what she hoped would be a happier life. She moved into an apartment building they all called Tortilla Flats. It was on Rose Avenue, right on the border between the barrio and the exclusively black ghetto known to the locals as Ghost Town. The inhabitants of the Flats were a loose band of teens and twenty-year-olds. Their numbers fluctuated, as people moved on, got busted, or found religion. There were even a few like Karen, Asia's birth mother, who had left in the back of a coroner's wagon. It was also at the Flats that Munch had met Sleaze John, Asia's handsome, dark-skinned Latino father, although he died somewhere else.

God, she hadn't thought of that group for a long time, Sleaze, New York Jane, Brian, Gypsy, Farmer, all the others. How many of them were now dead, in jail, or living under a freeway overpass and advertising their needs on pieces of cardboard?

Culley was much older than the rest of them, possibly as old as thirty. It only took a moment to relive what he did to her that afternoon, how it hadn't made sense. Just another experience that was way behind her now. So many things felt as if they had happened to another person, the person she used to be. It was easy to disassociate from all that stuff. She couldn't imagine what it would feel like to be sexually assaulted now. One thing for certain, she wouldn't be forgiving and forgetting. No, she'd be damned pissed.

The loudspeaker above her head crackled and then Lou's voice called her name, announcing she had a call on line two. She took the call on the extension at the service desk. It was Robin.

"What did you mean by we would do more than talk?" she asked.

Munch pictured Robin hunched over her phone in her dark house. "I was thinking it would be good for you to get out of the house." She picked up a pen and tapped it on the desk blotter. "But on the ride home, D.W. said you believe this guy is going to come after you again."

"He is." Her voice was dull, flat. "I know he is. He called me."

"Who?" Munch asked.

"The guy. The rapist."

"What did he say?"

"That the next time would be better."

"Did you call the cops?"

"The detective assigned to my case was out. I left a message." She paused. "Yesterday. I'm still waiting for a callback."

"Change your number," Munch said.

"I have. More than once."

"Then call the cops back. Demand that they do something."

"They said there was nothing more they could do. They suggested I move."

"That's it?" Munch asked. "You're just supposed to give up your life? What a bunch of shit." If Robin was expecting a soft shoulder, she'd rung the wrong person. Besides, Munch figured, this woman needed to fight back or risk being lost forever.

"What choice do I have?"

Munch drew a *V* for Victory and circled it. "I've got a friend who's a cop."

"But I've already gone to the cops. You've seen the results."

"Yeah, I know what you mean. But, believe me, they're not all assholes. I'll talk to my friend and see if he can put some heat on for you."

"Thank you. I've been feeling so alone."

"What about your family?"

"I didn't want them to . . . be upset."

"You haven't told them?" Munch asked.

"My mother would have a stroke or worse. She'd want to come out here and move in with me. I had a hard enough time getting away from her the first time."

"Still, a little moral support might help you right now."

"I just can't," Robin said.

"What's the name of the cop who's handling the investigation?" Munch asked.

"Peter Owen. That's not your friend, is it?"

"No, I've never heard of him. What division is he out of?"

"West L.A. That's what it said on his card."

"I was planning on seeing my friend after work today," Munch said. "I'll tell him what's going on and call you."

"No," Robin said. "It would be easier if I called you."

"Oh, right," Munch said, remembering all those unretrieved messages on Robin's answering machine. "Of course."

The faces of the women look down on him from his trophy wall. He figures any woman who gets these kinds of pictures taken knows what guys are going to do with them. Actually, he's just as interested— even more so—in what goes on with his women above the neck as below. Besides, what they choose to reveal below leaves little to the imagination.

He feels as if he's been on an extended leave but soon must return to duty. It's Nam all over again. When he first returned stateside, he went up to the Bay Area. It was all hippies then. Hippies and liberals. Seemed like everywhere he went the returning vets were accused of killing babies and massacring helpless civilians. As if any of those people had any idea what it all meant. What it had been like. He learned to keep quiet about what he'd been, what he'd done.

The result was a loneliness so deep he is only now beginning to touch it. It's been unbearable for so long. He's still not sure where he found the strength to live.

Now he feels as if he's in the eye of a hurricane. It is quiet. But for how long? He is incredibly exhausted. So much is at risk. At the very least, his freedom. Jail. Prison. A trial. His balls shrink from the fear of it. Forget the business. His customers—

his hard-won clientele—would desert him. He would be penniless—alone—reviled. Those few who call themselves his friends would never understand.

Nobody knows true compassion until they're forced to break all of their own rules.

He sighs and turns to the pictures pasted on the wall by his bed. He doesn't blame the women all the way. They got it and want to flaunt it. That's understandable. His fingers trace the curves of Robin's thighs in the photo. He keeps the ones of Robin closest to him. Robin with her one-hundred-watt smile.

He laughs at his own unintentional joke. Then sobers quickly. Feeling ashamed at this joke that comes at his beloved's expense. She will forgive him and she *will* come around. Resistance has its limits. Robin just needs time. She needs the security of being shown who is the boss. All women do.

And somebody else needs to mind her own business. He will not tolerate interference. Lady Mechanic, indeed. Who does she think she's fooling?

CHAPTER 8

St. John opened Diane Bergman's address book and turned to the B's. The closest Bergman listed was an Alfred in Pacific Palisades. Alfred Bergman's business number prefix was the same as his home number. St. John called the work number.

"Bergman Florists," a woman answered.

"Is Al in?"

"I can get him for you."

"No, don't bother. I was planning on coming in. Will he be there in an hour?"

"Yes, we're open until five."

St. John asked for the address, jotted it down in his notebook, and then called out to Shue, who was in the hallway doing hand-to-hand combat with the vending machine.

"Are you ready to go make the Bergman notification?"

Shue gave the machine one more shake and then said, "Sure, sure."

Ten minutes later, Shue was seated in St. John's passenger seat. While St. John maneuvered through early-afternoon freeway traffic, Shue systematically searched his pockets.

"I want you just to tell this guy that Diane Bergman is deceased. Avoid the specifics."

"Yeah, yeah. I know," Shue said, examining a tiny wad of paper that had apparently made the trip through the washer and dryer. "No mention of murder. You're just there as a formality. I make the notification and we see what floats up." He finally found the object of his search, a roll of breath mints. He brushed off the pocket lint, unwrapped the foil, and offered one to St. John.

St. John grinned and took one. Shue was the perfect partner for the initial phase of the investigation. His air of confusion, almost befuddlement, made people want to explain things to him. Even St. John himself easily forgot the man was competent.

Twenty minutes later, they arrived at Bergman Florists. The front window was tastefully decorated with Halloween wreaths, cornucopias, and pumpkins. They entered the front door and were greeted by a jingling bell and the sweet smells of jasmine and gardenias. Indoor waterfalls provided gentle background noise and a sense of tropical humidity.

A man with salt-and-pepper hair and the deeply bronzed face of a dedicated sun worshiper was standing patiently by while a lady in a knit suit studied a photograph album full of flower arrangements. He looked up and said, "I'll be right with you."

"Alfred Bergman?" St. John asked, already having decided he definitely wasn't an "Al."

"Yes?" Bergman gave St. John a long up-and-down. When he turned to Shue, his smile lost some of its life.

"This is Mr. Shue of the Los Angeles Coroner's Office. I'm Detective Mace St. John." He gave the man a quick flash of his badge. "Do you have an office or somewhere we can have a word in private?"

Alfred Bergman pursed his lips to speak but seemed at a loss for the proper response. The woman behind the cash register froze in place. St. John swore he could see her ears perk.

Bergman snapped his fingers, and the woman behind the cash register came back to life. "Betty, please help Mrs. Ghormley." He put a hand briefly on the back of Mrs. Ghormley, who was still deeply engrossed with the catalog of flower arrangements.

He lifted his eyebrows for St. John's and Shue's benefit, then said, "Take all the time you need, dear." He raised a tanned hand and beckoned the two men to follow him toward the back of the store. His white silk shirt, tucked into tight-fitting designer jeans, billowed as he walked.

A standing screen divided the shop space and concealed a large industrial double stainless steel sink. Wooden drain boards held buckets of baby's breath and fern fronds. Blocks of green Oasis, rolls of florist wire, and sphagnum moss were stacked on shelves above the sink. Glass-fronted coolers held additional buckets of long-stemmed roses, lilies, and carnations.

They passed a thin, long-haired blond man spearing bamboo skewers through hibiscus blossoms. The three men entered a small office. St. John shut the door behind them. There were only two chairs, the padded one on casters that serviced the crammed desk and a three-legged stool. Bergman pulled out the desk chair and turned it so that it was facing out.

"Please," St. John said, indicating that Bergman sit. "Forget I'm here." He took up a position against the wall and focused on Shue.

Shue lowered himself onto the stool and fixed Alfred Bergman with an apologetic smile.

"Are you a relative of Diane Bergman?"

"I have a sister-in-law named Diane. Why? What's this about?"

"I'm sorry to have to inform you. Mrs. Bergman has been found dead."

"Oh," Alfred said, his posture deflating as his breath left him. "Where did you find her? I mean, what happened? Was it some sort of a car accident?"

One point for Alfred, St. John thought. No audible gasp, no sharp intake of breath for the sake of the investigator. Alfred was either genuinely stunned or he was a clever actor.

"I need a family member to ID the body," Shue

said. "If you're not up to it, perhaps there are other relatives in the area."

"I'll do it. The only family she has is some crazy aunt in Palm Springs." He lowered his tone to sotto voce. "Lives in one of those trailer communities." He pressed his fingertips to his lips and snorted demurely. "I was certain she'd outlast us all." He didn't seem disappointed.

"Anyone else that she was close to?"

"You mean like a boyfriend?"

"Boyfriend, girlfriend." Shue shrugged.

"No," Alfred said emphatically. "I mean, I'm sure she had friends, she was on enough committees. But if you're asking if she was seeing anyone romantically, then I'm sure I don't know. I doubt it. She wouldn't have done anything to endanger her public persona. Besides, she lived for my brother. Poor soul."

St. John wasn't sure as to which soul the man was referring, but he kept his questions to himself for the moment.

Shue leaned forward on his stool and clasped his hands between his open knees. "One of my duties as coroner is to work with the family members on how they want to take care of the remains. Are you the man I should be talking to?"

"Oh, I suppose," Alfred said, sighing deeply. Tears filled his eyes. "You know, we've just been through all this with my brother. He passed six months ago. Diane started her personal war on lung cancer, spending all his money on that cancer center."

"And everybody loved her?" Shue prompted.

Alfred pursed his lips. "Oh, sure. She was the queen of the charity circuit. Not the first time a woman from her background has bought her way into society." He waved his hand in front of his face, as if to erase the last words he'd spoken. "I don't mean any disrespect."

St. John made a dismissive shake of his head as if to say, *No problem, perfectly understandable.*

Alfred turned to him. "And you're the police?"

St. John opened his wallet and fished out a business card. "I've been assigned to investigate the death."

"Was she murdered?" he asked, looking aghast.

"Yes, sir," St. John said, thinking how the expression of shocked outrage suited Alfred. St. John wondered if he practiced it in the mirror. "When is the last time you saw Mrs. Bergman?"

"Last week. Last Tuesday."

"And where was this?"

"At the attorney's office. We had probate business. Oh God," he said. "I guess this changes everything."

St. John said, "What's the attorney's name?"

"Logan Sarnoff. He's also the executor." Alfred spun around to his desk and found a business card.

St. John started to copy the information on the card into his notebook, but Alfred stopped him with an exaggerated wave of his hand. "Keep it," he said. "I have others."

"Did Mrs. Bergman ever tell you that she was being threatened by anyone?"

"No, nothing like that."

"Did she have any enemies that you knew of?"

"God, no. She lived in Brentwood."

"I might have some more questions later," St. John said.

"Whatever I can do to help," Alfred said. "God, this is just too unbelievable."

On the way out to the car, Shue hiked up his trousers and scratched his nose. St. John noticed he'd missed a belt loop.

"So, sounds like you got yourself a real who-dunit," Shue said.

St. John tried not to betray his excitement. The Bergman murder was his first hot case since transferring to West L.A., and he'd been here for months. "Let's get on that autopsy as soon as possible."

Shue ran a hand through his hair, which up to that point had threatened to look kempt. "I'll do what I can to clear a space."

"Good, I can't wait." He knew to the uninitiated, those words would seem odd. But years ago the population of the world had divided for him into the "they" and the "we." The "we" being all those select individuals who dealt in death.

At four-fifteen, Munch went into the bathroom and changed out of her uniform into some cleaner, and coincidentally, more flattering, Levi's jeans and a T-shirt. She also kicked off her greasy work shoes and put on white tennis shoes. The bathroom was small, with only one stall. She was tying her laces when she noticed there was a half-inch-round hole in the tile just above the toilet paper holder. She put her eye to it, wondering if the hole went clear through to the men's bathroom that shared this wall. She couldn't see anything, but just to be safe, she stuffed it shut with a wad of toilet paper.

Lou was going to love this. Last month, the phone bill had been through the roof. Ninety three-dollar-a-minutes had been racked up to one of those sex lines. Between gas pumpers, mechanics, and the car wash guys, it was hard to say who was responsible. Lou solved the problem by putting a lockout on 900 numbers.

Her GTO was parked in front of the office, glowing from a fresh wax job. Pauley had left her keys on the floor. She saw that his van was gone, so she would have to wait until tomorrow to thank him. She loaded her trunk with what equipment and supplies she needed for Mace St. John's air-conditioning, and then left to pick up her kid from school.

Asia attended a Catholic school on the corner of Bundy and San Vicente. St. Teresa's was close to Munch's work, had a great after-school care program, and owned a fleet of vans. Like the wax jobs on Munch's limo and car, most of Asia's tuition was paid for in trade. Another plus about the private school was that all the kids wore uniforms. That meant there was one less decision to make during the morning scramble.

When Munch was a kid, before her mother died but when she was still old enough to go to school and have overnights at her classmates' houses, she learned that other people lived differently. Her friends didn't have their morning cereal poured by strangers or wonder if their mom would remember to do laundry. They took a lot of things for granted. Which is how it should be. How it would always be for Asia.

She turned now into the alley that bordered the playground. The school was surrounded on all sides by businesses: two restaurants, three banks, a stationery store, and a dress shop. Across the street there was a gas station and a Westward Ho market. Shoppers and every sort of delivery truck used the alley as a shortcut in between the hours of kids being dropped off and picked up from school.

The attendant on duty, a middle-aged woman, waved and called for Asia. Asia came running. Her tight brown curls—her "curlies"—bouncing and shoelaces trailing.

"*Konnichi wa,*" she said as she climbed into the car and dumped her coat and schoolbag on the floor of the backseat. Asia had a Japanese teacher this year, who was teaching her students different phrases.

Mother and daughter strapped on their seat belts. Munch had to open her door to free the left half of her lap belt. Asia took note.

"Mom," she said disapprovingly.

Munch offered no defense. When you're busted,

you're busted. As open as Asia was to learning new things, she also had a real cautious side. She insisted on seat belts, knee and elbow pads when skating or biking, and to Munch's disappointment, refused to go on roller-coaster rides. Which meant, of course, that Munch, too, was doomed to endless repetitions of "It's a Small World" when they went to Disneyland.

"I got you something," Munch said, reaching into the backseat.

"October?" Asia asked, eyes sparkling.

"Hot off the presses," Munch said, handing her daughter the latest issue of *Bride's* magazine. Asia also had a private collection of wedding paraphernalia left over from limo runs and kept her Barbie doll permanently decked out in veil and gown, a tiny silk flower bouquet at the ready.

"Cool," she said now, running her small hand over the glossy cover.

"How was school?"

"We learned a new song."

Oh no, Munch thought. *Anything but that.*

"It's a Japanese song." Without further encouragement Asia demonstrated. Which wouldn't be so bad except that what the kid lacked in tone and pitch perception she made up for in full-throated projection. Asia wanted to be in show business. She had the confidence for it; now all she needed was some kind of talent. The song had an endless number of verses or so it seemed after two blocks.

Munch had no idea if her daughter was pronouncing the words right or just making them up as she went along.

She interrupted at the light on Wilshire. "We're going to see Mace St. John."

"Yeah!" Asia responded. "And Sammy and Nicky?"

"Sure."

Munch smiled. She knew going to see Mace St. John, and by extension his dogs, would meet with the girl's wholehearted approval. She was at that age when she wanted a dog. She wanted a little brother, too, but Munch explained they would take things one at a time.

The sun was low in the sky. The brisk snap to the air was quickly turning to a chill. Asia was dressed only in her short-sleeved white cotton shirt and plaid pinafore.

"Where's your coat?"

Asia didn't look up from her magazine. "In the back."

Munch reached behind her and retrieved it. A note had been pinned to the front. *"Mind your own business,"* it read. *"If I needed to hurt you, I could."*

Munch's throat went dry. "Where did this come from?" she asked as calmly as possible. Heat shot through her. She felt sweat form in her armpits, under her collar.

"What is it?" Asia asked, reaching for the note.

Munch held it back, away from her grasp. "Did

you see who pinned this on your coat?" *What sick, limp-dicked son of a bitch?*

"I didn't even know it was there until just now."

Munch stuck the note in her shirt pocket and struggled to bring her breathing under control. All she could think of was getting to Mace St. John. He'd know what to do and have the power to do it. God damn it. She looked over at her precious little girl and asked with as light a tone as she could manage, "So, uh, how does the rest of that song go?"

CHAPTER 9

Mace St. John was underneath the Bella Donna when Munch pulled into one of the parking spaces provided for his siding of track. The dogs were with him but romped over to meet the new arrivals.

"Where's your ball, Nicky?" Asia asked the border collie mix. Nicky understood and went bounding off to retrieve a tennis ball. Sam, the husky-Lab, stayed behind to lavish Asia's willing face with kisses. The new dog, tied by a rope to the train car's ornate platform, whimpered loudly.

"Always the bridesmaid," Asia said, breaking free from Sam and going over to the tethered hound, "never the bride."

Munch opened her trunk and retrieved her air-conditioning gauges, a case of Freon, and her evacuator pump. St. John waved to her, smiling around the half-smoked cheroot clamped between his teeth. His shirtsleeves were pushed up past his elbows. He had grease on his hands. She walked over to where he was working. Her composure lessened with every step. By the time she got to him she was breathing hard and fighting back tears of rage.

"What happened?" he asked.

She showed him the note. "I found it pinned to Asia's coat when I picked her up today."

"At school?"

"Just now."

"Okay, get ahold of yourself."

For just a moment, her agitation switched to him. The first order of business shouldn't be calming the little lady. Besides, he was only seeing a tip of how she really felt. She was already holding on to herself as hard as she could. Not trusting herself to speak, she glared at him until he continued.

"Let's call the school. No, better yet, I'll call the watch sergeant over at the station and have him dispatch a unit. What kind of security do they have at the school?"

Munch thought of the middle-aged woman who presided over day care. "None to speak of. I mean, they don't let kids leave with strangers, but it would be pretty easy for anyone to get in there."

"I'll have the patrol officer speak to whoever is there and see if anyone unknown to them was around the school today. That's all we can do for now."

"Should I keep Asia out of school tomorrow?"

"I'll have to think about that."

She looked over at her kid. Asia was still happily playing with the dogs. She'd made them all capes out of old beach towels and they were deep into a superhero fantasy. She was calling the new dog "Brownie."

Munch and St. John went inside the Bella Donna to make the calls. As always, she was slightly overwhelmed when she stepped inside the train. It was like being instantly transported to another world, another era. The walls were covered with red velvet flocked wallpaper. Doorknobs and light fixtures were ornate brass affairs. The top halves of the windows were leaded glass. The lime-green satin shades were up, letting in the light but more important, providing a clear view of Asia.

In the far right corner of the lounge section, behind the small antique practice piano, and across from the bar, was a small mahogany table that came out from the wall. As with most things on the train, this piece of furniture served a dual purpose. The table lifted out and the bench seats on either side slid down and together to form a bed. There were small brass hooks in the ceiling where the porter would hang a curtain for privacy. The phone was on the table amid a mass of paperwork.

St. John called the police station first and explained the situation to the watch commander. The desk sergeant promised to dispatch a unit immediately and to call back with any news. He would also run patrol checks throughout the day

and add the incident to the briefing items at roll
call.

Munch next called the school. The principal, Mrs.
Frowein, was still there and was understandably
upset when she heard what had happened. Munch
didn't reassure her that it was probably nothing, or
some kind of stupid prank. Whoever had done this
had crossed way over the prank line by bringing
Asia into it. Mrs. Frowein promised Munch unceas-
ing vigilance in the school yard from now on.

"Let's get to work on your AC," Munch told St.
John. She wanted to make use of the available light,
but even more than that, she needed to retreat to
the safety of work. Mechanical problems she knew
she could deal with. Unlike the rest of life, where
either the same issues kept popping up to haunt
her or brand-new shit hit that she didn't even see
coming. And only time would tell if she needed to
worry about something. By then, of course, it was
too late.

They walked back outside. She checked the AC
pump for oil and found it was filled to the proper
level. St. John hovered over her with his hands
extended, as if he, too, felt the need to do something. "Bring over your air compressor," she said.

He wheeled out his portable compressor and
plugged it into one of the extension cords he had
running from the storage building next door. The
spur of track that the Bella Donna rested on was
private property. Munch knew St. John had spent
many hours following miles of track to find such a

location. When he stayed there full-time, he was allowed unlimited access to water and electricity. His presence added security to the industrial park on the V of Exposition and Olympic. Even though it was five minutes from the Brentwood Country Club and the miles of professional buildings on Wilshire, you only had to go a few short miles south to run into serious homeboy territory. The flavor of the neighborhoods in L.A. changed just that quickly. Anyone who'd ever gotten lost downtown could tell you that. Even on the West Side you had Marina del Rey sharing boulevards with Venice Beach. Pasta and legumes on one side of the road, spaghetti and beans on the other.

She knew about both worlds now, she thought, as she hooked up her gauges to the fittings on St. John's air-conditioning unit and attached the outgoing hose to her evacuation pump.

"What does that thing do?" he asked.

"Sucks out all the air and moisture. This will also tell me if you have a leak."

St. John turned on the air compressor, and they waited while it built up enough pressure to operate the evacuator. The compressor's noisy pumping made small talk impractical.

She waited until the AC gauges showed fourteen inches of vacuum, then she closed the valves. She drew a finger across her throat and pointed at the compressor.

He shut it off and the air was filled with an abrupt silence. She looked for Asia, feeling a sud-

den, terrible panic. Asia was still where she had
been moments earlier when Munch looked. But
isn't that what they always say? *I only looked away
for an instant.*

"Now what?" St. John asked, meaning his AC.

Without turning to him she said, "I want to wait
about five minutes, make sure the system holds a
vacuum." Asia wandered over and sat near them
on the platform steps. The big dogs lay panting at
her feet. Brownie was in her lap. Munch thought
about Diane Bergman, still not quite believing her
death was real, that she'd never see her again. Then
she thought about Robin Davies and how shitty it
felt to have your peace of mind ripped off. Also,
how relatively easily somebody could do that to
you. "I need your help with something else."

"Oh?"

"A woman who lives near the station, a customer actually. She was assaulted." Munch looked
at Asia. The little girl didn't appear to be paying
attention to the conversation, but Munch knew
from long experience that little ears never closed.
"She was *personally* assaulted. Guy told her he'd
come back. She's living like a prisoner in her own
home. I told her we could help her."

"You mean like provide protection?"

"I was thinking more along the lines of getting
involved in the case."

"You were, huh?"

"Yeah. I mean, you could put in a word, right?
Make sure she doesn't just get swept aside."

"What's your part in this?" he asked.

"I like her and she's really hurting. Just let me introduce you to her. And you're going to need me there when you guys talk. At least at first. I told her to call me tomorrow morning at work."

"Did she make a police report?"

"Oh yeah, she got assigned a case number and everything."

"Who's the detective?"

"Peter Owen."

St. John made a noise through his teeth, like steam escaping.

"Do you know him?"

"Yeah," he said with a disgusted tone, "I know him."

"What? Isn't he any good?"

"He's about to retire. I tell you, once these guys pick a date, they should just pack their shit and go." He cast a guilty glance over to where Asia was sitting, but the little girl hadn't reacted. She was too engrossed in her mission to teach her new best friend Brownie to shake hands. "Most of these old-timers don't have a life outside of the department. They don't know what they're going to do with themselves. All they do all day once they know they're leaving is talk to other retirees."

"Kind of like an inmate fearing his release date?" she asked.

"Exactly. Guys get institutionalized. They start running scared, too, like getting superstitious, even if they never were before. Half of them die within five years of leaving the job. That's why I'm never going to quit."

"Where does this leave Robin?"

"Probably not in very good shape. I doubt if there's been any follow-through. It's like this: 'Big case, big headache; small case, small headache; no case, you figure it out.'"

"Great."

"I'll make some time tomorrow to swing by and talk to her."

"Thanks. I know she's feeling pretty desperate."

"I'll meet with her, but there might not be anything I can do. I hope you didn't promise her anything."

"Only that you were a great guy."

"Yeah, I'm a sweetheart," he said, his lips puckering in distaste.

"You are," she said.

St. John climbed aboard the Bella Donna and fired up the diesel generator. It belched out black smoke from its exhaust and then leveled out to a steady knocking idle. Diesel engines always sounded like they had a rod knock. They smelled bad, too, like oil and gas burning at the same time. Diesel-engined automobiles had been another reaction to the so-called gas shortage, and she hated the things.

Charging the AC system took another ten minutes. Miraculously, everything seemed to work.

"There you go," Munch said, picking up her tools. She turned in Asia's direction. "C'mon, honey. It's getting dark. Come inside."

"I'm hungry," Asia said.

"I ordered us a pizza," St. John said. "Should be here soon."

"You did?" Munch asked. "Is Caroline coming over?"

"Not tonight. She had meetings at work."

Munch felt a little thrill. So it would be just the three of them. Playing house. *Down, girl,* she told herself, *he's not the one.*

Fifteen minutes later the delivery guy showed up with the food. He didn't seem to have any problem finding the place. St. John had probably used the service a lot in the last year when he had been separated from Caroline. He paid the guy and must have given him a generous tip, judging from the bounce in the kid's step as he left.

They carried the pizza inside.

Munch brought out three plates from the kitchen and as many paper towels. She poured Asia a glass of milk and got a Coke for herself. St. John popped himself a beer.

Munch tore off a slice for Asia and set it down in front of her.

"Ah," Asia said, raising her right hand with her slim, brown forefinger pointing skyward. "*Domo arigato.*"

St. John raised an eyebrow.

"Don't ask," Munch warned.

He ate two slices before broaching the subject of the threat Munch received. "Have you, uh, come up with any likely candidates for your situation?"

"I've thought of a few, but they're all pretty thin."

He made each of the dogs sit and then rewarded them with pizza crust. "I'll see what impressions the lab can get off the paper."

Asia banged her milk glass down on the table. "You're acting like I'm not even here. What *are* you guys talking about?"

"Rescuing fair damsels in distress, m'lady," St. John told her. Then he grabbed her hand and kissed the back of it with a flourish.

"Yeah, right," Asia said, rolling her eyes, an expression she had begun using before she could speak. Munch wasn't fooled for a minute. Asia positively glowed when St. John turned his full attention on her. It was hard not to. Munch wondered once more what would have happened if St. John had stayed separated from Caroline. In matters of romance, timing was everything.

Still holding the little girl's hand, he said, "Honey, you know you're not supposed to talk to strangers."

"Yeah," she said, the seriousness of his tone making her drop her usual attitude.

"Even if that stranger has a cute little puppy, or a bunny, you don't go with him or near him if your mommy isn't around. Even if he *or she* says he knows your mommy, you go tell a teacher."

Asia nodded solemnly. Munch felt a deep resentment that this conversation had to take place. She didn't want Asia growing up any faster than she had to.

"Draw me a picture in school tomorrow," he said, letting Munch know he'd made the decision that Asia should attend her classes.

"And with that, we should be on our way." She shrugged at St. John and made the universal hand symbol for "I'll call you tomorrow."

Munch was exhausted when they finally got home. She made Asia wake up and walk under her own power. The little girl weighed fifty pounds now, too much to be carrying anymore. But Munch did bring in Asia's lunch box and knapsack of school supplies. The front porch was dark.

"I have to pee," Asia whined.

"All right, we're almost there." Munch shifted her load to her left hand and brought the key to the door with her right. Typically, the phone started to ring.

"Shi-oot," Munch said out loud when the key wouldn't go in the door. Even though this act of separating the door key from the rest on the ring was a rote task she performed nightly, tonight she had selected the wrong key. By the time she got the door open, the phone stopped ringing and whoever it was didn't leave a message. She found that more disquieting than she wanted to admit.

The phone rang again. Asia reached for it.

"No," Munch said, with more force than she intended. Asia jumped back. Munch picked up the receiver, tried to give Asia a comforting smile, and said, "Hello?"

"You have a nice house," the strangely distorted voice said. It vibrated, sounding like the voice of that robot in that old television show *Lost in Space*. The cadence was slow, as if the speaker needed an extra moment to prepare each word. "But you really shouldn't take the same route home every day."

She felt confused. Her mind grasped for a face, an identity to attach to this person. "Garret?" she asked, knowing immediately that she was wrong. Now the fear was setting in. She flashed to a quick image of one of those cop shows where some mob informant was being interviewed. You could only see the guy's silhouette. He was always in a dark room, with a baseball cap pulled low, and his voice electronically altered so none of the guys he was snitching on could identify him.

"Not Garret," the voice said. "Not the guy you fuck once a week."

"Who is this? What do you want?"

"Love. Understanding." He made a noise that sounded like someone humming on helium. She interpreted it as a sigh, especially when he added, "I'm doing the best that I can here. You, of all people, should understand that. So back off, bitch."

CHAPTER 10

WEDNESDAY

St. John got to work at six the next morning and went directly downstairs to the roll call room. Stacks of file boxes filled one corner. Bulletin boards displayed mug shots of the top ten predators currently at large in the area.

He leaned against one of the room's support pillars, near the front, close to the podium. Uniformed cops sat at the rows of tables facing a small stage equipped with video equipment and chalkboard. The scent of strong, black coffee filled the air.

He hated going to morning briefings, which were mostly for patrol anyway. Things had changed so much from when he was in uniform. In the sixties and seventies, the seating arrangement had been determined by the hash marks on your sleeve. One for every five years on the force. The old-timers sat in the back row, the rookies in the front. There was one color: blue.

Then, with this eighties decade, had come the racial polarization. Blacks sitting with their own, Hispanics banding together. Memos being handed out almost daily on the correct wording to use. *Negro* or *Neg.* was no longer acceptable, nor was *Mexican. Latino* was okay. *Chicano* was not. He rolled with it all. Just as long as they got to keep catching bad guys.

But the newest trend was the most disturbing yet. With the passing of new antidiscrimination laws, the department had lowered its height requirements. This had also paved the way for more women to join the force. In his day, a guy was a dwarf if he was only five foot ten. He'd wear built-up boots when he went on patrol. Now everywhere you looked there were, as his less sensitive colleagues referred to them, the C&R's: cunts and runts.

Truly, there was nothing more ridiculous than some little coppette or midget with a special-order twenty-two-inch-waist Sam Browne utility belt. Barely enough room to cram on all the required gear: Mace, cuffs, ammo, holster, nightstick, Handie-Talkie radio. The proportion of equipment to muscle was at a dangerous ratio and equally ineffective, in his opinion. Like some little kid playing dress-up cop.

The irony was that it was turning out that women made better patrol cops than men did, especially when the situation called for less than brute force.

Coppettes were better problem solvers, more prone to negotiation than intimidation, and they consequently garnered fewer civilian complaints. And, boy, wasn't that the name of the game, especially on the affluent West Side where every citizen seemed to know the mayor and wanted special consideration. Only the diplomats survived here.

The downside of this new order was that you couldn't get through roll call without singing happy fucking birthday to someone while he or she blew out the candles on a cake. It wasn't a police station, it was a goddamn sorority. Everybody hugging, announcing engagements and babies. He didn't even want to think about Valentine's Day. It was going to be a circus.

The watch commander, Sergeant Flutie, brought the meeting to order and called on St. John.

Mace walked to the front of the room and waited a moment for the scuffling of chairs and clearing of throats to die down. When he had everyone's attention he began. "Yesterday, at some time between two and four-thirty P.M., a threatening note was pinned to the unattended jacket of a young, female student at St. Teresa's elementary school on the corner of San Vicente and Bundy. There's an alley that runs along the south end of the school that separates the playground from the church and classrooms. I have no description of a vehicle or suspect, but to reach the area where the children store their coats, the suspect would have approached through that alley."

Sergeant Flutie stepped up next to St. John. "We've promised the principal, Mrs. Frowein, high police visibility for the rest of the week. Stop all suspicious characters. I expect FI cards and photographs."

"Thank you, Sergeant," St. John said.

"Any other business?" the sergeant asked. St. John held up the morning paper. The Bergman murder had made the front page, below the fold. There was a photograph of Diane Bergman culled from the paper's society page archive and a brief statement from St. John making all the usual reassurances. St. John wrote the license plate number of Diane's Honda Prelude on the blackboard and asked the patrol units to keep an eye out for the victim's vehicle. Nodding heads responded.

St. John was halfway up the stairway when he heard a female voice announce a patrol *officer's* pregnancy. He groaned and took the stairs two at a time until he reached the detective squad room on the second floor. Pete Owen wasn't at his desk so St. John left a note in his box and checked the time. The autopsy of Diane Bergman was scheduled for 7:30 A.M. If he rushed, he would just make it.

Dr. Sugarman was all business when St. John met him over the autopsy table. Diane Bergman's nude body lay before them. The tape had been dusted for fingerprints and then carefully peeled from her face on Monday. A light dusting of black powder still streaked the dead woman's cheek. St. John had not told Munch what the black residue was, because the tape had been the crime scene information he had chosen to withhold.

The negligee Diane Bergman had been wearing when her body was discovered had since been carefully removed, all loose particles shaken loose over clean white paper, and stored in an evidence locker. The flimsy negligee was described poetically on the coroner's inventory as robin's-egg blue. It was further described as rayon, size small, manufactured by Wacoal. Also listed on the property sheet were one diamond ring and one gold wedding band.

The medical examiner began his examination with a thorough visual inspection of the dead woman. He noted several hairline scars running the length of her face anterior to each ear and along the cephalic ridge of her forehead, the texture of her skin, and state of nourishment.

"Face-lift," he told St. John. "Looks like some liposuction, too." He spent a full minute on each of the burn sites, using a high-powered magnifying glass.

"The cop at Rampart was correct," Sugarman said, without looking up. He pointed to the damage on the victim's left breast. "You see the center of the wound is pale and how the peripheral zone is bright red. This is typical of electrical injuries. The heat generated by the electrical charge pushes the blood out into the capillaries. In essence, it boils." Sugarman directed St. John's attention to a second similar wound, this one on the victim's right shin. "This one will be the exit path of the current. You'll notice it's a larger wound." He placed a plastic ruler against the burn and announced its diameter in centimeters. It was larger than the other burn by sixteen millimeters. An assistant chronicled that fact with a camera.

Sugarman took a scraping of the white soot that peppered the corpse's torso and then swabbed the different orifices of the body for traces of seminal fluid, blood, or skin cells not her own.

"I don't see any signs of sexual penetration," he said. He pried open the corpse's mouth and looked inside. "Hmm."

"What?"

"The tongue isn't bitten through. That, too, might be a pertinent negative," Sugarman said into the microphone dangling above the body. The coroner and his assistant rolled the body over. St. John's eyes were drawn to the puncture wound created by the coroner's liver thermometer. The small opening had been circled, initialed, and dated with black ink to indicate origin. A rippled crease about a quarter inch thick encircled the dead woman's waist.

St. John pointed to it and asked, "Ligature mark?"

Sugarman glanced over. "You could say that. It's a panty hose line." He moved his magnifying glass up her spine. "Let's get a picture of this," he said, pointing to a rectangular indentation in the skin at the base of the neck.

"Label?" St. John asked, bending in for a closer look.

"Probably," Sugarman said, laying down his ruler

beside the impression. "As I'm sure you know," Sugarman began. He often started sentences this way. In his desire to be thorough, he was often redundant. He took extreme care to do his job correctly. St. John had long ago discovered that the only way to get Sugarman to arrive at his ultimate diagnosis was to wade through his personal flowchart of steps. One at a time.

"In death," Sugarman continued, "blood stagnates within vessels, muscles lose their tone, skin its elasticity, circulation ceases. The outer layers of the body take on doughlike qualities. Objects pressed against dead skin before full rigor and subsequent to fixed lividity create clear and lasting impressions."

He stepped back to allow the photographer in to chronicle the imprint on the back of Diane Bergman's neck. Then he turned to his assistant. "Bring back the article of clothing this woman was discovered in. I want to photograph that label side by side with this mark."

St. John exhaled through his nose and sneaked a look at the wall clock.

It was almost forty-five minutes later when Sugarman made the Y-cut and laid the body open, reflecting back the layers of fat and tissue as if he were unwrapping a macabre present. "See this?" he asked, poking at the heart muscle. "You see how swollen and hard all the muscles and deep tissue are? The body conducts electricity through veins and bone." He traced the path of the current with a gloved finger. The line of muscle and tissue between entry and exit wounds had a brownish tint.

"Would household current be enough to do this?" St. John asked.

"Two-twenty perhaps. As you probably know, regular one-ten household current is relatively low voltage. It can be fatal, but this is due to ventricular fibrillation, an interruption of the heartbeat. The damage I'm seeing here is much more brutal. The heart in this woman is virtually cooked."

"What else would produce this sort of damage?"

"High voltage, such as lightning, a transformer, high-tension power lines."

"Is there any way this application of voltage wouldn't be fatal?" St. John asked.

"Certainly. If it had been applied for a shorter duration or hadn't been directed through vital organs."

"What do you mean?"

"If the electrodes had been attached to either leg, the current would have followed femur to pelvis, never going through any vital organs. Current always seeks ground through the path of least resistance."

"Can it be directed?"

"Sure," Sugarman said. "That's the whole principle of the electric chair. Electrode plates are attached to the condemned prisoner's head and ankles so that the body becomes part of the circuit. Whoever did this left nothing to chance."

Sugarman lifted out the intestines. "You want anything special besides tox and stomach contents?"

"Whatever you think," St. John said. "Give me the works."

By seven-thirty, Munch was already on her third cup of coffee. Asia was in Lou's office, watching cartoons on the small television he kept in there. Usually it was tuned to the financial channel. Their routine never varied, Munch realized. A psychopath could set his watch by it. Monday through Friday during the school year, Asia rode with Munch to work. At eight-fifteen, one of the school vans arrived to collect her. At four-thirty on those same days, Munch picked Asia up at the school and went directly home. The weekends were another steady schedule of dance classes and ball games at the park. Saturday night was Munch's and Garret's date night, or as Munch had come to think of it privately, sex night.

She felt a pang of something resembling guilt when she realized her relationship with Garret was the last thing she thought of when she inventoried her daily life. She hadn't even considered calling him last night to tell him of the phone call and the threat to Asia. He got so pissy when she mentioned Mace St. John, and the cop's name would have surely come up.

A picture of Garret's bearded face came to mind with that sappy expression he wore when he looked at her. The knowledge of what he was feeling and what she could not feel irritated her. Life would be much simpler if their feelings for each other were more in balance. Maybe that was too much to hope for in any relationship.

They'd been going out for a few months, since the end of summer. He was such a great package. Sexually, they were more than compatible. He was the right age, had a good job, he didn't drink because he didn't care to, not because he couldn't. He even laughed at her jokes. What was it going to take? And why did the sound of his laughter have to grate on her ears?

She also hadn't called her A.A. sponsor, Ruby. Their relationship had been strained since August when Ruby suggested that Munch might want to go out with her son, Eddie. *Yeah, right,* she had thought as soon as Ruby said it. *It would be a great deal for Eddie, wouldn't it?* All three hundred pounds of him. Eddie lived in a room his mother fixed up for him in the garage. Eddie also had every ailment known to obese drunks including eczema and dandruff and high blood pressure. The last was evidenced by bulging eyes and his crimson, perpetually sweating face. And here was Ruby, the proud mother, Munch's sponsor, suggesting Munch give the boy a whirl. If Munch had presented such a catch in the form of another guy not related to Ruby, her sponsor and supposed friend would have wasted no time illuminating his many drawbacks. She'd be the first to point out that the guy wasn't self-supporting and at thirty didn't have any prospects. Much less that the most sobriety he seemed capable of stringing together was thirty days. But Ruby loved the big tub and felt responsible for his failed life. So much so that on top of enabling him she was willing to sacrifice Munch to him. Of course, Munch hadn't voiced any of these sentiments out loud.

Her thoughts were interrupted by the ringing phone and Lou's announcement over the loudspeaker that she had a call. It was Robin.

"Did that cop ever call back?" Munch asked after they dispensed with the hi's and how-are-you's.

"No, and I left him another message."

"All right. Forget him for now. My friend Mace St. John and I will stop by later to discuss your, ah, assault." She realized she was dancing around using the *rape* word. And again she wished that there was one person in her life with whom she could be unswervingly honest. More and more she was noticing that the path to happy destiny was strewn with countless eggshells.

"I'll call the gate and let them know you're coming," Robin said.

"Don't expect us before mid-morning," Munch told her.

"I'm not going anywhere." She made a short bark of a laugh that turned into a coughing jag.

Munch chewed her lip, and then decided against telling Robin about the note or the phone call—at least for the moment. It was still only a possibility that those two things had any relation to

Robin, yet she couldn't ignore the timing of the two incidents. "Robin, after we talked yesterday, did you tell anyone about it?"

"No, why?"

"How about when you called Detective Owen? What did you say in the message you left?"

"I just asked him to call me and gave him my number. Why?"

"I like to keep track of who knows what."

After hanging up with Robin, she paged Mace St. John. He called back within minutes and told her that he had made the morning shift aware of the situation and they were adding the alley behind the school to their patrol route. With luck, the police presence would be enough to deter any wrongdoer. She told him about the most recent call.

"You make a report?" he asked.

"I'm telling you."

"I'm not at the station," he said. "You need to document all of this, get the wheels of justice turning. When I get back to my desk, I'll call the phone company, have them put a trap on your line. One at the gas station, too. Don't tell anyone about it."

"Not even Lou?"

"Nobody."

"What should I do if he calls again?" she asked. "Do I need to keep him talking for any length of time?"

"No, it only takes a few seconds to trap the call. Let me know when and if it happens, and I'll handle it from there."

"Fine. I really don't want to give this guy any more power than I have to. I don't even want to think about it anymore. Last night, I scared the shit out of Asia. Every time the phone rings now, my heart races. But what really pisses me off is that rattling me is more than likely just what he wants."

"You're probably right. It doesn't hurt to take precautions."

"I am, I have, and believe me, I will."

When the school van arrived, Munch walked Asia to its door. How many times had she just let the kid run out there? And how many times when she was busy with a customer or on the phone had she scarcely given the driver or the van a second look?

After Asia climbed in back and strapped herself in, Munch came around to the driver's window. The driver was Mr. Mars, an affable black man with gold in his front teeth and a ready laugh.

"How you doing today?" Munch asked.

"Fine. Fine," he said. "Yourself?"

"Not so good." She lowered her voice so that Asia wouldn't overhear and then recounted the events of yesterday, beginning with the note found on Asia's jacket, and culminating with the threatening call.

Mr. Mars seemed to age a bit, with some of the light going out in his eyes, his usual smile fading.

"I tell you what I'm going to do," he said. "I'm gonna bring these children to school today and wait. I won't leave until each and every one of them is safely back in the arms of their parents."

Munch squeezed his arm, choked out a thanks. He patted her hand and told her to try not to worry.

At eight-thirty, she went on a test drive in a Chrysler New Yorker that had a noise in the rear end that worried the customer. The noise turned out to be a bad tire. The tread had separated, making a thump. There was also a bad shimmy at forty. It never ceased to amaze her what vehicle owners failed to notice.

A familiar black Mercedes was pulling into the station when she returned. She hoped it was there for gas only, but that wasn't going to be the case.

The Mercedes drove past the pumps and headed for the lube bay. She gave the Chrysler tire job to Carlos, who was happy enough to make the ten bucks. Not like Stefano, who felt changing oil and mounting tires were beneath his dignity.

Her first impulse was to duck into the storeroom and wait out the guy in the Mercedes. But, of course, she wasn't going to do that. She hated it when the other mechanics sat on their asses, putting out the thousand-yard stare when undesirable customers pulled in for service. Not dealing with a problem was the coward's way of making it go away and didn't always work. Besides, Lou had named her service manager and would expect her to handle this guy.

She stuck her grease rag in her back pocket and went out to see what "Frank" Fahoosy's complaint was this time. The name on his registration was Farhood Fahoosy. He told Pauley that his

family were friends of the Shah and had to flee
Iran five years ago when the Ayatollah took over
in '79.

And you believed him? Munch had wanted to ask
but didn't. It seemed like every Persian she met
claimed a close personal relationship with the
deposed ruler.

Fahoosy pulled up to the first lube bay, got out of
his car, and stood by his rear tire, his dark eyebrows
raised and lips pursed in an expression of exasperation. Like many of the Middle Eastern men who fre-
quented the station, Fahoosy was wickedly handsome. Black hair and eyes so dark that there was no
distinction where pupil ended and iris began. He
trained those exotic eyes on her now.

"Problem?" she asked.

Lou had also seen Fahoosy pull up and was
standing in the doorway of the office, waiting for
Munch to communicate whether she needed him
or not. She locked eyes with her boss and made a
slight upward lift of her head. Lou caught her
meaning and approached.

"This is unacceptable," Fahoosy said, pointing
to his rear tire.

She looked down at the chrome rim and wished
she'd never sold this guy a set of tires. The negotia-
tions for the low-profile Pirellis had taken half a
morning, and he had managed to get the spin-
balancing thrown in for free. At least she had
thought far enough ahead to pretend she charged
for valve stems, too.

Lou walked over and stuck out his hand. "Frank, how are you?"

Fahoosy took the proffered hand, his cuff pulling back to reveal a watch heavy with diamonds and gold chunks. According to his business card he was a producer. In Los Angeles that could mean many things, including nothing.

"This tire needs to be balanced again," he said. "It was not done properly and now bounces me all over the road."

Munch looked down at the wheel in question and noticed the lead wheel weight near the valve stem. She tugged at Lou's sleeve and pointed at the weights.

"Just a second, Frank," Lou said, and pulled Munch over to the side. "What?"

"I never balanced that tire," she told him, speaking softly so he would have to lean closer. "On a chrome rim like that, I always put the weights on the inside so they don't show."

"What are you saying? The guy swapped tires to get a free balance job?"

"That's right."

"Look, just go ahead and do it. It'll only take you a few minutes and it'll get the guy out of our hair." Lou was of the school that any customer was a good customer.

"That's not the point," she said. She was angry now . . . mostly at herself for letting greed overpower caution. When Fahoosy had first come in, she'd seen the obvious clues to the guy's nature: the wire coat hanger where the antenna used to be and the key scrapes up one door. She'd also seen four bald tires and gone out of her way to be nice to the guy. She had ignored the signs of his unpopularity, had given him the benefit of the doubt.

As a rule, Munch let her compassion to her fellow man go only so far, especially at the workplace. Fahoosy had also burned Pauley out of a wax job by stopping payment on his check—a fact that only surfaced with yesterday's mail. Now this.

"C'mon, Frank," Lou said, clapping the guy on the back as if they were old friends. He could do that, too. Pretend as if he liked someone for the good of the business. It hurt her face to smile at Fahoosy, but she did. Lou expected her to rise to any occasion.

"Let's let her work," he said now, "and I'll buy you a cup of coffee."

Munch waited until the two men were out of sight around the corner before she opened the trunk. The spare tire wasn't even bolted down. A mass of loose videotapes surrounded it. Movies with titles like *Naughty Nurses* and *Deep and Deeper.* Figured.

Munch thought of her own brief career in film. Flower George had set it up with this guy who drove a Corvette—a convertible. He was a young guy, too, and dressed sharp—not the regular sort of man who waved her to his car for a quick exchange of what he wanted for what she needed.

The guy said he could spot talent. Photogenic

gold. He said she had it, and she had let herself
believe for one brief, exhilarating moment that
maybe she had found a way out of her life. That he
was going to show her some magical escape from
old men's groping hands, her father's included.
His being the worst. She had been dumb enough to
go for the so-called filmmaker's line.

No, not dumb, she corrected herself. Take the
judgment out of it. If there was one thing she tried
to communicate to the women she sponsored, it
was to have compassion for their former selves and
to treat their current selves as if they were someone
they loved. Fake it till you make it, she'd tell them
when they would call, crying how difficult it was
to change so much about their lives. She counseled
her "babies" in the same manner she had been
counseled, by sharing her experience, strength, and
hope. She told newly sober women that they didn't
get screwed up all at once, and that they wouldn't
find their issues magically resolved all at once
either. When she told them these things, she was
also reminding herself.

So, no, she hadn't been dumb so much as she
had been naive back then. Oh sure, at sixteen she
had felt old enough for anything and plenty world-
wise. But now, with a twenty-eight-year-old
woman's perspective it was clear to her how young
sixteen really was. No match for some slick guy with
a pearly smile and earnest eyes, who, judging by his
car and clothes, had his shit pretty well together.
And he was telling her she was beautiful—had

something special. The very thing she suspected and was trying to convince herself of at the time. Somehow he had known how to prey on that.

She had gone with him to his "studio." He told her what to do and she let him direct her. Later, drowning her shame at the bar, she had wondered if there had even been film in his camera or if that was part of the lie. He never called back. For years afterward she had sneaked surreptitious glances at the covers of the sex rags they sell from the corner vending machines. She always looked at the girls' faces on the covers, scared spitless that one day she would see her own looking back at her with her tongue curled provocatively and eyes half-closed in a come-hither-and-do-me look.

How would she live that one down if the photos were to surface now?

It wasn't as if she didn't admit to most of her past life openly, especially when it would help someone else, like at an A.A. meeting. Even then she liked to work up to the worst parts. People liked to act as if they were cool with anything. Hey, it's the eighties, they'd say. But really you never knew. Of course, an audience of recovering alcoholics and addicts tended to be a much more tolerant crowd than, say, the PTA.

Garret knew. She would never enter into a close relationship with a man without telling h..n her history. He had taken the news of her past almost too well. She suspected it thrilled him a little, to be with such a former bad girl.

For the most part, it was safer to just keep your mouth shut about certain things. Flower George had taught her that, too. But then again, if the story of her past came out, so be it. Might even be liberating. One less thing to hide. Another advantage she had was that stacked against all she'd been through, there weren't that many big deals.

She slid the tire toward her and stuck her fingers through the center hub hole. Lifting a tire out of a trunk was awkward. No leverage could be applied; she had to rely solely on arm muscles. She could have asked one of the guys to help, but she never did unless it was something they would be asking for help with if the situation were reversed. Like putting a standard transmission back in after a clutch job or setting a cylinder head down over a new gasket. Nobody was ever going to accuse her of not pulling her weight.

Her size made it necessary for her to employ a variety of tricks when lifting. If a vehicle was on the rack, she could handle even one-ton truck tires by balancing them on her leg first and then bouncing them to the ground. But for now all she could do was grunt a little and heave. Fortunately the Mercedes rim was an alloy and lighter than its steel counterparts.

She leaned the spare against the back bumper and shut the trunk. The inside of the rim was dirty with old grease and road grit, further proving her theory that Frank had pulled a switcheroo. The shop's brand of wheel weights were still hammered firmly on the inside lip of the rim. She jacked up the back of the Mercedes, zipped off the lug bolts with her air gun, and put the wheel she had already balanced back on the car. It would have been less work just to balance the swapped spare, but there was principle involved, and that always took precedence over effort.

She rolled the tire that had been on the car into the office and leaned it against the wall. She was letting the jack down when Frank and Lou walked up the driveway holding Styrofoam cups from the bakery next door.

Lou had a cup in each hand. "All set?" he asked, handing her one already doctored just the way she liked it.

"Take it away," she said.

After Fahoosy left, Lou went back in the office to reconcile the morning's books and figure out his next gas load. A moment later he called Munch's name. She came to the doorway.

He pointed at Fahoosy's spare. "What's this about?"

"The detail guys must have forgotten to put that back into Fahoosy's trunk. They'll have to call him later. He can pick it up when he comes in to make good on the check he gave them."

"This is the kind of shit I'm talking about," he said. "You go out of your way to find trouble."

CHAPTER 11

Munch started to offer a defense but stopped when the phone rang. Lou answered with the standard "Bel-Air Texaco." She took the opportunity to walk away.

She grabbed the key to a Ford Mustang off the work order and read the customer's complaint. The engine was stalling at stoplights, cutting out on acceleration, and idling roughly. Sounded like it had a misfiring cylinder.

The Mustang was parked next to Pauley's wash stall by the north driveway. There was a hose there and it was in a far corner of the lot.

According to Lou, bad luck and financial reversals had hounded Pauley for years. He'd once even owned his own gas station but had lost it to the tax man. It must be pretty humbling for Pauley, Munch thought as she watched him run soapy mitts over the hood of a Lincoln Continental, to be merely leasing what amounted to three parking spaces and a wooden storage locker now.

During the summer, as soon as Pauley's business started to take off, the people in the apartment building next door complained of runoff. The city got involved and told him he had to install an asphalt berm around his wash area that funneled the water to a drain connected to the sewer. Lou split the cost with him, but it hadn't been cheap.

She gave him a little wave. He nodded in acknowledgment as he rinsed off the Lincoln. She started the Mustang, drove it over to the lube bays, and hooked it up to the scope. Pauley pulled the Lincoln over to his spot in the shade in front of Lou's office and began squeegeeing water off the hood and roof.

Spiking lines on the oscilloscope pattern soon informed her that the Ford needed spark plug wires. She shut off the engine and heard a woman's strident voice. The source was a well-dressed Brentwood matron. The object of her complaints seemed to be a mauve Jaguar. Pauley stood beside the gleaming car, looking conciliatory, as the woman pointed to the wheels.

"There are water spots on the rims," she said.

"Yes, ma'am," Pauley said. "I noticed that when the car came in. I rubbed them out twice."

"Well, it's not good enough. Are you telling me you can't polish chrome correctly?"

"No, ma'am." Pauley had a soft towel in his

hand and bent to demonstrate. "These stains are permanent."

Munch walked past the two of them on the way to the phone and shot Pauley a sympathetic look, but he was concentrating on trying to please the woman. She passed Lou's open office door and saw that he, too, was watching what was going on outside.

"And what about this?" the woman asked, pointing to a drip of water escaping from the gas cap flap. "I suppose you're going to tell me that this was here when I came in?"

Pauley said nothing. He used his rag to wipe at the water, then walked around the car and made several other swipes for show. The woman watched with lips pursed, one hand on her hip, while she checked her watch and tapped her foot.

Munch found the Mustang work order and called the owner's work number. She was in the middle of selling the needed repair when Lou suddenly slammed down his pencil and rushed out his door.

He came to a stop between Pauley and his unreasonable customer and lifted his hands high above his head in a gesture of exaggerated befuddlement. "What do you want him to do for you, lady," he asked in a voice that carried throughout the shop, "shit blood?"

Munch winced at the crudeness. The woman's jaw dropped. Pauley looked at his feet. The air around them all hushed with tension. Lou waited a moment for the woman to respond, then dropped his hands and returned to his office. Another moment passed and then time seemed to start up again. The woman paid Pauley and left. Munch finished her call to the owner of the Mustang. By the time she hung up the phone, she was grinning. Vulgarity aside, there were times when she really loved Lou. She walked back outside, thinking to share a laugh with Pauley, but when she caught his eye he was glaring at her with an emotion she couldn't fathom. She could understand his anger, but why was he directing it at her?

"What?" she asked.

He shook his head and walked off in the direction of the bathrooms. She decided he was embarrassed and left him alone.

By nine-thirty, the shop was caught up on all the jobs. The Mustang was running like new and the customer would pick it up when he got off work at five.

She looked at the deserted shop and sighed. She hated it when it got slow. That's when the idiots emerged, usually in the form of bored coworkers. There was nothing more annoying than men with time on their hands. Guys liked to tell stories, she noticed. And the fact that you'd already heard many versions of the same tale didn't stop them. It was like they had some sort of secret pact. You listen to my bullshit, and I'll listen to yours. Bikers did it, cops did it, dopers did it. If someone didn't have anything new to say, she often wondered, why didn't they ever consider just shutting up? Or reading a book? Or, God forbid, one of the service bulletins put out by the Bureau of Automotive Repair.

She also had to ask herself how much of her resentment stemmed from the fact that the majority of her stories couldn't be shared with the present audience.

Needless to say, she was more than relieved when Mace St. John's Buick pulled into the driveway. He parked in front of the office. She met him at his car.

"How are you holding up?" he asked.

"I'm about to go crazy. You could shoot a cannon through the back room and not hit anything."

"Let's go see your friend."

Munch let Lou know she was taking a break. He responded by looking at his watch.

They took St. John's car to Barrington Plaza Gardens. The gate guard asked them for their names, clipboard in hand. Before Munch could say anything, St. John flashed his badge. The gate guard shrugged and let them on through.

Fahoosy's black Mercedes passed them going out. She recognized the custom antenna and scooted down in her seat.

"Problem?" St. John asked.

"Just some jerk customer." She sat up again. "What am I hiding for? You've got a gun, right?"

He smiled. "What did this guy do?"

She told most of the story, only leaving out the part where she "forgot" to put the Mercedes's spare back in its trunk.

St. John found the guest parking spaces. He locked the Buick and the two of them walked up the path to unit 62.

Robin answered the door in a dark green jogging suit. The thick fleece managed to accentuate her thinness rather than conceal it, but at least she had changed out of her bathrobe and brushed her hair.

"Can we come in?" Munch asked.

"Oh, I'm sorry. Please."

Munch kicked off her shoes and left them by the front mat.

Robin directed her guests toward the sofa and settled in an armchair. Munch made introductions.

"Can I get anyone anything?" Robin asked. "A Coke? Water?"

They both declined.

St. John sat next to Munch on the couch and said, "I'm going to see Pete Owen later today. I'll offer him whatever assistance I can. I'm sorry this happened to you. I want you to know that we make catching these kinds of predators a number-one priority."

"I hope so," she said. The refrigerator made a loud, gurgling noise and Robin jumped as if reacting to a gunshot. Munch squeezed St. John's arm although she was sure he'd noticed. She was too honest with herself not to realize when she was making an excuse to touch him.

"I know this will be difficult," he said, using a gentle tone, "but I need you to tell me everything you remember about your attack and your assailant."

Robin perched on the edge of the chair cushion,

barely making a dent. She told her story in a mono-
tone, her eyes never leaving her hands. She told
them how she never saw it coming. She'd been on
her way home alone from an evening out. He had
come up from behind, wrapped his arm around
her neck, and choked her until she passed out.
When she came to, he had taped her eyes shut. He
told her he would kill her if she didn't do what he
said. She believed him.

"He talked to me." Robin rubbed the palm of
her hand down her thigh, stopping at her knee. She
did this repeatedly, as if it gave her some sort of
comfort. "He said he had been watching me. His
voice was disguised, like he was talking through
some kind of vibrating filter. He said, 'You don't
know how long I've waited for this.'"

St. John leaned forward. "What about the voice?"

"The only way I can describe it is to tell you it
was like listening to static, something that shouldn't
be human, forming words. Horrible words."

"Did you tell this to Detective Owen?" St. John
asked.

"I might have. I don't remember how thoroughly
I described everything. I was pretty shook up when
I spoke to him."

St. John's eyes had an intense glow to them. He
balled his fist and sank it into the cushion next to
him. "What happened next?"

She told them how he'd put her in her own car
and they'd driven in what felt like circles. She
didn't think they had ever gotten on the freeway,

but there was the sensation of going up and down hills. At last they'd stopped. He'd led her out of the car. Two steps up to the front door, across a floor that wasn't carpeted, and then down some stairs.

"Then he told me to remove my clothes," Robin said.

"His exact words?" St. John prompted.

"'Take it off, honey. Take it all off.'" Robin paused and took a deep breath. "When I hesitated, he pressed something against me that burned and tingled. He said he could adjust the level, that I'd stay conscious through the pain. I took everything off. The tape was still around my eyes. Every time I tried to cover myself with my hands, he'd put something cold and metallic to my chest and start to count to three. I never let him get past 'two.' I was so scared that I could only whimper as I felt the ropes tighten against my ankles and wrists."

Robin pulled at her fingers and looked to her right. Her face grew taut. Munch noticed a rash of red bumps on her face that extended down to her throat. Probably a result of malnutrition.

She told them how she'd heard a click and a whir. It took her a second to identify the familiar sound of a camera shutter opening and closing. Film forwarding.

"'Please don't hurt me,' I begged. I didn't even recognize my own voice. He said everything would go smoothly if I did what I was told."

Munch had listened to many women purge themselves, clean addicts that she sponsored. She'd heard stories of incest, child neglect, even one case of bestiality. She herself was no stranger to the cruelty people were capable of. None of it compared to what Robin told them next.

"Then I felt something being taped to my skin. Later I realized that they were wires." She lifted her pant leg and showed them the rows of red shiny scars.

"I heard a chair scrape across the floor and stop beside me. He was breathing hard. I could smell his sweat." Robin paused, bit her lip. When she continued her voice was much higher. "I heard a sound that I couldn't identify. I thought he was grinding coffee beans, only there was a little ringing noise going on as well—I had the impression of something spinning. The jolt came so suddenly, like a slide hammer pulling through my body. I heard something in my shoulder pop when I tried to pull away."

"He shocked you with electricity?" St. John asked; his voice was lower than usual. Munch saw him work his mouth as if it were dry.

Robin nodded. "After the first time, he only did it when I disobeyed him." She scratched at the side of her face until it grew red and raw. Munch wanted to grab her hand to stop her.

"He raped me for hours. Vaginally, orally, everywhere. The whole time he kept asking me if I loved him—if I could grow to love him. Did I feel the magic?" She paused and cleared her throat. "I told him yes. I would have told him anything. Afterward he had me take a shower. He even brushed my hair and gave me a nightgown to put on. He said because I had been such a good sport about helping him act out his fantasy he was going to take me back to my car."

Tears rolled down Robin's face before she made her final admission. "I actually thanked him. Up to that point I was thinking I was going to die. I didn't want to die."

Munch moved to sit next to her. "And you didn't. You made it. You're safe."

"Safe?" Robin asked. "I can't even remember what that felt like."

"You said something about him calling you?" Munch prompted gently.

Robin stood and walked across the room to her kitchen. Without another word, she pushed the play button on her answering machine.

There was a beep and then the odd, mechanical voice said, "I miss you." It paused. "Are you thinking of me, too? The first time is always awkward. I'm so glad we're past that."

The machine beeped again.

"We need to talk this out," he said. The longer he talked, the easier he was to understand. "Please don't ignore me. We have unfinished business, you and I."

Munch felt the breath leave her body. "That's him," she told St. John.

"Your guy?" he asked.

Munch nodded.

He held up a hand as if to put her on hold and then turned back to Robin. "What did you do when you got back to your car?"

"I drove to the hospital. They called the police."

"When did the calls start?" St. John asked.

"As soon as I got home from the hospital. The police have already tried to trace them. They weren't able to. Apparently the guy is using a mobile phone, and they have no way to trace it. Something about needing to know the origin of the call and then they can triangulate the signals. Well, shit. If we knew the origin of the call we wouldn't need to trace it, would we?"

Munch smiled. Her thoughts exactly. People could be so stupid. "I thought you changed your number," she said.

"I did. Somehow he got the new one." She picked up an envelope from the coffee table and handed it to St. John.

"What's this?" he asked.

"My discharge papers from the hospital and a copy of the police report."

St. John put the envelope in his breast pocket and asked Robin, "Do you have somewhere you can go? Somewhere else you can stay? Family? Friends? Preferably out of state."

Robin turned her dull eyes on him. "Won't he find me wherever I go?"

"No," the detective said firmly. "He's mortal. He can be stopped."

CHAPTER 12

Minutes later, Munch and St. John were back in the Buick. Munch waited patiently while St. John looked over the paperwork Robin had given him. When he finished reading, he rolled down his window and spat.

"Son of a bitch," he said. He lit one of his thin cigars.

"What?"

"I've never seen such bullshit."

"You mean the rape?"

"No, the fucking investigation. We've got no vacuuming of the car's interior for trace fibers. After four hours, eighty percent of fiber evidence is lost. As far as I can tell, nobody went back to where she was released and looked for other tire tracks or conducted any interviews." St. John fixed her with a look that demonstrated the intensity of his anger. Even though it wasn't directed at her, his expression made her cringe and pray to God she'd never be on the receiving end of his displeasure. "We've got no fiber scraping from the nightgown he left her in. In fact, the nightgown wasn't even taken into evidence."

"Where is it now?"

"The hospital lost it according to Owen's narrative. Shit," he said, stabbing the offending paperwork with his forefinger. "No mention of the duct tape over her eyes during the assault. What the fuck was Owen thinking?"

"What's the significance of the duct tape?"

"Everything is significant at this point."

She watched his jaw work as he gnashed on the white plastic mouthpiece on the tip of his cigarillo.

"This isn't the first time, is it?" she asked.

He looked at her a long moment before answering. "No, there have been others. Robin was luckier than some."

"Define lucky."

He grunted a laugh.

"How did this guy know to call me?" she asked. "Robin didn't tell anyone I was going to help her."

"What about you? Who did you tell?"

"Wait a minute," Munch said, seeing a telephone repair truck. "Pull this guy over."

"For what?"

Munch turned the window crank, but by the time she got her window down the truck had passed. "Turn around. Don't you have a siren in this thing?"

He pulled to the side of the road and asked, "What are you thinking?"

"The phone guy will know where the junction box for the building is. It could save us some time. Maybe our mystery caller has her phone bugged. Easiest way to do it is at the junction box, but they keep them padlocked."

"How do you know that?" he asked.

"You can see the lock."

"No, I mean about tapping into the line."

"That's not really the point right now, is it?" The truth was that Lou was a Vietnam vet. He had served in the army the same years as Mace St. John. The detective knew that. What he might not remember was that Lou's MOS—army talk for Military Occupational Speciality—was communications. This came in handy at the gas station. Especially when anyone who might be saying anything of interest used the pay phone around the corner. The phone block was conveniently located in the back room of the station. This same junction block had the pay phones on it in addition to the Texaco phone lines. Lou clipped on with a telephone repairman's handset when the need arose. She knew it was illegal as hell and saw no reason to burden St. John with this information.

"Okay," he said, raising a hand in mock surrender. "I don't care. But we can't do it that way. I'll call my connection at the phone company and have them send a truck out to make sure her line is secure."

"What else do you want me to do?" She felt curiously elated. She loved the irony of being on this side of a police investigation. Besides, it was exciting. Where was it written that she couldn't enjoy herself while helping someone?

St. John studied her for a moment. When he spoke, there was a warning edge to his voice. "Are you sure you want to get mixed up any deeper in this thing?"

"There's something else, isn't there? Something you're not telling me."

"When Diane Bergman's body was dumped, she was also dressed in a nightgown. We also found evidence of electrical torture."

"So you think it's the same guy?"

"I can't rule that out."

"So why kill one and not the other?"

"Who knows? You can't put your own logic on these guys. They're wired different." He stopped speaking. From the look in his eyes, she knew he had left her. Had gone somewhere with his thoughts and his secret knowledge where she couldn't follow. She waited while he pulled his notebook out and wrote something down. She pushed her head back into the headrest and glanced at the words he had written: *Duct tape to keep eyes from popping out?*

She didn't speak again until they had pulled back into traffic. "If this has to do with what happened to Diane, then I'm more sure than ever I want to help. Where do we start?"

"We look for whatever else Owen missed. That's where we fucking start."

When Munch got back to work, she went straight to her toolbox and grabbed her notebook. St. John stayed in his car to use his radio. She rejoined him as he was signing off.

"What you got?" he asked.

"Every day I write down the make and model of the cars I work on." She showed him the columns of license plate numbers, the customers' names, the service performed, and the amount charged. She turned back to the day in September that Robin had been raped, then checked the day before that. There it was. Robin Davies, Toyota Celica, Tune-up.

Then she pointed to the Peg-Board over the service desk where they hung the work orders and the keys. "Robin's bill would have been hanging there all day, with her keys on the hook as well. The work orders have all the customers' information on them, including addresses and phone numbers."

"So anyone who works here would have access," St. John said.

"Any customer as well," she said.

She looked back at her ledger and saw that the day Robin had her car serviced was also the day Fahoosy had his tires replaced. Could he have been the one? Copied down her phone number when no one was watching? Or did Munch just have it in for the guy? Like people who watch the FBI's Most Wanted list and see how closely their troublesome neighbor resembles an ax murderer from Detroit.

"C'mon," she told St. John. "I want to check something out."

She took him into the office.

Lou was watching the financial channel on his little television. "What's up?" he asked.

"I need to look through the old bills." She knelt down and sifted through the box that held the last few months' work orders. She went through them until she found the September invoices. St. John waited until she located copies of Fahoosy's and Robin's work orders. She handed them over saying, "Check this out."

Fahoosy also lived at Barrington Plaza Gardens. St. John copied down the phone number and address. When he was finished, Munch took the invoices back. She started to return them to the box and then stopped.

"This might be something," she said, taking out the next work order in the stack. "We put these in here in the order they were paid." She showed him an invoice with Diane Bergman's name on it. It was dated the day before Fahoosy's and Robin's invoices. "This is the last work I did on her car. I replaced her brakes. See, those are my initials in the corner." She scanned down the right-hand column. "She also had the car washed. That's the twelve-fifty charge under miscellaneous. She must have picked up her car a day after the work was completed."

"Or at least paid for it the next day, right?" St. John said.

She nodded, appreciating the way his head worked. He kept his mind clear of assumptions and crawled to his conclusions.

"Who worked on Robin's car last?"

"Me. She wanted only me to touch her car. Said she didn't trust the other guys."

"Feel like taking a little ride?" he asked.

"Sure. How little?"

"I've got a meeting with a woman at the DOJ."

"The what?"

"Department of Justice. Actually she's with the California Bureau of Investigation, sex crimes unit."

"How long will it take?"

"She's just over on Federal. Not more than an hour."

"Lou?"

"Might as well," he said, sighing loudly. "It's only money, right?"

She knew he had to act like his balls were being busted. The truth was he was probably a little relieved to have one less restless mechanic on his hands. Slow days brought out jealousy and back-biting. Especially with Stefano, who stomped around the shop when Munch had jobs lined up with her own customers. Like it was her fault she had developed a loyal following.

St. John took her over to Westwood, to the offices of the California Bureau of Investigation, sex crimes unit. Once they were alone in the car he said, "We can't overlook the fact that three out of four victims and potential victims of this guy are connected to your station. You got any bad feelings about any of your coworkers?"

"Oh, you know how it is," she said, suddenly uncomfortable about fingering anybody specific. It was one thing to complain to a friend. Another feeling entirely when that friend was a cop.

"Tell me anyway," he said.

"Lou named me as manager when he isn't there. That didn't sit well with some of the guys."

"Give me an example."

"Okay. There's this one guy, Stefano. He's from Yugoslavia or somewhere. Anyhow, he thinks he's really something. Lou hired him two months ago because he said he knew how to fix cruise controls and automatic transmissions. Come to find out, Stefano talks a good show but lacks a little in execution. Last month he worked on this guy's cruise control. Big Lincoln Town Car. Next day the guy comes in and says that it still doesn't work right. Stefano sticks out his chest and tells the customer that he doesn't know how to operate his own car. The customer says, 'I might not be a mechanical genius, but I know when I step on the brake that the cruise control should shut off.' I heard that and told Lou to give the guy his money back. Stefano's been shooting daggers at me ever since."

"You got a last name for this guy?"

"Barnevik." She tried to think. Did her caller have a slight accent? The electronic modification might be his way of disguising it.

"Write it down for me. Who else? What about your limo drivers?"

"I can give you a list of ex-drivers, but honestly I don't see any of them having the ambition to stalk me."

"Just humor me. Have you fired anyone recently?"

"I fire a driver at least once a month, but I don't make a big deal out of it. I just take them off the insurance policy and let 'em figure it out for themselves that I'm not calling anymore."

"Who else?"

"I've got a list of people I don't call anymore."

"Anybody who would dislike you enough to want to hurt you?"

Munch rubbed her forehead, feeling the beginning of a headache. It was a horrible thing to have to consider. "You mean like someone who seems sort of off?"

"You never know," he said.

And with that comforting thought, they arrived at their destination.

While waiting for their appointment, Munch picked through the brochures on the credenza. The first pamphlet listed myths about rape that needed to be dispelled. "First and foremost," it read, "you have to know and understand that it is not your fault—you didn't ask for it in any way—you did not provoke the incident by the way you act, dress, or carry yourself."

Not now I don't, Munch thought.

She turned to a second brochure about something called Rape Trauma Syndrome. The physical symptoms were loss of appetite, sleep disturbances, nightmares, difficulty functioning at normal everyday tasks, not wanting to leave the safety of your home alone. Everything cataloged fit with what Robin was experiencing.

There was also a list of emotional reactions broken into two categories: those expressed and those suppressed. Expressed emotions were feelings of fear, anger, and anxiety. A person suppressing emotions might display a calm, composed outward appearance but was probably not doing as well as someone who could express feelings outwardly.

Munch stuffed the brochures into her bag when the door to the anteroom opened.

They were greeted by a woman who identified herself as Special Agent Hogan. Emily Hogan. She had blond hair, which curled to her shoulders, and was wearing a tailored skirt suit and heels. Munch was surprised. She realized she had been expecting a bitter, angry, man-hating woman like the ones who led those incest-survivor workshops at the women's center. Certainly not someone who wore makeup and feminine gold jewelry at her ears and throat.

"How can I help you?" Agent Hogan asked.

St. John introduced himself and explained that they were looking for a rapist.

"You've come to the right place," Hogan said with a smile. "Let's go into my office."

When they were settled in matching upholstered chairs that faced the agent's desk, Emily Hogan said, "First, let's classify your assailant."

"Not *my* assailant," Munch said quickly, wondering why it made a difference to her that this woman know that immediately.

Agent Hogan didn't blink. "I was referring to your case."

"Right, the rape of our victim." Munch squirmed in her chair. St. John reached over and squeezed her arm. She wasn't sure if this action was meant to reassure her or quiet her. Probably both.

"Was it rape or sexual assault?" the agent asked.

"What's the difference?"

"Rape as defined by our penal code is an act of sexual intercourse accomplished against a person's will by means of force, violence, duress, menace, or fear of immediate and unlawful bodily injury on the person of another. Sexual Assault is a violent crime where sex has been used as a weapon to hurt and humiliate."

"It was both," Munch said.

"She was raped," St. John said simultaneously.

"What I can never understand is how anybody converts the act of sex into an act of violence," Munch said. She knew it happened, but witnessing—even being a part of certain acts—didn't mean she understood the why. She didn't have a man's equipment and could never fathom having such close personal interaction, joining your body with another's, in hatred. It didn't make any sense

to her at all. Especially now, with her new sensibili-
ties, living in a different world, being a different
person accustomed to sanity.

"Well, now," Emily Hogan said, "you've just hit
on the number-one myth. Rape is not about pas-
sion gone out of control. It's an act of destruction
and degradation. It's an act of ultimate power over
another."

Munch's head nodded, seemingly of its own
volition. She was acutely aware of St. John's silent
presence.

"I can't give you a why," Emily Hogan continued. "There are many things we'll never understand. What we do here is catalog and, hopefully,
put these offenders away as soon as possible." She
pointed to the file cabinets behind her. "Rape is one
of the most difficult crimes to prosecute, because
we have all the societal prejudices and myths to
overcome."

"I saw the pamphlets," Munch said.

St. John looked at her with slightly raised eyebrows. She felt exposed and wished she could just
get up and leave, forget this whole thing.

If Emily Hogan was aware of Munch's discomfort, it didn't show in her tone. She went on with
what was turning into a lecture. "A little historical
note: In the nineteenth century, when the crime of
rape was finally being pursued in the courts, there
was a seven percent conviction rate for successful
rapes, twenty-five percent for attempted rape.
When I started in law enforcement, it was the sev-

enties. A woman was expected to resist her rapist to her utmost ability. The more injuries she sustained, the more believable her case. I worked in a department where it was standard procedure to polygraph rape victims. If the woman failed her polygraph, the case was not pursued."

"But not now, right?" Munch asked.

"No, thank God, not now. But we still fight the wall of shame." She picked up a folder from her desk. "Listen to this. This is the first officer on the scene's evaluation." She read from the report, "'The assailant then made a demand for oral sex.'"

"Sounds plain enough to me," Munch said.

"Let me tell you something," Hogan replied. "No rapist ever stood before his victim and said the words, 'I demand oral sex.'"

She put down the file and addressed them both. "The first cop on the scene is usually a uniform. He's dealing with some poor woman who's just had a terrible, traumatic experience. He wants to get her help, take her to a hospital, hook her up with a rape counselor. The last thing he wants to do is make her relive the experience in explicit detail. But that's exactly what we need."

She picked up a packet of papers from her desk. They looked like applications. She handed one each to St. John and Munch. It was a questionnaire. "You're going to have to go back to your victim and have her fill this out to the best of her ability."

Munch started to read the questions.

"What did the offender call his sex organs?"

She hated it when guys named their dicks, as if that part of their body had a separate identity and a mind of its own. She'd heard it said more than once that a stiff cock had no conscience, but she didn't buy it. Man or woman, people had to take responsibility for their actions. She also thought it was weird when people named their cars.

"There's all kinds of rapists," Agent Hogan said.

Munch stopped reading and asked, "You mean they all have a distinctive MO?"

"No," St. John interrupted, "that's Hollywood bullshit. There's no such thing as a distinctive MO that lasts much longer than four months. Assholes update their MO constantly."

Munch was used to cop speak. "Asshole" meant criminal. When he said "Ass*hole*," on the other hand, with the emphasis on the second syllable, he was referring to a defense attorney. She'd spent enough time around him, hanging on his every word, to pick up the nuances.

"That's right," Agent Hogan said. "Modus operandi is learned behavior designed for the safety of the offender to ensure the success of his crime. And with every act the offender perpetrates, he hones his craft a little more. MO evolves with each crime."

"Constantly," St. John agreed. "Maybe the asshole gets ID'd and caught because he left fingerprints. The next time he wears gloves. Maybe he grabs his victims in a shopping mall. The woman screams and somebody comes to her rescue. The asshole runs off to his little cave, licks his wounds, and plans a way for that not to happen again. So next time he grabs his victim in an underground parking lot with nobody else around."

"So by looking at how the guy does his crime," Munch said, "the precautions he takes, you can figure how he was caught before. So maybe this guy disguises his voice because he was busted on a voice lineup."

The look he gave her was of approval. She struggled to conceal her pride.

"Anything else?" Munch asked Agent Hogan.

"We need to know exactly what this offender said and how he said it. Some rapists have a fantasy that the act is consensual. He might say to his victim, 'Tell me you love me.' Or he might ask her if it feels good. These offenders we classify as 'the inadequate rapist.' This is the type of guy who is socially withdrawn, who is unable for his various reasons to procure a partner. He generally collects pornography and has a complex fantasy life."

Munch had a quick mental image of the videotapes in Fahoosy's trunk. *Strike two, motherfucker.*

"He might even prefer to rape his victim once she's unconscious. Perhaps passed out from intoxication."

"You count that, too?" Munch asked.

Agent Hogan looked at her and blinked once.

Munch felt her cheeks go hot and wondered if the blush showed. "And the other types of rapists?" she asked quickly to get the conversation rolling again.

"That's what we need to figure out here," Hogan said. "We need to know how he subdued her. Did he put a knife to her throat? Did he cut her? How did he react to seeing the blood? Once she was complying, did he stop using force? Did he display a sense of entitlement? All this is important.

"Eighty to eighty-five percent of rapists are known to their victim," she added.

"I believe it," Munch said, pulling out her own experiences and holding them up to test against this woman's theories.

"This is true with the inadequate rapist," the agent continued, "or the weenie rapist as I like to call him, as well as the rapist who feels he's entitled."

"Entitled," Munch said. That would explain that time with Culley.

"Now we're talking about what makes this guy tick," Emily Hogan said. "What makes him feel good. What he needs to do to satisfy his needs. That's his signature. That's the part that doesn't change. Sexual fantasies are constant throughout your life. You might embellish them, dress them up, refine them. But whatever thing that imprinted you at whatever critical moment in your sexual development is your thing for life."

Munch studied the form in her hand. The questions came right to the point.

"What did the offender call the victim's sex organs?"
"What profanity was used?"

"Were other objects used for penetration?"

"And if so, what?"

A flashlight, Munch remembered. *Red plastic handle.* Later, at the hospital, the doctor extracted several minuscule flecks of chrome from the walls of her vagina. She hadn't wasted any time wondering what sick pleasure that guy got out of sticking this inanimate object up inside her. She also didn't understand why some men wore panty hose under their trousers or wanted you to hurt them. She did know that there were all types out there. Guys like Culley, who drove you out to a deserted graveyard and were so mad at you for hooking up with someone else that they demanded sex one more time.

"This goes in your mouth or in your cunt," Culley had said. What a choice. She chose the latter, staring at the headliner of his Chevy until he was finished. Then he drove her back to the Flats. And she told on him. Of course she told on him. She wasn't the type to go climbing into a hole and cower. She dealt with things as they happened and then got over them. Sleaze John and a couple of the other guys whipped him good. What she couldn't understand was why he drove her back. Not that he should have killed her or anything, but he could have made her find her own way home and gotten a head start. But then, he never planned to leave. Now she understood. Culley was one of those who believed he was entitled. Did Robin's rapist also now feel a sense of entitlement?

And there was that redheaded guy they all called Gypsy. He was a strange one, even by their standards. That incident happened even before the thing with Culley. Gypsy climbed into bed with her one night. Woke her up from a sound sleep with a knife under her chin. He was stoned on something. Reds most likely. He didn't smell like he was out-of-his-mind drunk. He told her things, told her how much he wanted her, wanted to make love to her. All this with the blade of his hunting knife resting on her throat. She had gotten mad, pinned as she was under the covers with his weight on top of her, his breath in her face. She heard her next-door neighbor, Brian, through the thin wall. He was strumming his guitar. He stopped playing when she said in a loud voice, "Well, then, you may as well kill me, *Gypsy,* instead of just showing me your goddamn knife." Brian had not kicked in the door as she had hoped he might. Instead, Gypsy had put away his knife, mumbled something that was halfway between an excuse and an apology, and staggered away. Brian, a big, tall, strapping guy, told him he wasn't being cool. He said this from the doorway as Gypsy stumbled down the street never to be seen again. They were both weenies.

"Man," she said, her fist clenched. Nothing like anger arriving ten years after the fact.

"What?" St. John asked.

"Oh, um, I was just wondering about this last question. 'What was the order of sexual encounters?'" she read out loud.

Emily Hogan looked at her. "Fellatio, oral sex, followed by anal penetration is a much different assault when carried out in the reverse order."

"I get it," Munch said, almost sorry she had asked for clarification. She folded the questionnaire and put it in her purse, next to all the other disturbing literature.

"And this brings us to the third classification of rapists, the sadists. Fortunately, this is a very small group. These are the kinds of guys who should have been drowned as pups. As the name implies, their pleasure comes from another's pain. You'd be looking for a man who is probably in his mid-thirties; it seems to take these guys that long to work themselves up to the point where they act out. And with most of your rapists, like serial killers, you're going to be looking for someone from the same racial background as his or her victims."

St. John told Emily Hogan about the electrical torture, the disguised voice, the use of duct tape over the eyes, and how the guy had dumped two of the women on the freeway when he was done with them, one of them dead and one alive, but had taken a third, Robin, back to her car.

"And now our offender has been making follow-up phone calls to that victim, Robin Davies." He read Emily Hogan the transcript of the calls. Then he put a hand on Munch's arm. "Munch is starting to receive calls and we have good reason to believe it's the same guy."

Hogan nodded and fixed Munch with a sympathetic expression. "Sounds like this guy believes he's in love with Robin and he perceives that you're trying to come between them."

"Tell me what I can do to help you all catch this guy," Munch said.

"We'll set up both you and Ms. Davies with tape recorders," the agent said. "Turn the recorder on with every incoming call until you see who it is. Sometimes these creeps have a friend or even a stranger start the call so that the intended recipient is caught off guard. This way we ensure that we don't miss anything at the beginning of the call. We'll give you enough tapes to make certain that you don't run out. Don't erase the beginnings of the calls that turn out not to be from the bad guy."

"Why?"

"Two reasons. First, to show that nothing was erased, and second, in case the creep has someone else call and then chickens out."

"I know," Munch said. "Think weenie."

Hogan smiled. "Now, when he does call, see what you can learn about him. Give him open-ended questions. We don't want yes-or-no answers, but something that will get him to launch into free narrative."

"Like what?"

"Like: 'Why are you doing this? What will it take to make you stop?'"

"So you want to get into his head?"

"I want anything he'll give us," Hogan said. She reached under her desk and pulled out two tape recorders. From her drawer she retrieved two unopened six-packs of cassette tapes. She gave Munch quick directions on how to attach the machine's microphone to her handset at home. She also instructed Munch to keep a log of the time of the calls.

"As soon as you hear from him, call me," St. John added.

"Should I try to set up a meet?"

"Only if he suggests it. If you bring it up first he'll probably suspect a trap."

On the way home, they stopped at Robin's. The gate guard didn't want to let them in, but St. John flashed his badge again and told the guy to open up. Minutes later, they knocked on Robin's door.

"Yes?" she called from inside.

"Robin, it's Munch and Mace St. John. Can we come in?"

She opened the door a little more quickly than she had before. Progress measured in inches.

They gave her the questionnaire and explained that they needed the answers filled out in detail. While Robin looked the questions over, St. John hooked up the tape recorder and instructed her on how and when to use it.

"I brought you some brochures," Munch said.

Robin reached out for them but then grabbed Munch's hand. "I never wanted to end up like this," she said.

"You won't. You haven't. It's not over."

Robin held up the list of questions she was to answer. "I'll have these for you tomorrow."

"Call me when you do," Munch said. To seal the deal she gave Robin a hug. The woman had the body mass of a child. "Meanwhile, eat something. We are *not* going to let this bastard win."

CHAPTER 13

Munch returned with St. John to the Texaco station in time to see the mailman hiking up the sidewalk. "Hey, Phil," she said. "Anything for me?"

"As a matter of fact . . ." His voice trailed off as he sifted through the bundle in his hand. "Here you go," he said finally, handing her a white envelope. The return address was the Bergman Cancer Center. Munch felt a sudden weight around her heart when she recognized Diane Bergman's handwriting.

"Mind if I use your phone?" St. John asked.

"Go ahead," she said, ripping open the envelope. Inside were several pages of paper, folded in thirds. A Post-it note stuck to the center read, "*As promised. Good luck. Hope this does you some good and thanks again. D.*"

Munch didn't fight the tears. In fact, she welcomed the relief of them. She unfolded the papers and saw that they were a list of names, addresses, and phone numbers printed on Bergman Cancer Center stationery. The top center of the papers still bore indentations from a clipboard, most of the names had small check marks next to them, and there was some scribbling in the margins, numbers and letters written in pencil: *100,000s CARC 35¼ –23* followed by the date *10/1/84.*

St. John noticed and looked at her questioningly. He started to say something but then spoke into the phone, "This is Detective St. John with the LAPD. Is Mr. Sarnoff in?" He covered the mouthpiece with his hand. "I'm on hold. What is this?"

"The guest list from last Friday night. Diane sent it to me."

"Tell the mailman to wait."

She ran after Phil. "We need to ask you a few questions."

Phil put the mailbag pull cart in an upright position. "What's up?"

She looked back at St. John, who was finishing his call. He held up a finger, said his good-byes into the phone, and walked over to them.

Munch made introductions

"How can I help you, Detective?" the mailman asked.

"Can you tell me where and when this letter was mailed?"

Phil looked at the envelope. "It's got a return address."

"How about the cancellation stamp?" St. John said. "What does that tell you?"

"It's stamped with yesterday's date and the local zip code. That means it came through the Brentwood substation. It was probably posted sometime yesterday."

"How about if it was mailed from a residence?"

"You mean someone's personal mailbox? Depends on when the delivery truck got it."

St. John consulted his notebook and read off Diane Bergman's street address.

Mailman Phil thought a moment. "They get their mail midday, around noon or one."

"Even on Saturday?"

"Even earlier on Saturday," Phil said.

"So if the postman picked up outgoing mail on Saturday, when would it be processed?"

"Monday."

"So if this letter was mailed from the house on Chenault, it was probably put in the homeowner's mailbox after the mail had already arrived on Saturday morning, picked up on Monday, and processed Tuesday."

"Yep, or mailed at a curbside box or at the post office on Tuesday."

St. John took out his notebook and wrote down Phil's name and number. "Thanks for your help."

Phil said no problem, and left.

St. John turned to Munch. "Are you all right?"

"Yeah," she said, wiping her face, "just sad."

He pointed at the list. "I'm going to need that."

She held it out to him. The Bergman Cancer Center stationery listed its officers in the left-hand margin. "Is this the same Sarnoff you just called? Logan Sarnoff?"

"Yes, it is. Do you know him?"

"I know who he is. I'm going to a thank-you reception at his house on Friday. He's the first vice president of the Bergman Cancer Center Foundation."

"He's also the family attorney. I'm on my way to meet with him now."

"I do know this guy, the treasurer, Ken Wilson," she said, pointing to the third name down. "He's a customer."

"Was he at the party?"

"Yes, and he's on the guest list, too, with his name checked off."

"What does he do?"

"He's a stockbroker. Lou uses him. He drives a red Jeep. Funny vehicle for a white-collar guy, don't you think? He lives in Encino and has an office on Wilshire. When does he need four-wheel drive?"

"Do you know the address on Wilshire?" St. John asked.

Munch reached under the service desk and pulled out the phone book. She could find no individual listing for Ken Wilson. "I'll have to get it from Lou's Rolodex."

She copied Ken Wilson's office address on a sheet of paper and brought it back to St. John.

"Hmm," he said. "I'm heading over there now. This is the same building Logan Sarnoff's office is in."

"I'm not surprised. Birds of a feather and all that."

* * *

Fifteen minutes later, St. John was ushered into the comfortable office of Logan Sarnoff. It was on the eighth floor of a modern office building on Wilshire Boulevard. An oval window looked out toward the Pacific Ocean. Catalina Island was a vague lump on the orange-brown horizon. He sat down in a plush leather chair opposite the attorney, a trim, clean-shaven man in his sixties, wearing a suit that probably cost as much as the detective's privately owned vehicle.

"I'm investigating the death of one of your clients," St. John said without preamble.

The attorney didn't speak immediately and when he did, he spaced each word theatrically. These guys charged by the hour.

"Yes, Diane Bergman. Alfred called me."

"I understand that Mr. Bergman preceded his wife in death. What did he die of?"

"Pulmonary cancer. It came on very suddenly. His loss still saddens us all."

"I'm sorry," St. John said.

"But you're here about Mrs. Bergman—Diane." The attorney looked thoughtful. "The newspaper reported that an autopsy was scheduled."

"Yes, and I've been assigned to investigate the death," St. John said. "When was the last time you saw Mrs. Bergman?"

"That would be last Friday night. There was a charity function in the Palisades that we both attended. I'm not even sure if I spoke to her that night. She was so busy with all the arrangements."

"Did she seem upset?"

"More like harried, which was to be expected."

"Did Mrs. Bergman have a will or life insurance policies?"

Again, the attorney paused before replying. "I'm sure you're familiar with the concept of quid pro quo, Detective," Sarnoff said at last. "Before I can give you any information, I need to know that I'm not compromising the interests of any of my other clients. I don't expect you to reveal to me all aspects of your investigation, but I will need to know more than what you've told me so far. Do you have any suspects?"

This time it was St. John's turn for contemplation. He balanced the attorney's offer in his time-honored fashion, weighing what he stood to gain against possible losses. "This is to be kept confidential."

The attorney nodded sagely.

"Diane Bergman's body was discovered on the shoulder of the San Diego Freeway early Monday morning."

Sarnoff nodded. "I knew that much from the media reports."

"We are ruling the case a homicide. To date we have neither suspects nor a motive. Anything you can tell me that you think would be pertinent, I would appreciate. I've been to her house. I know she was widowed earlier this year. I need to know what her financial assets were and who might profit from her death."

The attorney closed his eyes, but neither his expression nor his tone wavered. "Mrs. Bergman did make arrangements with me," he said. "In the event of her death, her entire estate reverts to the Bergman Cancer Center."

"Where is this?"

"At UCLA Medical Center. It's a remarkable facility. Quite state of the art. The latest in diagnostic tools. Early detection often means the difference between life and death. It most certainly would have made a difference in Sam's case."

"Any life insurance?" St. John asked.

Sarnoff nodded. "Again, the Cancer Center was the beneficiary. Diane wanted our work to continue."

"And who controls those funds?"

"The foundation is fully incorporated and governed by a board of directors."

"Yourself being one of them?"

"Yes. I and eight others."

"And what about Alfred?"

"He wasn't on the board."

"Were provisions made for him in either of the Bergmans' wills?"

"Between you and me?"

St. John made reassuring noises.

"Sam and I discussed this very thing and decided against splitting the estate. Alfred Bergman has his own money and no dependents. Sam wanted to pass on knowing that Diane would be well provided for."

St. John nodded and made a pretense of checking his notes. Logan Sarnoff steepled his fingers and let them come to rest on his nose. The room was quiet enough to hear the secretary typing at her desk in the reception area. Finally the attorney seemed to come to some inner decision.

"There was one other thing."

"Yes?"

"Sam Bergman left burial instructions in his safety deposit box. A box that was in his name only. His illness prevented him from retrieving these instructions before he died, but he did alert me to their existence. Acting in the role of his executor, I met with the bank president and presented the situation. Because I could show cause as to why I needed access, I was able—in the presence of one of the bank's officers—to enter that safety deposit box. My privileges only extended to the document I was there to retrieve. However, I did see other things." He stopped talking and looked at St. John. "I wouldn't mention this except in these extraordinary circumstances."

"Yes, sir."

"There were photographs in the box. Photographs of Diane. Compromising. Pornographic. Who knows? Perhaps grounds for blackmail."

"Are these photographs still in the safety deposit box?"

"Yes, no one else would be able to open the box. Even you would need a court order. Sam's estate is still in the probate process."

"Yes, sir." St. John was well aware that flashing his badge wouldn't get him far at the bank unless he was willing to pull his gun as well.

He took down the name of the bank branch where Diane Bergman's husband had had his safety deposit box and thanked the attorney for his time.

"I hope you'll be discreet," the attorney said as he ushered St. John out the door.

"Don't worry," he said. "I have to live with myself, too."

St. John left the attorney's office, took the elevator down to the fifth floor, and found Ken Wilson's office. He showed his badge to the receptionist and was pointed to an open cubicle in the corner. The broker was on the phone but glanced up at the detective and nodded to a chair.

Wilson had no sooner completed one call when his intercom buzzed and he was alerted to two more. The broker looked at St. John with a helpless smile and took his calls.

St. John waited one more minute and then pulled out his badge and held it in front of the broker's eyes.

Ken Wilson's face went pale. "Let me get back to you," he told his caller.

St. John introduced himself and explained he was investigating the death of Diane Bergman.

"How can I help you, Detective?"

"Were you at a party with her last Friday night?"

"Yes. It was a fund-raiser for the Cancer Center. I'm on the board of directors for the foundation."

"Did you speak to Diane Bergman at the party?"

"Briefly."

"Were you aware of any arguments she might have had with anyone?"

"The only annoyance I was aware of at the party was the man we hired for security. He was an off-duty police officer and he kept cornering guests and talking their ears off."

"About what?"

"I believe he thought he was networking. He said he was retiring soon from an important chief of detectives position. He was telling all the lurid details of his cases. I guess he thought we'd be interested or impressed or something. I know he wanted references from us, the board members."

"Do you remember the guy's name?"

"Owen. Peter Owen. Do you know him?"

"Yeah," St. John said. "I know him, all right."

The hardware store down the street makes keys, but he never goes to the same locksmith twice. That would be stupid. You get a routine going and people start recognizing you. All he needed was some nosy hardware clerk to ask why he needed so many keys duplicated. Ask him what line of work he's in that requires so many different car and house keys. He has a strategy prepared if anyone ever recognizes him from another time. He'll just start asking them questions about themselves. People never noticed you were being evasive if you got them talking about their own lives.

Well, regular people anyway, not cops.

But it isn't going to come to that, he's reasonably certain. West Los Angeles has too many places where they make keys. Even some of those private mailbox places made them, although he doesn't quite trust their expertise. The other secret to his success is his ability to blend in. The trick there is to act bored. You sure don't accomplish anonymity by pulling a hat brim over your face or wearing dark shades indoors. That only attracts attention and he's learned his lessons well. Like what you leave behind can nail you, whether it's something as nebulous as suspicion in some witness's mind or something more concrete, like a footprint or strands of hair or semen.

He's also grateful for the abundance of Radio-Shacks. He always pays cash for his purchases of resistors and transformers. To date only one clerk has tried to get chummy, asking him what he was going to do with the toggle switches, twenty-gauge wire, and box of alligator clips. He mumbled something about picking the stuff up for his boss; then he looked at his watch so the guy would take the hint and his money and let him out of there.

He isn't exactly on the clock, but his absences are noted by some and he doesn't need that kind of attention.

His dream is to invent something. He knows a guy who got rich just from one stupid idea. The guy worked at some Styrofoam plant and one day noticed all those curly shavings that they swept up and threw away every day. The guy gets the idea that they would be good packing material, takes out a patent, and the next thing you know this guy is living in a mansion, driving Italian sports cars, and dating babes young enough to be his daughter.

Just one good idea, that's all it takes. He's been playing around with one gizmo for a while. It's simple, like most brilliant concepts. He took a piece of two-by-four and drove two ten-penny nails through it. The nails are six inches apart. He has soldered wire to the heads of each nail. The other ends of these wires are connected in series with a common, everyday desk lamp. He's got a field generator, found it in an army-navy surplus store in Santa Monica. When he spears a hot dog—an ordinary raw hot dog—on the tips of the two nails, cranks up the generator, and flips the switch: voilà! Within only ten seconds the hot dog is thoroughly cooked. The beauty of his invention is that the device can be used over and over.

That night Munch woke from what must have been a nightmare. She opened her eyes as soon as she was conscious. As wide awake as if she'd had a jolt of adrenaline. She got up and checked on Asia, then read, then turned out the light and just lay there. In the dark. Feeling unnamed and unwarranted panic. It was three in the morning. She had to get up in the next few hours. If she didn't get some more sleep, she'd be brain-dead all day.

She tried lying quietly, so at least her body would be rested. She realized she was clenching her fists and relaxed her fingers. Her neck and shoulders were also taut, so much so that she was barely using the pillow to support her head. She pressed fingertips to her wrist. Her pulse was still accelerated; it was as if whatever flight-or-fight impulse her dream had triggered would not shut off.

She thought about the act of rape, about what Emily Hogan had said about conviction rates being so much higher in attempted rapes as opposed to the completed act. Was that still true today? It would sure be nice if she could believe what that pamphlet said about women not being to blame for their rape. The thought was comforting in some ways but terrifying in others. Maybe she and Asia should move to a security building.

Perhaps all this free-floating anxiety had its root in unresolved issues. Had she repressed her emotions all those years ago? Did that kind of psychoanalyzing even apply to practicing drunks? She could barely remember what Culley looked like. Kind of square-jawed, wasn't he? And cleanshaven. And strong. He had been much stronger. Even if she had gotten away, where was she supposed to run in a graveyard?

Gypsy had lots of hair, down to his shoulders. It was red and curly. Full beard, too. Who knew what he looked like under all that? She remembered he used to wear Levi's everything, kept his keys on a clip that he wore at his side, and that stupid knife of his strapped to his leg like he was some kind of desperado.

They'd all been pretty full of themselves back then. The farther she got away from that life, the more she wondered what she'd ever found to like there. All the men, the lifestyle of selfish partying. All right, enough of that, she told herself. The war was over. She'd surrendered eight years ago, sweating out her addictions in the backseat of her car.

Someone was trying to hurt her. She needed to focus on that.

Trying to figure out who wanted to hurt her led to thoughts of anyone she'd ever done wrong, how her own greed always got her into trouble. She thought of that nice guy who used to come in a year ago. He had an old Caddy convertible. She sold him an intake manifold gasket job. She had been convinced at the time that it would solve his rough idle problem. When it didn't, she charged him for the work anyway and sent him off without a word of explanation. If she knew then how that act would still be haunting her at—she sat up and glanced at the clock—three-ten in the fucking morning, she'd gladly give him his money back.

But that was just the point, wasn't it? You weren't supposed to wait until the consequences of your sins threatened you before you were sorry for them.

She tried to direct her mind to more pleasant memories but could find none. She couldn't derail her past sins from her thoughts. Logic told her that she must have done something right sometime in her life. She just couldn't put her finger on anything at the moment. Whatever small act came to mind, she could easily tie to some self-serving motive. Like Garret. How long was she going to keep up the charade with him? Wouldn't it just be kinder to end it now? To free him to find someone who'd appreciate him? Was she being selfish? Keeping him around until someone better came along? Or was what they were going through now a phase? Were relationships like sobriety? Did you need to hang on and keep on keeping on even when you forgot all the reasons why?

She threw off her covers and swung her legs out of bed. Now she was standing in the bathroom. She locked the door behind her even though she was alone in the house save for Asia, whose sweet snores were loud enough to penetrate the walls. She faced the mirrored medicine cabinet and crossed her arms over her chest, hugging herself. This exercise worked only with direct eye contact. She looked deep into her own hazel eyes and said with as much conviction as she could muster, "I love you, self."

Then she said it again, and once more after that. She returned to bed and recited all the prayers she knew to shut out whatever self-destruct committee members were still gunning for her. Her last prayer to God was for the strength and wisdom to do the right thing.

And then the phone rang.

CHAPTER 14

Munch reached for the receiver, her heart beating so hard it hurt. Before she picked up the phone, she flicked on the tape recorder.

"Hello?"

"Couldn't sleep either?" the caller's mechanical voice asked.

"What do you want?"

"I never meant to hurt her," the voice said.

"You mean Robin," she asked. "Or Diane?"

"Diane? Don't go putting ideas in her head."

She remembered how St. John had coached her not to be confrontational. They wanted her to develop a level of intimacy, let him do the talking.

"So you mean Robin. You didn't want to hurt Robin."

"I love her. I know this sounds crazy. I'm not saying I understand it myself."

"Were you the one at the school?" she asked.

"I don't mind her having friends," he said. "But I can't have her being poisoned against me, not before I get a chance to win her over. Haven't you ever been so drawn to someone that you would do anything to be with them?"

"I understand irresistible urges," she said.

"Of course. Like so many of these girls, you were a drug addict. It's probably very similar."

She felt a little trill of fear in her stomach. "How did you know that?"

"You don't consider it a big secret, do you?"

She saw her opening then. "It's not something I'm proud of. I don't deny it. I don't pretend it didn't happen."

"Have you told Garret everything? Does he know about the drugs? How you would do anything and I mean anything to get a fix?"

The implied threat of his words triggered her anger. "What is this? You think you have something on me? You think you can blackmail me?"

"So you don't care who knows?"

She realized she was quickly losing control of the conversation. "How is it that you know so much about me?"

"I've made it my business to know. You should be flattered."

"Then you should also know I sponsor other addicts and alcoholics. And the thing is, I've never talked to anyone yet who didn't have a logical reason for what they did. You're obviously a smart guy, to know all you do about electricity and telephones. Can you help me understand what you want?"

"I want the normal things."

"Meaning what?" she asked. "Normal is such a relative term."

He answered with one of those odd chipmunk-sounding noises that she interpreted as laughter. Encouraged, she pressed on. "Can I ask you one thing? Why Robin?"

"She's the one. We have a connection. Her and I. I felt it the first time we met. I know her and I got off to a rocky start."

"That's what you call it?" she asked, unable to contain her incredulity. "If you truly cared for her, you'd leave her alone now. She doesn't want to see you anymore. You left scars on her body. She's completely traumatized. How can you call that love?"

"Why are you putting yourself in the middle of this?" he asked, his volume rising. "It's not as if you wanted me."

"I didn't?" she asked. Her stomach turned queasy. There was also a ringing in her ears. For a long moment all she could do was watch the tape recorder spools turn. "What makes you say that?" she finally asked.

"I know."

I know. The words, even in their strange distorted form, echoed with certainty. She believed him. "Diane didn't want you either, did she?"

"If you're going to play games," he said, "I'll hang up."

"You're the one playing all the games. A real man would use his own voice."

"You think you know what real men want? You think you're some kind of expert?"

"No, but I would like to understand what you're getting out of this. Maybe if we figured it out together—"

"It's not just about getting my dick wet. Maybe someone like you can't understand beyond that."

"I understand about doing things I can't help. I understand feeling bad afterward and wishing I could change. Is that what you're hoping for?" She paused. They said to develop intimacy, to learn whatever details she could. A name seemed like as good a place as any to start. "What should I call you?"

"Daddy," he said. "Every little girl needs a daddy."

She felt an overwhelming wave of revulsion. As if his breath were in her ear and he would reach over any second and touch her. His words ripped loose the scabs on her memories, and all the maggots wiggling beneath the surface were exposed. She hung up, needing to sever the connection with this sick intruder. Then she regretted her action, knowing she had given away too much. You should never let an adversary know when they'd scored. It just made them come back and hit that found weakness with all they had.

Asshole, she thought, staring at the phone. She pushed the stop button on the tape recorder with more force than was necessary.

She had to admit the anger she was left with felt much better than the guilt she'd been grappling with just moments before. Anger felt powerful, made you want to get up and do something. Not just lie in the dark and feel bad. Ruby always said anger was a secondary emotion, that people used it to block out deeper unpleasant feelings. Like betrayal? Munch would like to ask her now. Because being sold out really sucked.

She picked up the phone again and called St. John.

He answered on the first ring.

"It's me," she said. "He just called." She filled him in on the gist of the conversation and how she had ended the call. "I blew it, right?"

"Why do you think that?"

"I hung up on him."

"No, I think your instincts were right. He was testing you."

"So if I hadn't gotten angry at him, he would have known I was just stringing him along?"

"Exactly. I'm going to have a policewoman answering the phone and staying at your house from now on. This has gotten too heavy."

"That'll never work. He knows me. He'll know if it isn't me."

"You want me to come over?" he asked, sounding fully awake now.

"No, I'm all right," she lied. "But until this thing is resolved I'd like Asia to come stay with you guys."

"Sure," he said. "We'd love to have the little rugrat."

"Is Caroline awake?"

"Yeah, you want to talk to her?"

"Please." She waited while the phone was passed. She could hear muffled hushed whispering and then Caroline came on the line.

"Hey, kiddo."

"Hi, sorry to wake you."

"No problem. You sure you want to be involved with this creep?"

"I want to catch him. I'm sure of that."

"Don't worry about Asia," Caroline said. "I'd love to play mom for the weekend."

"She's got a ballet class on Saturday and softball on Sunday. If it's a hassle she could take a weekend off—"

"Don't be silly. Just write me out directions and I'll get her where she needs to go. It'll be fun. Really."

"She loves an audience."

"She'll have one. Do you want me to pick her up at school tomorrow?"

"Thanks. I'll tell them to expect you."

"All right, honey. Try not to worry, and be careful. Do you want to talk to Mace again?"

"Sure."

St. John came back on the line. "I'll stop by in the morning."

"Sorry to wake you," she said.

"No problem."

She hung up feeling a curious mix of emotions: relief for Asia's sake; anger at this intruder in her life; the melancholy of looking in the window of another's life and wishing it was your own. The last was that old demon jealousy raising his ugly head. Then she had one more thought that chilled her blood. She realized that Robin's "secret admirer," and very probably Diane's murderer, was at that very moment feeling much the same things.

Mace St. John watched his wife hang up the phone. She had to stretch to reach the nightstand. He appreciated the way her satin nightgown twisted at her middle and accentuated her waist. He ran a hand up her leg, stopping at her thigh.

"What's on your mind?" she asked.

"Have I told you lately how much I love you?" he asked.

She rolled on her back. Her blond hair spread out on the pillow as she pretended to contemplate his question. "I don't think you have."

He leaned over and kissed her cheek. "I love you," he said. Then he pushed back the covers and swung his legs out. "I'm going to get up for a while."

"Are you all right?"

"Yeah, yeah. Stomach's a little sour." He stood, smiled down at her. "You go back to sleep. I'll be to bed in a while."

She smiled at him, blew him a kiss, and then burrowed back into the covers. He went into the kitchen and poured himself a 7UP. A cold sweat beaded his forehead. He wiped it away and then stared at his hand for a moment. He knew he shouldn't let himself get so upset. Maybe that old adage applied here, that you shouldn't mix business with friendship. Your judgment clouds.

He walked through the house, enjoying the quiet. He chased the soda with half a bottle of Pepto-Bismol. Had to be the guacamole, he decided. He made a note to himself to tell Caroline not to fix it anymore. Not if this was the price he paid.

THURSDAY

The next morning Munch packed a small suitcase with Asia's clothes. Asia only needed one more clean school uniform to see her through the week. Munch also packed the little girl's tights, leotard, ballet shoes, softball uniform, and wedding scrapbook.

"Where are we going?" Asia asked.

Munch put on a bright smile. "You've been invited to spend the weekend with your godparents starting tonight."

Asia's shoulders slumped. "Ahh, do I have to?"

"You can show them all your new ballet moves. I know they'd love to see them." Asia needed very little encouragement to perform for a live audience. She still spoke wistfully of the curtain call and standing ovation the cast of *Pinocchio* had received last summer.

"I can sing for them, too," she said, warming to the idea.

"Yep, you do that. But right now I need you to get ready as quickly as you can." While Asia dressed, Munch changed the cassette in the tape recorder Agent Hogan had given her, taking the time to make herself a copy of the tape she would be handing over to the authorities. Her hands shook as she boxed and labeled the used tape containing her early morning call. She was running late, which was making her rush. She spilled her coffee, put too much milk on Asia's cereal, and when she looked down she saw she had misbuttoned her shirt.

Oh great, she thought. *This is going to be a wonderful day for working with heavy machinery.* She didn't even get the time to look at the morning paper and read the three things she never missed: her horoscope, the comics, and the obituaries.

She called Robin as soon as she got Asia off to school. The answering machine picked up, but instead of a personally recorded message, there was only a beep.

"Robin," Munch said. "It's me. Give me a call at work."

At nine o'clock she called again, then once more ten minutes later. She hung up when she saw St. John pulling into the station. She met him at his car, before he had a chance to get out. "We've got a problem."

"What?" he asked.

"Robin isn't returning my calls. I think we better get over there and see if she's all right."

Stefano walked past them on the way to the bathroom.

"Stefano," she said. "I'm taking a test drive. Be back in ten minutes."

"Okay," Stefano said, his tone peevish as if taking this information were some burden on him.

She stared at him a long moment, wondering if he didn't have another reason for his irritability. But Stefano just kept on walking in that way of his, as if he was very aware of his ass.

They took St. John's Buick to Robin's. The gate guard recognized them this time and waved them through without a hassle. Robin's Toyota was gone.

"Maybe she went shopping or something," St. John said.

They walked up to the front door and tried to look in the windows, but the curtains were drawn. Munch shaded her eyes with her hand and peered through a small gap between the drapes. The house was dark and seemed empty. St. John rang the doorbell. There was no response from inside.

He knocked on the front door. Three sharp authoritative raps that just screamed "cop."

"Do they train you guys how to do that?" Munch asked.

"Yeah, the same week we learn how to swagger."

She laughed, but then quickly grew serious when she spotted the transom window over the front door. "Give me a boost," she said.

He laced his fingers together. She kicked off her greasy shoes and stepped into his hands. He lifted her until her fingers could grasp the sill of the transom. It was slippery with dust.

"See anything?" he asked.

"No." She noticed that there were no trash bags stacked on the kitchen floor, waiting for some Samaritan to remove them. Maybe Robin had ventured out into the world again. St. John lowered her. Was it her imagination or did he hold on to her a second longer than was necessary? She searched his face for the hint of a blush, a nervousness in his eyes, but no, his expression, if anything, was impatient. She sat at his feet and reached for her shoes.

"Let's leave a note," she said, tying her laces. "You got a piece of paper?"

He handed her his notebook. While she looked for a clean sheet, he checked his watch. A notation in his handwriting caught her eye. *"L.S. says photos of D.B. at bank. First Federal on San Vicente."*

"Who's L.S.?" she asked, showing him the page. "D.B. is dead body, right?"

He reached for his notebook irritably.

"No, wait," she said, relinquishing it without a struggle. "D.B. is Diane Bergman, right? Just nod if I'm right."

He ripped out a blank piece of paper without giving her an answer. She wrote a brief note and wedged it in the crack of the door. She twisted the knob, but the door was locked.

"Is L.S. Logan Sarnoff? The attorney guy you went to see yesterday?"

"She probably took my advice and went to stay with relatives," he said, completely ignoring her question.

"Without telling us?"

He made an open-palmed shrug and they walked back to his car.

On the way out, St. John stopped at the gate. The gate guard stepped out of his kiosk to see what they wanted.

"Did you happen to notice Robin Davies leave today?" St. John asked.

Munch leaned across the front seat. "Gold Toyota Celica?"

The guard stared off to the right for a moment and then shook his head. "But she might have gone out the Montana exit."

"There's another exit?" Munch asked.

"Sure." The guard pointed down a street to their left.

"Thanks," St. John said.

"Are you feeling all right?" Munch asked, noticing his pallor.

St. John put a palm to his forehead. "I must have a bug or something."

"Don't breathe on me," she said. "I can't afford to get sick."

"Me neither."

When they arrived at the alternate gate, they found that it operated automatically—opening as soon as their car passed through unseen sensors. One-way spikes stretched across the exit driveway accompanied by signs warning of severe tire damage. What made the scene laughable was the entrance gate to the right. Not only was it open, but judging from the bougainvillea stems twined through its bars, it had been in the open position for weeks, possibly months.

"So much for high security," Munch said.

"It was always an illusion anyway," St. John answered.

CHAPTER 15

St. John dropped Munch back at the gas station and pondered his next move. Robin's disappearance worried him more than he wanted Munch to know. He also knew that pursuing leads in the matter was going to require diplomacy. If he called the department liaison at the phone company and asked them to check the lines going to Robin Davies's apartment, he would have to make a report of his request. On that report he was also obliged to list a case number. Since Robin Davies was not his official case, he was left with few options.

He headed back to headquarters. On his way he stuck one of the cassette tapes of Munch's calls into his tape deck. Replaying the tape only reinforced his agitation. This was one sick fuck they had on their hands. He opened his glove box and pulled out the large jar of antacid tablets. Three-quarters gone. He'd purchased the bottle only two weeks ago.

He parked in the police lot and entered through the side door, climbing the stairs to the detective squad room. He didn't go directly to his desk. Instead he stopped at the cluster of desks that comprised the Major Assault Crimes unit, or MAC as it was called.

Pete Owen was sitting in a cloud of cigarette smoke, talking on the phone. Owen was a gaunt, pale man with thinning brown hair. Sunken everything: eyes, chest, shoulders. He looked up at St. John, then made a quick, furtive gesture for St. John to take a seat.

Owen's eyes darted from St. John to a pad on his desk. "Let me get back to you on that," he said into the phone, pulling a report file over to cover his notepad. He concluded his telephone conversation with "Tomorrow, before five. Sure thing." He hung up, covered his face with both hands, and exhaled noisily. "Man," he said, letting his hands drop, "everybody's in a big hurry. What can I do for you?"

"Robin Davies," St. John said.

"What about her?"

"Rape case. Early last month."

Owen started to nod and sift through the midden of paperwork on his desk, exposing the notepad. Three questions were scrawled across it: *Medical insurance? Vacation time? 401k plans?*

Owen flipped the pad over.

"Looking for work?" St. John asked.

"I've got something lined up," Owen admitted. "But I'm keeping my options open. You know Charlie Long out of South Central?"

"Oh, sure. Retired two years ago."

"He was all set up to take over security at this lodge up in Big Bear. He and the wife sold everything, bought a cabin. Charlie was going to spend his golden years hunting and fishing."

"Sounds like Charlie."

"Then his wife gets allergies. Can you beat that shit? She can't take it up there. So what happens to Charlie? He's got to move to the desert. Now he's counting golf carts at some la-la-land golf community in Palm Springs. Hates it. Just hates it. Says Frank Sinatra is an asshole."

"So this Robin Davies."

"The one in Brentwood? Calls herself a model? You know her?"

"Friend of a friend. Anyhow, she's gone missing."

"Since when?"

"This morning. She tell you she was going out of town?"

"No. You think there's a reason to worry?"

"You know she's been getting harassing phone calls?"

Owen's face grew cautious. "Yeah. I took the report. We trapped her line but couldn't trace the call."

"So she said. The caller was using a mobile phone."

"Sounds like your interest is more than casual."

"Several months ago another woman was raped and dumped on the freeway. Rampart handled the case. Vic's name was Veronica Parker. Her rapist also shocked her into compliance and then later provided her with a nightgown."

As St. John talked, Owen had located the case file for Robin Davies and opened it. He looked up now and said, "Yeah, I know about that one. Sounded to me more like a case of a whore getting beat out of her fare."

"According to the Rampart dicks, the suspect used an electrolarynx. Whether he's missing his vocal cords or just uses it to disguise his voice, I don't know. You might want to check into that."

"Yeah, I just might," Owen said, but he made no move to make a note to himself.

"There's also a possibility that your UNSUB," he said, using cop speak for *unknown subject*, "might also be responsible for a homicide I'm investigating. White female named Diane Bergman. Her body was recovered Monday morning—"

"Diane Bergman as in widow of Sam Bergman?" Owen interrupted.

"You know her?"

"Yeah, she's on the board of the Bergman Cancer Center out at UCLA. That's where I applied for a job as head of security. Shit." He sank a little farther into his chair, ran bony fingers through his thin hair.

Obviously, St. John realized, Owen didn't bother reading twenty-four-hour crime reports or the newspaper, or this homicide wouldn't be such a surprise. "When's the last time you saw her?" he asked.

"Last Friday. I handled security at this party they gave in the Palisades. Big estate. Lots of people roaming around. We kept an eye on things, made sure no one went in any of the bedrooms, or nicked any pricey little doodads."

"Any problems at the party?"

"Nah, none to speak of. When was she killed?"

"Sunday evening sometime. I have a witness who saw her arguing with a middle-aged white male at the party on Friday night. You know who that could have been?"

Owen threw his hands in the air. "That describes most of the men there. Man," he said, pushing back in his chair and throwing his pen on the desk. "I think she liked me for the position, too. You know who's taking over her duties on the board?"

"No. Was she seeing anyone?"

"Not that I know of. She had the look though."

"What look is that?"

"You know, on the hunt. Giving guys the slow up-and-down. Like she's sizing you up for a cock ring."

"She come on to you?" St. John asked.

"Nah, I'd be way out of her league. What about her lawyer?"

"Sarnoff? What about him?"

"I should give him a call. I bet he's running things now. He was at the party, too."

"So I understand."

"Yeah, it was a real who's who, if you know what I mean. All the high and mighty of the West Side. Makes them feel good about themselves, all this charity shit. You gotta notice that they give the most time and money to diseases they have a chance of catching."

St. John nodded.

"And they can't get enough gory details," Owen went on. "Love to ask questions about the job, you know. What it's like to see dead bodies, all that shit."

"What are your thoughts on the guy calling Robin Davies?" St. John asked.

"Robin . . . ?" Owen started his sentence as a question and then stopped himself. But not before St. John caught the fact that he had already put her out of his mind even though her file was still open at his fingertips. "What more can we do? I told you the guy calling her couldn't be traced. In fact . . ." He looked down quickly at his notes. "Yeah, here it is. I told her to change her number and leave it unlisted."

"That didn't make a difference. He got her new number right away. I need you to call the phone company and check her line for other taps."

"I can do that," Owen said, closing the file.

"I'll wait," St. John told him, sitting back in his chair.

Owen gave an annoyed chuckle but picked up his phone. He was still shaking his head derisively when he asked St. John, "How good a friend *is* this friend of yours?"

Now it was St. John's turn to feel defensive. Owen couldn't know how close to the bone he'd struck with such a casual question. How good a friend was Munch? Sure he felt a bond with her. She'd saved his life. Literally. You don't ever feel casually about someone after that. But she was a kid. Well, maybe not so much anymore. The waif he'd first met had transformed herself in the last seven years. He was not immune to the softness that had emerged in her, the femininity that colored her moves, whether under a car or delivering a batch of cookies she'd made him for his birthday. Another curious development in her personality was her recovered innocence. Or, perhaps, innocence never lost despite all she had lived through. She shed her unholy childhood like the husk of a cocoon, not using it as an excuse. No, she was much too involved in living now. He loved that about her, how enthralled she was in everything he told her. It played to his ego, her appreciation of his ingenuity in adapting equipment on the Bella Donna. The way her large hazel eyes absorbed his every word when he spoke. This was a new age. Men and women could be friends. Hell, Munch knew he was happily married. Wasn't she the first one always to ask about Caroline?

Owen looked up from his phone call, hearing St. John let out a small groan. *How could he be so blind to all the signals that had been passing between them?*

"What?" Owen asked, hanging up.

"Nothing," St. John said. "I'm just an idiot sometimes."

"Yeah, me too," Owen said. "Just ask my wife."

"What did they say?" St. John asked, nodding toward the phone.

"They'll check the junction box for tampering and get back to me. You want to wait?"

"Nah, I've got to run over to the Federal Building and drop off some tapes. You might want to come. I've been working with Emily Hogan in sex crimes over there. She's building a database on sex offenders."

Owen looked at his telephone. "Maybe another time."

"Yeah, sure."

"Oh, hey," Owen said, opening the bottom drawer of his desk from which he retrieved a *Penthouse* magazine. "I bet no one mentioned this." He turned to a dog-eared page. St. John looked down at the spread featuring Robin Davies.

"What issue is this?" he asked.

"August," Owen said. "This year. Not quite the innocent little girl next door, eh?"

St. John didn't dignify the comment with an answer.

Robin woke disoriented. At first she thought she was home, then she remembered. A stab of adrenaline-charged fear brought her fully awake. The strap around her ankle prevented her from turning over. She sat up. Next to the bed was a vase of fresh roses. Their scent permeated the damp, dark room. Candles flickered on a table against the wall. Gradually other forms around her took shape. She wasn't alone.

"Morning, Sunshine," he said. He was sitting in a straight-back chair at the foot of the bed.

"What do you want?" she tried to ask, but her voice came out in a barely audible croak.

"Thirsty?" he asked.

She nodded, watching his every move, knowing she was completely at his mercy. The tops of her eyelids seemed to be pushing into her brows. Her eyeballs felt overly large and distended, bulging like some cartoon character's when they pop out looking at something fearsome. He handed her a cup of coffee. She took a sip. It was warm and sweet. Coffee had never tasted so good. The next thing she felt was an inexplicable surge of gratitude to be alive, to be feeling anything.

"Thanks," she managed, offering him a tentative smile.

Emily Hogan was at lunch when St. John stopped by her office. He left the tapes on her desk with a brief note and then returned to headquarters. Not surprisingly, Pete Owen had nothing new to report. St. John popped his head in the office of the Special Investigation Team lieutenant, Joe Graziano, and briefed him on what he was up to. By one o'clock he had his approved warrant to search Sam Bergman's safety deposit box.

The bank manager at First Federal helped St. John personally. He was a tall black man with short cropped hair showing signs of silver. He introduced himself as Felix Tornay.

"We'll all miss Diane," he said as he ushered the detective into the safety deposit vault.

"Did you work with her?" St. John asked.

"Yes. We still saw her at least once a month." Tornay removed two keys from his pocket. "What's the number again?"

"Three twenty-eight."

Both men scanned the walls until they located the box. Tornay slid the keys into their slots and turned.

"When was the last time she was in?" St. John asked.

Tornay paused, looking up to his left. "Early last week. She made a deposit, I believe. I can check our records if you need the exact day." He lifted out the box and set it on the freestanding table in the center of the room.

St. John slipped on a pair of latex gloves and raised the lid. There were several thick documents in the box. Vehicle titles, a deed to the home on Chenault, and an unsealed white envelope. St. John saw the rectangular bulge of the photographs. The warrant was written for seizure of the entire contents, but he knew the bank manager would want a written inventory.

"Ready?" St. John asked.

Felix Tornay poised his pen over his pad. "Go ahead."

"One ownership certificate to a 1982 Honda Prelude." He dropped the document into the brown paper shopping bag he'd brought. "Title to the house on Chenault."

Tornay wrote without looking up.

St. John lifted the thick white envelope, parting the opening for a quick peek inside. Diane Bergman, in a full-frontal naked exposure, pouted seductively at him, each hand cupping a full white breast. "White envelope full of Polaroid photographs," he said as nonchalantly as possible.

Tornay stopped writing and looked up. St. John grabbed another document and continued. "Ownership certificate for a 1980 Mercedes." It took another few minutes to empty the box. St. John thanked the bank manager and left.

Don't ever get murdered, he wanted to tell the guy. *We find out everything about you.*

Munch had problems concentrating. She chalked it up to more than just lack of sleep. Last night's caller knew she was sober, knew she had been an addict, knew she was dating a man named Garret. And, if she could trust what he said, she had spurned his advances. By ten-thirty, she knew she needed more caffeine if she hoped to last until five. Ducking her head into Lou's office, she asked, "Want a cup?"

He lifted the half-full mug on his desk and sniffed it. "Yeah, sure."

He started to reach in his pocket for money, but she said, "I'll get it."

Crossing the lube bays, she studied her coworkers. Carlos was on the phone with his back to the driveways, head tilted and shoulders hunched. No doubt speaking to his wife of two months. She was already pregnant, Munch knew. No way this headcase rapist could be Carlos, her buddy. They'd been together for years. She helped him all the time. He helped her, too. Though in her case it was usually helping him diagnose a problem, and the help he returned was more along the lines of lifting or pushing.

Since her promotion, the dynamics of their relationship had changed. She now had authority over him, but that wasn't the whole story. She took her position as service manager seriously. Owning her own limo business had raised her consciousness as to the concerns of management: rent, price increases, taxes, credit card chargebacks, and customer complaints. Unless the shop was making a profit, there would be no jobs. She knew she was right when she chewed Carlos out for being late or Stefano for not repairing a car correctly and then trying to bullshit his way out of it. She was also conscious of their unhappy looks. Especially Carlos's unspoken accusation that she had changed—as if she had somehow betrayed him.

She stopped by where Stefano was standing. He was spraying his tool box with WD-40, rubbing the fragrant lubricant across the red paint with a shop rag until it gleamed beneath the fluorescent lights. The freestanding tool chest was a monstrous thing, the most expensive model Snap-on tools made, and that was saying a lot. She wondered now if perhaps his obsession with his tools wasn't some symptom of inadequacy or overcompensation on Stefano's part. She would have to check with Emily Hogan on how well he fit the rapist's profile.

Certainly calling him a loner wasn't too much of a stretch. He always ate his lunch out, and never offered any explanation of where he went when he fired up his noisy little Alfa Romeo midday.

He stopped spraying and looked down at her. "Yes?"

"I'm making a run to the bakery. You want anything?"

An arrogant little smile played across his mouth. He lifted both eyebrows and stuck out his chest. "Well . . ."

Oh God, she thought, *you give these guys one little opening and they think you want to get between the sheets with them.* "C'mon," she said impatiently.

"Tea," he told her. "Black."

"You would have to be different," she said, then smiled to soften the words.

He smiled back. Even that was slimy.

She was almost down the driveway when she saw Pauley coming to work in his van full of detailing supplies. How much did she really know about him? Or the mailman, for that matter, if she was going to start looking at everyone. Talk about paranoia. This could get crazy quick.

She was still laughing at herself when she cut across the rows of metered parking to reach the bakery. D.W.'s van was parked in front. She stepped into the bakery and saw him standing at the counter. Shoelaces dangling, counting out his money. The cashier was putting two cups of coffee in a white bag already bulging with muffins. He finished his transaction and turned.

"Morning," she said.

"Oh, hi," he answered. His ears colored a little and he looked down at the bag in his hand.

"On your way to work?" she asked, wondering at his discomfort. Then she put it all together. "Two cups, huh?"

He smiled sheepishly.

She felt a funny twinge of something almost like jealousy. "I wondered what happened to you this morning," she said with a knowing smile at his double order. What on earth did she feel jealous about? The spiritually correct emotion would be happiness for him. She neither expected nor wanted him to wait for her. He was free to pursue somebody else, somebody more receptive to his charms. She shook her head. Funny how vanity and accompanying delusions sneak up on a person.

"Yeah, well," he said, pawing the linoleum with his big work boots and not meeting her eye.

Had she made him feel guilty? As if he were cheating on her? She reached over and grasped his arm. His muscles were solid under the flannel of his work shirt. "Have a good day," she said. "I mean it."

"You, too." He walked past her.

"Oh, by the way," she said. "Have you heard from Robin?"

He stopped and turned. "I won't see her again till Tuesday. Why?"

"She's not answering or returning my calls."

"Well, she can be funny that way."

"I stopped by, but she didn't seem to be home."

"Maybe she left town," he said.

"Could be. Her car was gone. Wouldn't she have notified the Meals-On-Wheels people?"

"I'm sure she would have," he said. "I'll call the office and check if you like."

"Yeah, I would. Let me know as soon as possible, okay? I'm worried."

"Well, uh, I gotta get going now." He lifted the bag of coffee by way of reminding her that she wasn't the only woman in the world.

"Talk to you later," she said.

She put in her order for the coffees and tea. The smell of brewing coffee made her think of A.A. meetings and her sponsor, Ruby. She hadn't called her in weeks. She missed the sound of Ruby's soft Ozark accent. That voice had helped her through many a rough time. Now she had to ask herself, *Had someone else in Ruby's household been listening in to those calls?*

CHAPTER 16

St. John arrived at Century Entertainment in the early afternoon. The club where Joey Polk and rape victim Veronica Parker aka "Ginger Root" worked was close to the San Diego Freeway, highly visible to the traffic going to LAX. LIVE GIRLS, the sign above the windowless building proclaimed. ALL NUDE. Then to stress the point, XXX. And finally the redundant, but grammatically correct, NUDE NUDES.

In the fifties the club had been a bowling alley with a little coffee shop in front. The walls were still painted in alternating wedges of green and pink. The coffee shop had been supplanted with a retail outlet that sold all manner of sex supplies for the discriminating adult.

He had to circle the block several times before entering the entertainment complex off Century Boulevard. When it had been Century Bowl, there was access to the grounds from the side streets. But now all those other entryways were barricaded and the long driveway running alongside the main building was mined with steep speed bumps.

He parked his Buick in a space in front reserved for customers in search of X-rated videos or a battery-operated dildo for that special someone. A group of businessmen jostled toward the entrance. One of the guys whipped out a credit card.

St. John followed, paid the cover charge, and walked through the curtained entrance. The place was dark and loud. Up on the stage a naked woman lay on her side, facing a customer in the front row. She raised her leg and gave the guy a full shot. St. John averted his gaze, embarrassed for them both. He thought of his wife, how much she would hate a place like this. And, hey, he didn't exactly approve either. But as he often explained to Caroline, he had to go where the job took him. Crimes committed in hell were not witnessed by angels in heaven.

An Asian girl in a bikini stopped at his table. "Can I get you a drink?" she asked, all smiles, small tits, great ass.

He reached for his wallet. "Bring me a Coke." The place was beginning to fill up. Men on their lunch breaks, he imagined. He feigned interest in the floor show while keeping an eye out for Joey Polk.

His drink arrived several minutes later followed by a voluptuous, tall redhead dressed in a leopard-print sarong.

"Six dollars," the waitress said and waited.

He pulled out a ten. "Give me a receipt, will you?"

The redhead put a hand on his shoulder and leaned over so that most of her tits showed. "Looking for some company, honey?"

"Is Ginger working today?" he asked, using Veronica Parker's stage name. The waitress returned with his change and a wet register receipt. He gave her a dollar tip.

"No, honey, but I can fix you up," the redhead said. "My name's Sunny. Sunny Delight. What's yours?"

"Mace."

"What's your pleasure, Mace?"

"Think we could go somewhere a little more private?"

"Sure thing," she said. "Individual private dances are fifty dollars. We do accept American Express, Visa, and MasterCard."

He unfolded his badge holder and gave her a quick peek. "I just want to ask you a few questions. Won't take long."

She sighed and called over her shoulder, "Lenny."

A large, no-neck bald guy approached. He was wearing a navy blue T-shirt with the word SECURITY written in white block letters across the back.

"Cop," she said.

Lenny stuck his chest out belligerently. St. John took his measure. Fat, muscle-bound morons didn't impress him. They were slow and clumsy. He pretended respect anyway. "I don't want trouble. Just a little information."

Lenny's face was blank of all expression. His posture—legs slightly spread, hands crossed and covering his groin—showed his San Quentin breeding. That and the predominantly blue, home-grown jail tattoos adorning his muscular arms. "What can we do for you, Officer?"

"I'm following up on an assault report. The victim's name is Veronica Parker. You might know her as Ginger."

A flicker of recognition crossed Lenny's eyes. "She stopped working here after what happened. I don't know where she went. I'm sorry I couldn't be of more help to you."

St. John seriously doubted the sincerity of Lenny's remorse. He gave them both business cards. "Call me if you hear from her. She's not in trouble. I'm trying to catch the guy who raped her."

Sunny let her hand trail provocatively across St. John's chest. "Sorry you couldn't stay and enjoy the show."

"Yeah," Lenny echoed. "Real sorry." His tone made it clear that as far as St. John was concerned, the show was over. The detective stood and started to walk toward the entrance.

"You gotta exit through the bookstore," Lenny said, pointing toward the shop of sex supplies.

"Bookstore?" St. John realized this was a marketing ploy. Obviously Century Entertainment had taken a lesson from Disneyland, herding everyone getting off the rides through the souvenir stand. He pushed through the one-way door of the attached shop, past mannequins with spike-studded leather bustiers and the rack of porn magazines. He stopped and bought a copy of each of the latest issues. The cashier was surprised and a little offended when St. John insisted on a receipt.

D.W. called Munch at a couple minutes past three. "Robin's fine," he said.

"Did you talk to her?" Munch asked.

"She left a message at the hospital that she was going away for the week."

"The hospital?"

"Yeah, she talked to some volunteer with the Meals-On-Wheels program."

"I wish she had called me," she said.

"She probably will."

That afternoon business picked up. It more than picked up. It flooded in. Sometimes Munch wondered if all those customers waited huddled behind some starting line and at a prearranged signal all agreed to come in at once.

She didn't even get a chance to use the bathroom until just before she left. The wad of toilet paper she had jammed into the hole above the dispenser was on the floor. Whether it had fallen out or been pushed from the other side, she didn't know. She picked it up and stuffed it back in. Whatever was going on here would have to wait until tomorrow.

She washed up and then went into Lou's office to use the phone.

"Who you calling?" Lou asked.

"The school."

"St. Teresa's," a woman's voice answered.

"Mrs. Frowein?"

"Yes, this is she."

"This is Munch Mancini. Do you know if Asia was picked up yet?"

"Yes. I waited with her myself. I even made Mrs. St. John show me her driver's license."

Munch smiled. "Thank you."

"My goodness, dear, it was the least I could do."

The house was quiet when Munch got home. She turned on the television and took a long bath. The phone rang at six-thirty. She switched on the tape recorder and then lifted the receiver.

"Hello?"

"Hi." Asia's high voice was breathless.

"Are you having fun?" Munch asked.

"Caroline and me are making cookies," Asia said.

"Caroline and I," Caroline said in the background.

"Caroline and I," Asia dutifully repeated. "And I saw a rabbit at school today."

"What kind of cookies?"

"Chocolate chip."

"Are any of them making it into the oven?"

"Yesss," Asia said in that long-suffering tone of hers.

"I miss you."

Munch heard the phone drop and Asia saying, "Sit. Sit. Good girl."

Caroline's voice came on the line then. "Sorry about that," she said. "Were you through talking?"

"Yeah. She sounds like she's having a good time."

"How are you?" Caroline asked.

Lonely, jealous. "Fine."

"Do you want to come over?"

"No. Really, I'm fine. I'm going to have some soup, and then climb into bed with a good book."

"We're here if you need us," Caroline said.

"I know that. You always have been."

After hanging up, Munch felt too exhausted to worry about Robin anymore. Asia was safe, that was what mattered most. She double-checked all the doors and windows before going to bed. Sleep was a long time coming.

CHAPTER 17

FRIDAY

Friday at work was even busier than the last part of Thursday. Munch was grateful for the pace. Even Lou was less than dour. The workload forced him to roll up his sleeves and perform two tune-ups and a carb overhaul.

He actually grinned at her when she drove past him on her way into her lube bay to service a Chevy Luv. Feeling good, she set the hoist and lifted the pickup into the air. After draining the oil, changing the filter, and squirting grease into the zerk fittings, she inspected the rear axle assembly. Checking the differential fluid level involved unscrewing the fill plug and sticking her finger in the hole. After confirming that the axle housing was full, she brought her finger to her nose. She loved the pungent smell of the molasses-thick ninety-weight gear oil. She would always groan if it spilled into her hair or down her shirt, but secretly she really didn't mind. It was the smell of her making her own living, doing a job she loved. What did she care if someone else had gone to some college so that he or she could spend a life at a desk inside an eighteen-story office building, window view or no?

The rest of the day breezed by with all of the back-room crew running from job to job, making horns blow, air-conditioning colder, and stumbling idles smooth. The only hassle was some guy in a Suburban who claimed to have an appointment with Pauley for a detail. Munch had to tell him that Pauley had called in earlier to say he was spending the day mobile. This meant that instead of working out of the station, Pauley loaded up his various supplies and went to his customers' homes instead. The guy in the Suburban wanted to make another appointment, and Munch had to explain that Pauley was an independent contractor. She didn't have a home phone number for him. The guy in the Suburban didn't leave before giving Munch a whole ration of shit about how that was no way to run a business.

When she arrived home that evening, Munch left her GTO idling in her driveway as she got out to unlock the padlock on the chain-link fence. She arched her back to relieve her stiff muscles, now aggravated by cold and the commute home—the first time she had sat still all day. She knew she had cleared close to three hundred dollars. If only every day could be so profitable!

A movement by the house caught her eye. It was Garret, waiting for her on her front porch. She raised a hand in greeting. He must have hopped the four-foot chain-link fence encircling the front yard. They had plans to attend a cocktail reception at Logan Sarnoff's home in the Palisades. Tonight's party was a thank-you to all the vendors and volunteers like Munch who were contributing to the Charity League–sponsored fund-raiser to find a cure for cancer. Most of the funds raised were already earmarked for the Bergman Cancer Center, though it seemed to Munch that if they spent less time and money on all the thank-you and congratulations parties, they'd have a lot more for the charities. She wished the party had been canceled out of respect for Diane. The only appointment she wanted to keep was with a hot bubble bath and maybe some good boom-boom with Garret.

Her fingers refused to cooperate. The numerous tiny cuts on her knuckles broke open anew as she fit first one key then a second into the dual padlocks on the gate. Black-stained lines delineated the calluses on her thumbs and forefingers where they had gripped countless bolts. Her cuticles were hopeless: split at the quick and encased in grease. She knew that even if she soaked for an hour, her hands wouldn't come completely clean. That would take a week—it only happened on the last day of one of her twice-a-year vacations.

"Sorry," she said, taking in Garret's scrubbed face and newly pressed slacks. "I'll try to be quick.

I got tied up at work with a Chrysler; the customer wanted it back for the weekend." She paused before opening the door and smiled at him. "Man, what a day."

"How about a kiss?" he asked.

She obliged him, then opened the door. After kicking off her shoes, she strode across the living room. Garret followed. "I'll get cleaned up," she said, "and we'll go."

"No problem," he answered. "What can I do to help?"

"Turn back the clock," she said, shedding her greasy uniform as she headed for the laundry room. She threw her uniform shirt and pants in the diaper pail she kept for that purpose. At the end of the week she took the dirties in to work for the uniform company to launder and replace with a clean set. Until then, she didn't want her house to smell like the shop. Once she was home, she preferred gardenias.

"Don't stress," he said. "It's actually fashionable to arrive a little late."

"We're going to fashionable, all right." The washing machine was full with a load of towels and sheets. She had meant to run it that morning. She picked up a box of laundry soap and began to scatter it on the dry wash.

"I'll do it," Garret said, taking the box from her. "You go. Make yourself pretty . . . er."

She wished he would stop trying so hard to flatter her. She didn't need it. "Thanks," she told him, forcing a smile. Just because she was feeling rushed and irritated, she shouldn't take it out on him. Maybe he gave her so many unasked-for strokes because he was hungry for them himself. The problem was, she hated to offer him any extra encouragement. She was already granting him as much as she felt comfortable with. But she couldn't very well explain that, could she? That she was willing to share her bed a night a week but drew the line at emotional involvement.

She walked through the kitchen in her underwear, grabbed the dish soap, and took it into the bathroom with her. Squeezing a liberal dollop under the rushing water, she waited for the tub level to rise in a fluffy layer of lemon-scented bubbles that would cut the grease from her body and prevent a bathtub ring.

She usually allowed twenty minutes for her evening bath. She needed the time to herself, a decompression period to give her a chance to unwind and make the transition between work and home. Ruby had suggested this when they were still speaking regularly.

With a small X-Acto knife Munch carefully scraped away as much grease as she could from under her fingernails, letting the curls of black grease fall into the open toilet. She then finished undressing, undid her hair, and sank into the steaming bubble bath with a sigh of short-lived relief as Garret joined her.

"Need me to wash your back?"

"More like watch it," she said, hunching her shoulders forward.

"Something happen?"

"Remember Diane Bergman? The nice lady I told you about who hired the limo last weekend?"

"Yeah, the one you're helping raise funds for cancer research. She'll be there tonight, right?"

"No. Haven't you seen the news? She died."

"She did? She was only like fifty, wasn't she?"

"It wasn't natural causes. And another customer of mine, Robin Davies, who lives down the street from the station, got raped last month."

"Jesus," he said, stunned. He closed the toilet lid and sat. "Did they catch the guy?"

"No." She soaped up a washcloth and started working on her knuckles. "The guy is still out there. He's been calling Robin and we think he's the same one who called me."

"What?" Garret jumped to his feet. "When was this?"

"Tuesday night."

"Why didn't you call me?"

"It was late."

"And you probably figured it was just some prank," he said. His expression was so hopeful she didn't want to deflate him by mentioning the note on Asia's coat or the second call.

"Yeah, right. But then I was at Robin's house with Mace St. John . . ."

"When did you see him?"

"He came by the other day."

"So he's the 'we.'"

She hesitated before answering. "He's involved in the case."

"He wants to get into your pants."

"No he doesn't. We're friends, Garret. You knew that when I met you."

"That's what you said."

She felt the tension increasing in her neck and shoulders. "I've told you a million times, he's not like that. He's Asia's godfather, for Chrissakes. You know I help him with the Bella Donna."

Garret snorted. "And I suppose you're the only mechanic around."

"Maybe he just recognizes genius."

"Yeah, I'm sure that's it."

The bubbles around her were beginning to pop. She covered her face with the washcloth and inhaled.

"Why were you at Robin's house with him? For that matter, why are you even involved at all?"

"I thought he, we, could help her. While we were there she played a message the rapist left her and it sounded like the same guy who called me."

"Why didn't you tell me?"

"I've been trying. And now to make matters even more complicated, Robin has disappeared."

"Are you in danger?"

"No, I don't think so. The cops gave me a recorder to tape the calls."

"How many times has this guy called you? What does he say?" He ran his fingers through his hair and paced the small floor.

"You can hear for yourself. I dubbed the tapes before I handed them over."

He stopped pacing and looked at her as if something had just occurred to him. "Where's Asia?"

"Just to be on the safe side she's going to stay with the St. Johns for the next few days."

"I'm not leaving you alone," he said. Then he made a self-satisfied nod. "Bet you're glad you're moving, though."

Munch had forgotten all about their plans to look at a house this weekend. But she did remember that she hadn't committed to anything, yet. She was saved from having to respond when their conversation was interrupted by a banging in the laundry room. Garret got up to investigate. Munch opened the drain and stepped out of the bath. In the time it took to dry herself, the thumping hadn't ceased. She wrapped herself in a towel and followed Garret.

She found him in the laundry room clutching both edges of the bucking washing machine, attempting to hold it still. She pushed him aside, lifted the lid, pulled apart a clump of wet towels, and rearranged them. When she shut the lid the washer resumed its cycle. Quietly. She wanted to ask him how he had managed to live almost forty years on this earth and not know how to deal with or recognize the symptoms of an unevenly loaded washing machine. She bit back the words. Someone once said you could tell the people who were in the most successful relationships by the bite marks on their tongues. To be honest, she was more concerned with her character than her relationship. She didn't want to be a bitch.

Perhaps that would be the excuse she would use when she finally ended it with Garret. Last Sunday morning had been a prime example. They had been watching TV, and she came in and sat on the edge of the bed. She knew she was blocking his view. She was trying to give him an opportunity to stand up for himself. That's all she wanted, him to be his own man and not some meek little puppy dog. Instead he had just moved aside and not said anything, leaving her to feel like a shrew and wondering why she couldn't appreciate this guy.

She also knew that if it had been St. John there in the laundry room playing Billy Bronco to the bucking washer, she would have thought it was cute. Maybe with the right guy, she wouldn't have to be a bitch.

She was pulling on her dress when Garret called to her from the living room.

"Where's the tape?"

"Still in my tape deck."

"Mind if I play it?"

"Go ahead." She heard the clicks of the sound system being turned on and took a deep breath to calm herself. "His voice is gonna sound weird. He does something to disguise it."

Garret didn't respond. She came out of the bedroom and stopped in the doorway of the living room. He had put the headphones on to listen to the tape. She saw the spools turning and his expression darken. When it was over, he ripped the headphones from his head and said, "How does he know my name?"

"I don't know," she said. "It's like he reads my mail or listens to my telephone conversations."

"Maybe you should start keeping more to yourself."

"Whatever happened to, 'You're only as sick as your secrets'?"

"Forget about all that. What I want to know is who is this guy?"

She shook her head. "If we knew, he wouldn't be roaming the streets."

Twenty minutes later they were in Garret's Camaro heading for the cocktail party in the Palisades Highlands. While he drove, she painted her short nails with dark red lacquer. The sharp scent of acetone filled the car.

"You know everyone's going to be talking about Diane Bergman's death tonight," she said.

"Let's see what we can find out."

She smiled in his direction. Sometimes he was all right.

The house was elegant. A glass cabinet in the foyer held porcelain figurines painted in delicate pastel shades. The sunken living room had a fire going. A camelback antique clock kept time on the mantel. White sofas stood out on richly colored Persian carpets. Tuxedo-clad servers wove among the guests with trays of hors d'oeuvres and drinks.

Munch felt a sharp cramp in her stomach and wondered if her body was already telling her it was time to leave. Garret brought her a soda and announced that he was going to mingle. He seemed right at home. She watched him make the rounds, drink in hand, smiling, shaking hands, and chatting it up. He could be a regular little social butterfly when necessary. She knew he wanted to own his own independent repair shop one day and be a fixture in the community. Good for him. Ambition was an admirable thing.

He was soon swallowed by the crowd of local philanthropists. Business cards flew like confetti. She backed into a corner of the room and tried to act as if she were having an interesting time. A half hour crept slowly by and then her stomach grumbled. She hadn't eaten since around ten. The line by the food table had died down. She walked over to the impressive array of finger foods and reached for a canapé. Her nails felt weird, like they couldn't breathe. The dark color she'd used to cover the grease stains seemed to draw extra attention to her hands. This suspicion was only confirmed when a well-dressed man at her elbow said, "Aren't you the mechanic?"

"Yes, sir," she answered. "And you are?"

"Logan Sarnoff."

"Ah, our host. You have a great house."

He made a modest gesture of acknowledgment. "Did you study auto mechanics in high school?"

She'd only gotten as far as ninth grade but to this man she said, "It wasn't offered to women then."

"Was your father an auto mechanic?"

She considered briefly telling this guy the whole truth, imagining the shock on his face when she announced that her father had been a pimp—also not a profession offered in high school. She went with a milder truth, saying only, "No, he wasn't mechanically inclined. I just figured it would be a good trade wherever I wound up."

"And do you work on your own car?"

This was not the first time she had been asked this question. Still, the blatant stupidity of it always surprised her. "What sort of law do you practice?" she asked. "Criminal? Defense?"

"No, I do the occasional litigation but mainly I'm a family attorney specializing in estate planning."

"And did you write your own will or pay someone to do it?"

To his credit, he chuckled and said, "Touché." He took a sip of his drink and added, "Say, I could have used you a few months ago."

"Did your car break down?"

"No, I had a litigation involving an automobile transmission. I had to learn all about the darn thing so I could argue whether the new transmission was rebuilt or reconditioned. That determination is based on how many parts had been replaced as opposed to merely cleaned and greased."

"And the difference was?" Munch asked.

"A couple thousand dollars." He shrugged as if it were small change.

"That must be a cool part of your job," she said, "always learning about new stuff."

"It can be."

Munch looked down, swirled the ice cubes in her Coca-Cola. "Isn't it sad about the Bergmans?"

"Yes," he said. "I knew them both. Terrible thing."

"I still can't believe it." She pulled an envelope out of her purse. Diane's name was written across the front. "I meant to give her these pictures the last time I saw her."

"Pictures?" he asked.

"Of my limo," she said, returning to her purse for a business card. "So the people at the auction can see what they're bidding on." She handed him two cards, in case one of his rich friends wanted one, too. "Have you heard anything more about what happened to her?"

Sarnoff took a sip of his cocktail and fixed her with gin-glazed eyes. "I have friends in the DA's office. I know the police are expending every effort to catch the killer. They have reason to believe he has struck in this area several times in the last few months, although this is the first murder."

"As opposed to . . ." She let the statement linger open-ended.

"Rape," he said.

"The rapist that uses a cattle prod or something?" she asked.

"I'm not sure how much I'm at liberty to say," he said.

"It's been on the news," she lied to salve his conscience. There was no reason for him to know she was privy to inside information. She didn't have time to convince him she could be trusted. St. John told her once that a good way to get a guy to talk was to lead him to believe he wasn't the first or only source.

"Well then, yes," Sarnoff said, "Diane's murderer was most probably the sick bastard who has been raping and torturing women with electrocution. In Di's case, he went too far." His face crumpled and he made a high, keening noise as if he were going to cry.

She put a hand on his arm. "I know the homicide cop on the case. Don't you worry. He'll find the killer and bring him to justice."

"Let's just hope that happens before another innocent woman has to suffer," Sarnoff said.

Garret rotated back toward them. His face made her think of a satisfied chipmunk, the way his round cheeks were flushed red and his brown eyes glowed. He must have made some gratifying contacts. She introduced him to Sarnoff, who removed a white handkerchief from his pocket.

"You've got quite a woman here," the lawyer said, dabbing his brow with the hankie and seeming to have set his grief aside. "A real go-getter."

"Yes, sir," Garret said, hugging her to him. "She's something, all right."

Sarnoff nodded and wandered off. The doorbell rang, followed by shouting and laughter. She heard glass breaking from the direction of the kitchen, but nobody registered alarm. Garret still held her. His thumb rubbed repetitive swirls on her arm until her flesh burned. She put a hand over his to stop the growing friction. The room felt close with body heat and exhaled air.

"Hear anything interesting?" she asked, having to raise her voice a bit to be heard above the growing din.

"Sam Bergman had big bucks and no kids. He and Diane met at his bank. She worked there as a loan officer."

"He owned the bank?"

"Among other things. He was thirty years her senior. You didn't tell me that."

"Are you saying she was a gold digger?" Munch asked. "People aren't saying that, are they?"

"More like wondering who gets the money now," he said. "Best bet is they left it all to their charity unless some long-lost relative shows up."

She sneaked a look at her watch. It was nine o'clock. Surely they had made enough of an appearance here. Someone jostled into her back. The beginning of a headache was forming behind her eyes.

She pulled him into a corner. He stood beside her, facing the crowded room. "Garret?"

"Hmm?"

"If you could be anywhere in the world right now, where would you be?"

He fixed her with a particularly sappy look. "Right here with you."

Her stomach spasmed again. It wasn't the answer she had been looking for. She was thinking more in terms of at the beach on a sunny day, or even at the movies. "Would you mind if we left now?"

"Not at all."

He put a protective arm around her shoulder and they fought their way to the front door. She couldn't tell if he was guiding her or holding her back.

CHAPTER 18

Mace St. John was looking forward to a quiet evening at home. He'd spent the whole day talking to friends of Diane Bergman and visiting the stores where Diane shopped. Everyone gave him much the same story. Diane Bergman was a nice woman, unpretentious, caring, but somewhat private. Nobody he spoke to had seen her after the party last Friday night.

Her car still hadn't shown up. Chances are it was already south of the border being fitted with new VIN tags and license plates or being parted out at some chop shop. The toxicology results from the coroner weren't in yet. He was told he could expect them the middle of next week.

He read the mail addressed to Diane Bergman that had arrived since her death, listened to her voice on her answering machine, and spent a few more hours at her house on Chenault. He was starting to feel as if he knew her. It was a common phenomenon when investigating a murder as the victim's life and habits took shape. Their voices, faces, even desires, became part of his memories. That part of the job didn't get to him so much. It was the living who gave him the problems—recalcitrant witnesses, pushy reporters, and the frequently small-minded, always self-interested brass.

Now it was time for him to leave all that at the office. Caroline had a meat loaf in the oven. Asia was at the kitchen table, cutting out pictures of brides from a magazine and pasting them into her scrapbook.

"Why do you like weddings so much?" Caroline asked.

"Well," Asia said, pausing in her work to turn and address Caroline. Her brown eyes glowed with enthusiasm. "When you get married you get to have a big party with all your friends."

"With a cake," Mace said.

"Uh huh," Asia said, nodding. "And everyone brings you presents and it's not even your birthday."

"Oh, I see," Caroline said. "So you like the party."

"What about the groom?" Mace asked. "You have one picked out?"

"Oh no," Asia said solemnly. "I'm much too young for the responsibility of a husband."

He ruffled her hair as he passed, loving the way she wrinkled her nose in annoyance.

"Lay off," she said, swiping at his hand.

"What?" he asked, dropping his jaw in mock astonishment.

"Don't mess up my curlies," she said, lowering her voice to sound more menacing.

He picked up the pair of scissors she was using. "I'm going to cut those curlies off."

"No, no!" Asia screamed. The dogs jumped to their feet and barked.

"All right, all right," Caroline yelled as the noise level increased.

Mace laughed. "I'm going to get you," he warned and waved the scissors over his head. Asia's shrill screams masked his own unexpected grunt of pain. He lowered the scissors and grabbed at his shoulder with his free hand.

Asia screamed again. Samantha jumped up and nipped his arm. Mace looked at the dog in amazement.

"Good dog, Sammy," Asia said.

"Serves you right," Caroline said wryly.

"I don't believe it. First my dog turns on me, now my own wife. What's next?" He massaged his cramping chest and shoulder muscles, trying to make the gesture appear casual.

Caroline pushed a beer into his hands. "Go watch TV or something. I'll call you when dinner is ready."

He went into the living room and sat in his father's old recliner. He didn't turn the television on, preferring instead to listen to the happy noises coming from the kitchen. It had been a trying week, doing the legwork of two men, this thing with Munch. Rumors of more budget cuts were circulating at the station. Just yesterday he had heard that the brass was going to eliminate take-home vehicles. *Fuck,* he thought. *What next? Would they be expected to pay for their own gas?*

There was a clatter of flatware and then Caroline's calm, low voice telling Asia where to place the forks and spoons.

He sipped his beer, hoping it would calm his stomach. Caroline joined him after about ten minutes.

"Rub my shoulders, will you, honey?" he asked.

Caroline gripped either side of his collarbone and began moving her thumbs over his muscles.

"No," he said, moving her hands more to the top of his shoulder joints. "Up here. It burns."

"Both sides?" she asked.

"Yeah, and then down my arms."

"How long has this been going on?" she asked. Something in her tone alerted Asia, who looked up from her scrapbook.

"The last couple days," he said.

Caroline came around to the front of him and looked at his face. "Your color is terrible. Is your stomach still upset?"

"A little. But I don't think I have a fever."

"And yet you're sweating. I think we should go to the hospital."

"The hospital?" He sat up. "I got a little burning in my arm and you think I need the Emergency

Room?" He stood up and crossed the room. "You know what they're going to want to do, don't you?" He started to throw his hands up in the air for emphasis, but then remembered the pain he'd felt in the kitchen. "They're gonna want to run a bunch of tests." He glared at her, daring her to deny this.

Asia stood in the doorway, absorbing every word.

Caroline just looked at him with that stubborn calmness of hers and said, "I'll shut off the oven."

"You're going to get everyone all worked up over nothing," he said. "You know that, don't you?" Hot saliva filled his mouth. For a moment he wondered if he was going to puke.

"Asia," Caroline said, "go get your coat, honey."

"Oh, shit, Caroline. You're going to drag the kid down there, too?"

"Put your shoes on," she said.

"This is crazy," he told her, sliding his feet into his loafers. "It's probably just some Asian flu bug."

"Hey," Asia said, "I don't have no flu bug."

"*Any* flu bug," Caroline said, "and he didn't mean Asian you, he meant Asian as in place."

"Oh," she said.

"Or it's food poisoning," Mace continued. "That can be nasty. Make a guy feel off for days. That's probably it." Asia was already by the front door. Caroline gave each of the dogs a biscuit and told them to be good. Mace pulled on his coat, wincing as his arms lifted to find the sleeves.

He reached for the keys but Caroline grabbed them first.

"I'll drive," she said.

He didn't argue, which surprised them both. The truth was he really did feel like shit.

They all climbed into Caroline's Monte Carlo. Asia got in the backseat and strapped herself in. "What's happening?" she asked, wide-eyed and on the verge of tears.

"I think Mace should see a doctor," Caroline explained as she started the car. "And the only ones that are open right now are at the hospital."

"Is this an emergency?" Asia asked.

To St. John's surprise Caroline replied, "Yes."

Didn't she know you weren't supposed to scare kids? Saliva filled his mouth again. He rested his head against the window glass and tried to collect his strength.

Their destination was Marina Mercy Hospital on Lincoln, only several miles from their house on the canals. By the time they reached the first stoplight, he had remembered what his dad always used to say about how the hospitals themselves made you sick. He forced a smile and said in his most innocently surprised voice, "Huh. You know what? I think I'm feeling better."

Caroline didn't look at him. As soon as the light changed she gunned it across the intersection.

He wiped away the cold sweat on his forehead. "Look," he said. "There's a nice coffee shop up here. Let's go get a piece of pie, some coffee. We can talk this over."

"Can we?" Asia asked.

"No," Caroline said. "We're going to the hospital."

"Pull over," he said. "Right now. I mean it. God damn it." He meant to put more volume in his voice, but his stomach was churning butter. "This is a waste of time."

"If I were you," Caroline said, "I wouldn't get myself all riled up. You're just making it worse."

"Oh, yeah? What is it *you* think is wrong with me?"

She reached over and grabbed his hand. Her fingertips were cold. "I think you're having a heart attack." She let go of his hand to maneuver the car into the Emergency Room parking lot.

Her words hit him as only the truth could. "But I'm only forty-two," he said.

Caroline shut off the car and came around to help him out. "Maybe they'll go easy on you seeing as how this is a first offense."

"You're a bitch," he said.

"I know," she answered softly.

He gripped her hand.

"C'mon, kiddo," she said to Asia.

Asia climbed out of the car and grabbed Caroline's other hand. Her thumb was in her mouth. Together the three of them progressed through the sliding doors and up to the counter.

"Can I help you?" the nurse asked from her chair.

"Yes," Caroline said. "I think my husband is having a heart attack."

Asia was very quiet. Her large eyes searched the adult faces above her. Mace winked at her, tried not to wince while she was looking.

The nurse came around the counter and had Mace sit. She put a blood pressure cuff on his arm and her stethoscope to his chest.

"I've got our insurance card," Caroline said, thumbing through her wallet.

But the nurse wasn't interested. She rushed past Caroline and grabbed a wheelchair. "Get in," she told Mace. "How long have you been experiencing these symptoms?"

"A couple days," he said. "It's the flu, right?"

"The one from Asia the place," Asia volunteered.

The nurse turned to Caroline. "Wait out here, ma'am. Someone will be out to talk to you in a minute."

"Is it his heart?" Caroline asked.

"Oh, yeah," the nurse said. "But don't worry."

His last words to his wife before they wheeled him to the examination area were, "Don't tell anyone."

Caroline located the bank of pay phones with her eyes. She had no intention of keeping this to herself. Mace would just have to understand. This was happening to her, too.

"Is Mace going to die?" Asia asked.

"No. He's going to be all right," Caroline said. She picked dimes and quarters out of her coin purse, and put them in her pocket.

"Can I call my mom?" Asia asked.

"Let's wait until we know more," Caroline said. She sifted through the stack of magazines on the low table in front of them until she found a children's magazine. "Come here, kiddo." She lifted Asia onto her lap and opened the magazine to an article about static electricity. "Here," she said, "you read to me."

While Asia stumbled over the text, Caroline waited for the nurse to return from the hallway leading to the examination rooms. On the entire drive to the hospital she had been certain she was acting appropriately. Now, as she sat here in the blaze of the hospital waiting room lights, she wondered why she wasn't more upset. Because we're here, she told herself, and he's too damn cantankerous to let anything be seriously wrong. There was no sense in getting worked up until the facts were in. For now, all she could do was wait here for the next task, which would probably entail filling out a bunch of paperwork.

A different woman emerged from the double doors where they had wheeled Mace through. She was wearing green surgical scrubs and was carrying a clipboard. "St. John?" she called out.

Caroline put aside the magazine and slid Asia to her feet. "Yes?" She stood, gathering her purse and Asia's coat.

The woman in the green scrubs walked over to them. There was a white plastic name tag pinned over her left pocket that identified her as *Gomez, R.N.* "Are you the family?" she asked.

"Yes. I'm his wife."

"You can come in and wait with him," she said.

Caroline and Asia were led to a one-bed examination room. Mace was lying on a bed, attached to several monitors. Oxygen was fed to him by a nasal cannula. The plastic tubing ran to a wall valve with a floating ball indicator. It hovered at six liters a minute. She didn't know how good or bad that was.

Mace's eyes were wet and bright with fear. Caroline realized she had never seen him afraid before. She tried to smile encouragingly but the sight of his emotion was too much. He moved his body to one side and she sat at the end of his bed. Asia leaned into her legs.

This is really happening, Caroline realized. She lay down beside him, buried her face in the sheets bunched over his stomach, and allowed herself to cry. He found her hand and gripped it tightly.

"We've given him an EKG," Gomez explained in a loud, careful voice. "The ER doctor has read the results and sent for the cardiologist. She's on her way. We're still waiting for results of the blood work."

Caroline sat up, waiting for the words *"He's going to be fine."*

Instead Gomez handed her a tissue and said, "We know he's had a heart attack. The blood test will measure his levels of creatine phosphokinase. CPK is an enzyme in the muscle cells that leaks into the bloodstream when the muscle is damaged. This happens when there's been a heart attack."

"I thought you were certain of that," Caroline said, wondering how many times Nurse Gomez was going to repeat the words *heart attack*. It was as if she were trying to make a point or something.

"We still need to do the test. What we're trying to determine now is if the heart attack is still going on."

"And then what?"

"Your cardiologist will determine the best course of treatment. There are drugs we can administer that will attack clots. And if those don't give us results, an angiogram is possibly in order."

A second woman, dressed in white and carrying a metal clipboard, came into the room and conferred with the woman in scrubs. Gomez looked over the chart and then made a notation.

"Wait a minute," Mace said, sitting up in agitation. "What's this test?"

Caroline studied the monitors above him, wishing she knew what they all meant.

Gomez also glanced at the monitors. She turned to the woman with the chart and said, "Doctor said to give him two milligrams of morphine." She addressed Mace in that same overly loud voice she'd used earlier with them. "Sir, the cardiologist is on the way. Your wife and daughter can stay with you until she gets here. Try to relax and let the medicine do its work."

Caroline watched Mace's face soften as the morphine inserted into his IV entered his bloodstream.

"Don't tell anyone," he said again.

"Okay," she said, looking into his eyes and understanding him thoroughly. If there was one thing Mace strove for, it was control, especially over himself. He had to be feeling terribly vulnerable. "Let's just get through this night."

On the way home from the party, Munch remembered she was out of milk.

"Can we stop at the store?" she asked. "There's a little mom and pop place at the bottom of Chautauqua. I just need to run in for a minute."

The only parking was across the street. Garret locked his Camaro before following her to the store. She grabbed a quart of milk and headed for the register, where there were two customers ahead of her. While she waited, she picked up a copy of *Auto Trader* magazine and flipped through the import car section. She was considering buying a Honda with a blown engine at work, and she wanted to check what that year's model sold for running.

Garret, meanwhile, picked up a copy of *Sports Illustrated*. Munch noticed with amusement that the sports magazines were placed next to *Penthouse* and *Playboy*. Munch's eye wandered to the cover of *Penthouse*. She gasped at the face of the model draped coyly around a grinning scarecrow.

"I know her," she said, picking up the magazine. Garret looked up. "Who?"

"This is Robin," Munch said, pointing at the magazine. "The one I told you about. The customer that got raped." She stared. "I've got to call Mace."

Garret stuffed his magazine back into the rack while Munch took the *Penthouse* to the counter.

"You're going to buy that?" he asked.

"Yeah."

"So you can show it to your cop friend?"

"What's your problem?"

"What's *my* problem? Oh, I don't know. Maybe I'm weird. Why should it bother me that my girl-friend wants to share some porno with another man?"

"This could be evidence or something," she said.

"Yeah, right."

Munch paid for the milk and the magazine. They stepped outside. The night was balmy with Santa Ana winds. Three teenage boys dressed in white T-shirts and baggy pants ran across the street. Munch watched them closely. The angle of the boys' path led directly toward Garret's Camaro. She and Garret were stuck on the oppo-site side of the street, waiting for another break in traffic.

The boys reached the sidewalk, jostling one another, looking over their shoulders. Suddenly, one of them darted to his left and picked up a ficus tree in a huge wooden planter from the front of a pottery store. He ran down the street with the leafy branches resting on his shoulder, potting soil spilling on the sidewalk.

"Hey!" Munch yelled in a guttural tone, her best imitation of a cop voice. A voice that said, *Stop, punk.*

The boy dropped the tree. Unfortunately, the wooden planter split open on contact with the ground. The kid was still bent over when he turned to the direction of her voice and said in a high, almost hysterical voice, "I was just . . ." Then he stopped speaking, probably realizing that there was no excuse, no innocent explanation for what he had done. His two friends up ahead gestured for him to join them.

"I knew they were up to something," Munch said, feeling excited and powerful. Even heroic.

"Shut up," Garret said quietly.

She didn't look at him. They were both facing the street. Traffic still hadn't slowed. The three boys were moving away at a walk—too cocky to run. She realized that her challenging the kids had automatically involved Garret, too. She didn't have the right to front him off like that. She had assumed that he'd be proud to do the right thing. She was wrong.

CHAPTER 19

As soon as they got back to her house, Munch noticed the empty space on the dinette table. The tape recorder that Emily Hogan had given her was gone. She looked quickly over to the shelves housing her stereo system. The receiver, turntable, and tape deck were all there.

"The tape machine is gone," she said out loud.

"What?" Garret said. "You mean the one the cops gave you?"

"Yeah," she answered, striding over to the table. "The box of tapes is gone, too."

"The TV's still here," he said.

"That isn't what he was after."

"How'd he get in?"

"I don't know." She picked up the phone and dialed the St. Johns' number, but to her surprise got their answering machine.

"Where would they all be at—" she checked her watch "—ten-thirty at night?" she asked Garret.

He took off his coat and threw it on the couch. "Maybe they went to a movie or something." He walked past her, through the kitchen, and checked the back door. "It's locked," he reported. Together they inspected all the windows. None of the screens had been disturbed and none of the sills showed signs of being jimmied, pried, or broken.

Munch used the phone in her bedroom to call the police. She dialed 911. A woman's voice answered and asked the nature of her emergency.

"I've been robbed," she said.

"Robbed?" the woman asked in a patronizing, almost jovial fashion. "Or burglarized?"

Munch stared at the phone in amazement. She was a fucking victim here and this woman was going to play semantic games? "Someone broke into my house and stole a tape recorder. I guess that makes it a burglary."

The woman read back Munch's address and asked if that was where she was calling from. Munch confirmed that the information on the woman's screen was correct.

"And who are you?" the lady asked.

"Miranda Mancini," Munch told her, giving her seldom-used Christian name.

"We'll send an officer out to take a report."

Munch hung up and called the beeper number on Emily Hogan's business card. She was still waiting for the agent to return the call when the black-

and-white patrol car pulled up in front of the house.

The officer was a dark-haired woman whose name plate identified her as L. Ducatee. She sat at the small dining room table and wrote down everything Munch told her, including the facts that there had been no sign of forced entry and that Munch was already the victim of menacing calls that were under investigation. Officer Ducatee advised her to lock her doors, then gave Munch a pamphlet with her name and badge number filled in at the top.

"A detective from Burglary will be getting in touch with you," Ducatee said. "If you want, we have a home safety program. One of our counselors will come to your house and perform a safety inspection. It won't cost a thing."

"Thanks," Munch said. "I'll give it some thought."

The cop left. Munch locked the door after her, looked down at the phone that still hadn't rung, and then said to Garret, "What is this? Everybody's disappearing on me."

"I'm not," he said.

She took off her coat, the movement concealing her expression. His words were meant to be reassuring. So why did she feel exasperated? What more did she want from a guy? Maybe this was as good as it got. There was no Sir Galahad on his white steed, no such thing as a soul mate. She wasn't perfect and had no right to expect perfection from another. You had to take the good with the bad. The alternative was to be alone, which wouldn't be the end of the world, but for Asia's sake she'd like to have a more regular family with a positive male role model.

"Let's go to bed."

She didn't have to ask twice.

The cardiologist's name was Dr. Cameron Krueger. She stood about five feet two inches tall, had short gray hair, and was surprisingly obese. She waddled into the room out of breath and sat or rather leaned into the lone chair in the examination room. St. John realized that her excess fat made bending more than ten degrees at the waist a physical challenge. He waited for her verdict as she sat across from him, shaking her head over his lab results. The padding on her thighs forced her legs apart so that there was a distance of some two feet between kneecaps.

"So," she said, sweat beaded on her forehead, "how much did you smoke before you met me?"

"I don't really smoke," St. John said. "Just cigars."

He saw Caroline rolling her eyes and it pissed him off.

Dr. Krueger looked up from his chart. "You're having a heart attack. Your CPK levels haven't started to go down yet and your EKG still shows a pattern of ischemia, or insufficient blood flow, in the anterior or front wall of the heart muscle. We need to get you into a treatment room upstairs and see what's going on in there. The best way to see inside you is with an angiography. We basically inject dye into your blood vessels and film the results."

"Then what?" Caroline asked.

"That depends on what we find. Sometimes an angioplasty is enough to clear out the blockage. Other times, surgery is the answer."

"As in a bypass?" he asked.

"We'll know more after the procedure." The doctor handed him release forms to sign.

He looked at Caroline. "What do you think?"

"We have to find out what's going on. I think you should do it."

He signed his name at the bottom of the consent forms.

Asia tugged at Caroline's shirt and said, "Excuse me, I have to go to the bathroom."

"Can you hold it for a minute longer?" Caroline asked.

"No, that's all right," St. John said. "Take her now."

Dr. Krueger looked at Caroline and said, "You can meet us upstairs. The cardiac unit is on the third floor. I'll come find you in the waiting room."

The attendants came in and kicked off the wheel locks on the gurney. St. John realized they were going to take him away now, just roll him out. He fought back sudden terror. The monitors betrayed his quickened pulse.

"We'll see you upstairs," Caroline said. She bent down and kissed him on the lips.

"Go," he said again. "I'm in good hands here." When Caroline and Asia had left the room he looked in the doctor's eyes and said, "Give it to me straight, Doc. Is this it?"

"I've seen worse," she said. "The important thing is to get you into treatment."

They wheeled him into an elevator and took him to the third floor. In the hallway they were met by a swarthy-complexioned man wearing surgical scrubs.

"This is my associate, Dr. Patel," Dr. Krueger said. "He's going to be performing your angiography."

"How do you do, sir," Dr. Patel said in a post-colonial British accent common to educated East Indians.

"Just peachy, Doc."

"Yes, quite," the doctor said with a knowing but not unsympathetic smile. "I assure you that you will receive the best possible care. I have per-formed this procedure hundreds of times."

They all entered a large room filled with people in surgical gowns. The sign on the door identified this place as the cardiac catherization laboratory. St. John was helped out of his clothing and onto a motorized table. There he was strapped in and harnessed to var-ious machines. A nurse brought out a shallow bowl of hot water and a razor with which she shaved the inside of his right thigh all the way to the groin. When she was done she swabbed the area with a reddish-brown solution that smelled like iodine.

"This isn't going to hurt, is it?" he asked the nurse, only half joking.

She replied with a weak smile. It didn't take a rocket scientist to read between the lines.

"You going to knock me out for this, Doc?" St. John asked Patel.

"Oh no, old boy. You'll be with us for the duration. Not to worry. You'll be getting a local anesthetic. Here." He touched the crease where St. John's abdomen met his upper leg.

St. John closed his eyes. The image that came to him was of his father, years ago. St. John was eight, maybe nine. It was a warm summer evening. The back door was open and the orange trees his mother had planted before she died were in bloom. Their sweet scent washed over him as he sat on the front porch holding their cocker spaniel, Fluffy. Digger was standing in the kitchen, ironing. Harry Caray was on the radio. The Cubs were winning for a change.

He opened his eyes again and saw that they had erected a surgical tent around his lower body. Dr. Patel kept up a patter as he worked, explaining how he was inserting a needle into the femoral artery, followed by a guide wire. The guide wire would be inserted only a small distance, just enough to get the plastic catheter tube on its way to the aorta.

One of the surgical nurses shuffled over to his side and checked his pulse. He noticed that she was wearing blue surgical booties. They were identical to the type criminalists wore when they were trying not to contaminate a crime scene.

He always knew when looking at crime scene photographs if the techs had been there already. The booties left their own distinctive marks, fuzzy, oversized. He'd seen photos like that just the other morning, but something about them wasn't right.

Dammit. He knew he'd hit on something important to think about. He just couldn't connect the dots through the cloud of whatever drugs they had him on. He closed his eyes to help him concentrate and the next thing he knew, Dr. Krueger was talking to him. He must have dozed off for a minute, because now the room was cleared of everyone but him and the cardiologist.

"The angiogram showed a ninety-five percent obstruction in your left anterior descending artery," Dr. Krueger said without preamble. "If we do nothing besides pharmaceutical therapy, there is a fifty percent chance that you'll have a heart attack in the next five years." She paused. "And there's a ninety percent chance that that heart attack will be fatal. When I was in medical school, they had a nickname for this particular lesion."

"What was that?"

"Widow maker."

"So what's your recommendation, Doc?" he asked. His tongue felt thick and furry, like his brain.

"We're going to review the film and discuss the best method of treatment. We've left the sheath in your groin in place. We'd like to do a procedure called an angioplasty. Dr. Patel will go into your femoral artery again with a catheter. Only this time there will be a balloon attached. He will snake the catheter all the way to your lesion and then inflate the balloon. Hopefully, he'll be able to get past the plaque and reestablish good flow through the artery."

"Hopefully?"

"We have a ninety percent success rate with the balloon."

"What are the risks?"

"There's a two percent chance of rupturing the artery. And in that event we'll have to go in and do immediate surgery. But don't worry, we'll have a team of cardiac surgeons on standby in case of that eventuality."

"You said a ninety percent success rate. What happens the other ten percent of the time?"

"We can't get the balloon into the artery that is obstructed. In that case, you still have the option of surgery."

"Some option," St. John said.

"We've done this procedure hundreds of times. Dr. Patel is an excellent interventional cardiologist."

St. John smacked his dry lips. "Have you talked to my wife?"

"I'm going to speak to her now."

"When do you want to do all this?"

"Sometime tomorrow after we've all had plenty

of time to discuss our best plan of attack. Meanwhile, we need you to stay quiet."

"I'll be good," he said.

Caroline looked up when Dr. Krueger entered the waiting room. Asia was asleep on the Naugahyde sofa and snoring loudly.

"How's he doing?" Caroline asked.

"Fine, fine. He's sedated. The procedure went well." Then Dr. Krueger went over with Caroline what she had just explained to her patient.

"I don't know what he told you," Caroline said, "but he smokes a box of those little cigars a day."

"Don't worry," Dr. Krueger said. "Whatever a patient tells us that he smokes and drinks, we know to automatically double it."

"Can I see him?"

"Sure. He's going to be groggy. You can leave your daughter here. I'll have the nurses keep an eye on her."

Caroline stroked Asia's cheek and didn't bother correcting the doctor. Maybe they'd all do a better job if they thought Mace had a young child.

The ICU was protected by electronically locked doors. Caroline had to identify herself by speaking into an intercom before they would buzz her in. Mace was in an alcove near the center of the ward. His color was better, but not by much. She lifted his hand to her cheek and willed health to his body, his heart. He started and grimaced, then opened his eyes. She saw him struggle to get his bearings.

"Does it hurt?" she asked.

He smacked his mouth. She found the water bottle on his bedside table and lifted the straw to his lips. He drank.

A nurse bustled into the room and headed right for him, speaking in a loud voice. "Mace?" she practically shouted.

Caroline jumped back out of the woman's way.

St. John fixed a bloodshot eye on the woman. "I'm here," he said.

She wrapped a blood pressure cuff around his arm, rather roughly, Caroline felt. "How are you doing?" the nurse said. "Better?"

St. John looked at her with an expression of annoyance bordering on contempt. "You don't get it, do you?" he said. "I feel like shit."

Caroline stifled a giggle and said, "He's pretty out of it."

"You should hear the names they call me after I pull out the breathing tubes," the nurse said with a smile.

Caroline decided she wasn't so bad after all.

After the nurse was gone, Caroline picked up her husband's hand, being careful not to tangle the wire clipped to his index finger. "What do you think?" she asked.

"I guess we go for it," he said.

"I'll sign the forms," she said.

"Yeah, and call my dad."

Caroline didn't remind him that his father had been dead for almost a year.

CHAPTER 20

Robin's first steps were tentative. Her limbs felt watery from lack of use.

"Protein," he said. "You need more protein in your diet. Don't worry. I'll take good care of you."

He grabbed her arm, but gently, and helped her to the bathroom. All her makeup, soaps, creams, and hairbrushes were already there, lined up neatly on the counter.

"You'll feel better," he said, "when you clean up a bit."

"Can I please have some more light?" she asked.

"Coming right up."

She leaned in the doorway and watched him set up his apparatus. He had some sort of machine with a crank handle on it. Wires trailed from the machine. He showed her how they were fitted with tiny cylindrical sockets made of what looked like copper. Each socket had a rubber insulated boot that slid along the wire. He lifted a multicolored hank of wiring from the floor. Each of those wires had solid extensions soldered to their ends. He selected three from the harness on the floor and plugged them into the sockets on the wires attached to his box, being careful to slide the rubber insulators over the mated ends.

"You want to try it?" he asked.

"What do I do?" she asked.

"Kneel down," he said.

She forced her knees to bend. Her legs collapsed. He caught her before she fell and pushed the box between her legs.

"Just turn the crank here, like you're winding up a jack-in-the-box." He took her hand and placed it on the handle. "Don't be afraid," he cooed into her ear. "I love you. I won't hurt you if I don't have to."

His warm breath against her ear raised goose bumps along her arm. He hadn't lied to her yet. He had his principles. She turned the crank.

"Faster," he urged.

She complied. The machine offered resistance that seemed to drop off as it gathered momentum. It made a jingling noise; she felt it grow warm. The lightbulbs above the bathroom sink glowed dimly at first and then turned bright white.

"*Voilà*," he said.

"You're amazing," she said. He had to pry her fingers loose from the crank.

When St. John awoke he was shivering. They had him hooked up to all the machines. A plastic tube blew oxygen gently into his nose. The white, round adhesive EKG leads with the snaps in the center were still taped to his chest and abdomen. Colored wires trailed from the leads to the heart monitors just out of his line of sight. Another contraption with a trailing wire was clipped on his index finger. Clear fluid dripped into his arm via an IV needle inserted there. He tried to read the label on the bag of fluid hanging from the IV pole but couldn't seem to focus.

The sheath in his leg throbbed. It felt as if he'd been stabbed with a knitting needle. His chest felt different. There were new, scary burning sensations streaming out in all directions from his heart but particularly from under the left side of his rib cage.

He pushed his head into the pillow and pictured those damaged, fragile blood vessels. They had looked like dark spaghetti on the monitor. His legs cramped, but when he shifted positions he was rewarded with a sharp stitch in his side. He let out a groan.

The nurse on duty poked her head through the doorway. "Everything all right?" she asked.

"Yeah," he said. His tongue felt twice its normal thickness. "No more dope, though." His voice cracked. He tried to clear his throat.

"Want some water, hon?" the nurse asked.

"Thanks, yeah."

She put a straw to his lips and told him to go slow.

Any slower I'd be dead, he thought. There was something he needed to think about. Something important about footprints and photographs of dead women. Had to be the Diane Bergman case.

He coughed suddenly as the water went down the wrong tube. The sudden jerk brought sharp pain. He waved away the nurse, closed his eyes, and visualized the crime scene on the shoulder of the freeway. He saw Diane Bergman's body with the legs spread open. Her face, depersonalized with silver duct tape. And around the corpse . . . the footprints.

Footprints, something about the footprints. He felt his consciousness slipping away and tried to hold on just a few more seconds. He was so close to completing the thought. His body seemed to weigh a thousand pounds. He sank deeper and deeper into the bedding. His thoughts slowed to a floating blackness.

He felt a cold hand on his forehead and jerked in response. He immediately regretted the suddenness of his action and the renewed pain it brought to his chest.

"Sorry if I startled you," he heard Caroline's voice say.

He opened his eyes. The nurse was gone. It was just Caroline standing there. The clock on the wall read seven o'clock. He didn't know if it was A.M. or P.M. It was three-something last time he'd checked. His utter helplessness annoyed him and he goddamn didn't need or want her pity.

"Where have you been?" he said.

"They only let me in here a couple of minutes at a time. Hospital policy."

She smiled down at him as she spoke. She looked tired.

"What about the kid?"

"She's fine. I called Munch. She'll be here in a little while."

"I guess you had to do that."

"I should call Lieutenant Graziano."

"Let's wait a day on that," he said. "I'm not on call this weekend."

"But you have an ongoing case," she said.

"I'm still working on it," he said, tapping his temple with his forefinger.

"Uh-huh," she said, sounding skeptical. "Do you want to see Munch when she gets here?"

"Yeah, sure, send the little munchkin in. We've got a few things to straighten out."

Munch and Garret parked in the lot for visitors. She stopped briefly at the information desk and was directed to the elevators that would take her to the third floor and ICU. They went to the waiting room first. Caroline and Asia had set up camp in one of the corners. Asia had a new coloring book with the gift shop's price tag still pasted to the front cover. Caroline was reading a mag-azine, but put it aside when she saw Munch and Garret.

Munch went to Caroline first and hugged her. "How is he?"

"The same, we're just waiting now."

Munch introduced Caroline to Garret. He shook her hand and offered his sympathies. Munch wanted to tell him that nobody had died yet.

Asia gathered her crayons and stuffed them back into their box. Munch crouched in front of her. "And how are you this morning?"

"We slept here all night," Asia said. "Mace had a heart attack."

"So I heard. Was it scary?"

"A little, but the doctor said they would take excellent care of him."

Munch smiled, always pleased when Asia used any three-syllable word besides "whatever."

"He asked to see you," Caroline said.

Munch put her arms around Asia. "I'm going to go say hi to Mace and then we'll go get your stuff and take you to softball."

"All right," Asia said.

Garret stayed with Asia while Caroline walked Munch over to the intercom. She pushed the button and after a moment a voice said, "Yes?"

"This is Caroline St. John, I have a visitor for Mace."

"Come on in," the voice said. The door buzzed and Caroline pulled it open.

Caroline held back, though. "You go in," she said. "I'll wait out here."

St. John was in a bed near the nurses' station. His eyes were half open, his mouth slack. Munch studied the monitors surrounding him. The raster patterns on the oscilloscope were very similar to the ones she saw every day when diagnosing automotive problems. St. John appeared to be firing on all eight with no fouled plugs or faulty plug wires. She came up to the side of his bed and picked up his hand. His eyes rolled open but didn't look focused.

"Hi," she said.

He worked his mouth a few seconds, looking like someone just waking from a deep sleep. "Hi," he croaked back.

"Caroline said you asked for me."

"Give me a minute to get it together here." His eyes rolled back and his mouth hung open.

She started to think he had gone back to sleep and then his eyes opened wide. "That guy call you anymore?"

"No, I haven't heard from him since I talked to you last. Don't worry about him. I'll be all right. You just rest now."

"No, something I need to tell you." He smacked his lips again. One of his hands patted at his chest. "You got a light?"

"You can't smoke in here," she said, smiling a little in spite of the gravity of the situation. It was bizarre to see him so stoned. "What do they have you on?"

"Morphine or something," he said. "I told them no more."

That explains it, she thought. *Some people just can't hold their opiates.* "Try to enjoy yourself," she said.

"Fuck that," he said, shaking himself awake. "Tell me what's going on."

"I was in a liquor store last night and I was looking at the magazine display. Robin's picture was on the cover of *Penthouse.*"

"Diane Bergman, too," he said.

"Diane was on the cover of *Penthouse*?" Munch asked, not able to hold back a smile. "Which one was that? The senior issue?"

"No, no," he said. He closed his eyes. Once more his mouth went slack, then he jerked suddenly and let out a groan. She tightened her grip on his hand and put her other hand on his forehead. It was damp and cold. A shiver ran through his body, then he blinked and said, "Whew," as the pain passed.

"You okay?" she asked, wishing she could take his pain into herself.

"Yeah, yeah. Where were we?"

"Diane in *Penthouse*?"

"No. Pictures of her. I saw pictures of her. They all had pictures taken."

"Who all?" Munch asked, leaning closer. "All the women who were raped?" She remembered something odd the rapist had said in his last phone call. He made a reference to "*many of you girls.*" Is that what he meant? Girls who had their photographs taken nude?

St. John put a finger to his lips and said, "Shhh. Loose lips sink ships."

"Is that what you wanted to tell me?" she asked. This was like talking to someone in his sleep.

He shook his head no. "I wanted to tell you that you're a beautiful woman," he said. "You're smart. You care. Some man is going to be very lucky to have you someday."

She smiled. She liked where he was going, stoned or not.

His eyes cleared and when he looked at her she knew that he was all aware. "I can't be that man," he said. "And I'm sorry."

She felt her expression freeze on her face. At the same time, her scalp went hot. "I know that," she said, bristling, throwing a perimeter around her vulnerabilities. Then she let down, softened her tone, taking this opportunity to address openly the subtext she'd been dancing around for months, if not longer. "I've always known that," she told him. She smoothed back his hair and kissed him on the lips. For just a fraction of a second, he kissed her back. "I'm going to go now," she said. "Do you want me to send Caroline in?"

He nodded and she left him.

When she reentered the visiting room, she stopped for a second to study the three people sitting there—each represented ghosts of past, present, and future. Garret had an arm around Asia's shoulder and was speaking to Caroline in low tones. She was lucky to have each of them—Garret included. When the call had come at 6 A.M. from Caroline, explaining where they were and what had happened, Garret had sprung into considerate mode—offering to help in any way he could.

"Can I get you some more coffee?" he asked Caroline now.

"No," she said. "I'm fine." She looked up when Munch approached. "How is he?"

"In la-la land, but strong. You can tell. He asked to see you."

Caroline dug in her purse and handed Munch a house key. "I know you'll want to get Asia's softball uniform and dance clothes." She turned to Asia and said, "Sorry, kiddo, I was looking forward to seeing your game today."

"That's all right," Asia said.

Munch took the key, proud of Asia's show of maturity. "When will you know more?" she asked Caroline.

"This afternoon, I think."

"We'll stop in later," Garret said.

"Thank you," Caroline said. "I'll need you to feed the dogs, too."

"No problem."

Munch gave her a hug and they left to go pick up Asia's things.

St. John smiled at his wife. "Hi, babe."

"Hi, yourself. How are you feeling? Can I bring you anything?"

"A bottle of scotch would be nice."

"I'll see if it's on the approved list."

"I guess you'd better call the office. Tell them what happened."

"I'll go do it now. How was Munch?" she asked. Her eyes told him that he had no secrets from her even when he managed to keep them from himself.

"She'll be okay," he said. "The kid's a survivor."

CHAPTER 21

Munch let herself into the St. Johns' house. Sam and Nicky greeted them at the door, tails thumping the wall. It was kinda nice how they were always so happy to see her again. Maybe after they were settled in the new place she'd take Asia to the pound and pick out a dog. The new dog, Brownie, was not as friendly, hanging back in the kitchen and barking.

"It's okay," Munch told her. "We're the good guys." To prove it she went to the pantry and retrieved cans of dog food and the bag of kibble.

Asia's suitcase was in the living room, but her stuff was scattered throughout the house. Her scrapbook of wedding photographs and assorted memorabilia lay open on the kitchen table.

"What's all this?" Garret asked.

"These are mine," Asia said.

"Yeah," Munch said, "don't get any ideas." She put the dogs' dishes on the floor and turned to her daughter. "Have you had breakfast?"

"Caroline bought me some yogurt and a banana at the hospital."

"Okay, good. Change into your uniform now. After you wash your face and brush your teeth."

While Asia ran off to comply, Munch and Garret gathered her things. St. John's sports coat hung over the back of one of the kitchen chairs. Munch lifted it and felt the weight of his notebook in the breast pocket.

"I'm going to hang this up," she told Garret, and went into the master bedroom, which smelled strongly of his cologne. She looked down at the king-size bed and felt like the intruder she was. The notebook in his pocket called to her.

Fuck it, she thought. *I have an investment in this.* She walked toward the closet. Out of Garret's view, she stuck her hand in the coat pocket and pulled out the notebook.

St. John's printing was neat if rather cryptic. *Veronica Parker aka Ginger Root. Prior victim. Dt. Rosales, Rampart. Century Ent. on Century Blvd. Known Assoc. Joey Polk* Attempted interview 10/9. Uncoop. witnesses.*

Century Ent. had to be Century Entertainment, the nude dance club in Inglewood. And Veronica Parker had to be a dancer there. Judging from his notes, St. John hadn't had much luck.

"You get lost or something?" Garret called from the other room.

Munch started guiltily and jammed the notebook back into the pocket of the sports coat. "Be right there."

Garret had Asia's uniform laid out on the couch and seemed rather proud of himself for doing so. Munch gathered the jersey, pants, and shoes and brought them to Asia in the bathroom.

"Honey," she said, after closing the door, "would you mind if I took off for a little while during your game?"

"Is Garret staying?" she asked.

"Yes. He's really looking forward to it."

"What are you going to do?"

"I have to run a favor for a friend. It shouldn't take long."

"All right," she said as she squirmed into her clothes. "Whatever."

St. John watched helplessly as the nurse injected his IV. He felt the wave of numbing narcosis sweep through his brain. When Lieutenant Graziano strode into the ICU, Mace could do little more than smile wanly.

"How are you?" the lieutenant asked. Deep lines of worry creased his forehead.

"I'm cool," St. John said. It sounded as if he were speaking underwater. He struggled to surface. He was lost in the corridors of his brain, wandering, trying to follow a path of thought to its logical conclusion. But then, like a dream, just when he felt as if he was getting somewhere important, the thread of his reasoning evaporated and no amount of effort could bring it back. He kept having the same dream about surgeons dancing around a corpse.

"The important thing is to rest, get well," Lieutenant Graziano said. "The bills will be covered, Caroline will be looked after. We take care of our own."

"The Bergman murder," Mace said.

"I've already got another detective on it. He's got your notes. If there's any questions he'll come see you for clarity. Don't worry. We're on it."

"Who's on it?"

"Owen," Graziano said. "He said the two of you have already talked."

"Oh, shit," St. John groaned. "The guy is useless. He already compromised the case with his big mouth."

"Which case?"

St. John licked his lips. He was confused for a moment. Owen had screwed up and talked about his rape case, not the Bergman murder. "Robin Davies. Ask him about Robin Davies."

Graziano patted St. John's shoulder. "Don't worry. Everything's under control. You just get well."

"Wait a minute." St. John meant to hold up his hand, but when he looked down, it was still lying across the blanket. "The blue fibers that I found in the footprints. Check them against blue disposable booties like the kind criminalists and hospital personnel use. The person who dumped Diane Bergman's body on the side of the freeway might have been wearing hospital booties over his shoes."

Graziano walked out the door without reacting and St. John wondered if he'd even spoken aloud.

* * *

Munch dropped off Asia and Garret at the ball field and then headed over to the Bella Donna. She had her own key and used it to enter the lounge section of the train car. She went straight to the small table covered with papers, knowing St. John had a habit of bringing work over to his big-boy fort.

She soon found a folder marked BERGMAN HOMI-CIDE. Taking a deep breath, she opened the file and stared at the photographs. There were pictures of Diane's body as it was found on the freeway. Silver duct tape covered her eyes. Her legs were spread open obscenely, the nightgown hiked up over her thighs, exposing the dark patch of pubic hair. Numbered yellow markers were placed next to evidence surrounding the body. The killer, assuming this was who had dumped the body, had left footprints in the muddy silt.

Munch turned to the next photograph. It was of Diane's face with the tape removed from her eyes. It was the same picture St. John had shown Munch on Tuesday. Page after page of eight-by-ten glossies recorded every inch of damaged skin. The body was stretched out on a steel gurney. Several photographs of Diane's back showed specific close-ups of a blanched rectangle of skin at the base of her neck. In one shot the label of a negligee was positioned next to the patch of skin in question. The two weren't an exact match, but there were probably a lot of things that would account for that. But then another inconsistency struck her. The negligee had spaghetti straps; the top and bottom edges were trimmed in lace. If the label of the negligee had left a mark on Diane's skin, according to the crime scene photograph, it should have been positioned much farther down her back. Munch flipped back to the crime scene photographs to confirm this and then read the accompanying report from the coroner.

No evidence of rape had been found. Toxicology reports were still pending, but stomach contents were verified. The medical examiner reported that shrimp had been one of Diane's last meals.

Funny, Munch thought, *they were serving shrimp at that party I worked in the Palisades.* She looked over St. John's notes and discovered he hadn't been able to find anybody who had spoken with or seen Diane after the party last Friday, yet they believed she had been murdered sometime Sunday.

Munch found a Xerox of the guest list with the unexplained inscription in the margin: *100,000s CARC 35¼ –23.* Something about it seemed familiar. She copied the numbers and letters onto a business card and stuck it in her wallet.

In separate plastic evidence bags Munch discovered another packet of photographs. They were Polaroids, nude Polaroids of Diane. This must have been what St. John was mumbling about. Diane was smiling seductively at whoever was holding the camera, a dark-nippled pendulous breast cupped in each manicured hand. She was obviously posing for her lover. According to the evidence tag, St. John had recovered these pictures from Sam Bergman's safety deposit box.

Garret had wanted to take similar-themed Polaroids of Munch and she had let him. She wondered now if she should ask for them back when they broke up. *When,* she realized the word she had voiced in her head. Not *if.*

It also occurred to her, as had no doubt also occurred to St. John, that they had found another common thread between Diane and Robin.

It was almost ten when Munch pulled into the parking lot of Century Entertainment. Two men stood in the doorway watching her park. She studied them back, secure in the anonymity of her dark glasses. Both men were in their thirties, dress shirts bulging with fatty muscle, ties knotted around thick necks. Short, no-nonsense haircuts. She got out of the car and walked toward them, stopping when she was close enough to read the signs plastered to the walls of the anteroom. Tuesday—according to the posted notices—was porn star night. Another hand-lettered placard announced that for ten dollars you could have your picture taken with one of the girls. An example was included of a middle-aged man looking sheepish as some vamp in Tina Turner hot pants wrapped herself around him.

A larger black-and-white sign listed the dress code for patrons. It was very specific: no hats, no open shoes, no holey shirts or pants, no gang attire. Shirts must be tucked in.

"Why the shirt-tucked-in rule?" she asked. "You worried about weapons?"

The smaller of the two doormen, a guy with Neanderthal eyebrows and a florid complexion, looked at her primly. "This is a gentlemen's club," he said.

Oh, please, she thought while keeping her face impassive. She pointed to the sign by the cash register and then reached into her purse for her wallet. "Five-dollar cover?" she asked.

The guy with the eyebrows spoke again. "And a two-drink minimum. But women are not allowed in by themselves," he said.

"You worried about hookers?" she asked in a confidential tone.

"No," the guy said, looking at her as if she was dense. "Wives."

Yeah, wives could be a problem, Munch knew. "I'm looking for a friend of mine," she said. "A girl that dances here."

"Which one?"

Munch read the banner under a glossy photo of the Tina Turner look-alike. "Testarosa."

"All right, wait here," he said, "I'll see if she's free."

Munch doubted that very much.

The guy returned a minute later and crooked a finger at Munch, indicating she could enter.

The club was dark. She was enveloped by the blackness as soon as she passed through the heavy curtains, following the doorman/bouncer, who said his name was Dirk. Obviously a pseudonym. She was also momentarily assaulted by the music—rousing rock—played loud as it should be so that it took over your senses and made you feel like moving. Chairs were arranged in rows pointing toward the stage where a naked woman strutted toward a chrome firemen's pole. X-rated videos played on the televisions mounted high in the room's corners.

Half of the tables were filled, especially those closest to the runway. Gang-banging Cholos with shaved heads sat next to businessmen in suits and housepainters in coveralls. Most of the men's attention was focused on the show in progress. The woman up there was now rubbing herself on the chrome pole with an enthusiasm Munch was sure she'd regret tomorrow. The guys around the footlights waved five-, ten-, even twenty-dollar bills at her.

Dirk led Munch across the floor to a majestic black woman in a long, straight wig. He had to crane his head up to say something in her ear. Testarosa nodded, giving Munch a once-over.

Munch felt like a wren among peacocks. She jammed her grease-stained hands in her pockets.

Testarosa was clothed only in a thin negligee that was slit up the thigh. It was clear that her full round breasts often made good their threat to spill all the way out the front. Even without her high heels she probably stood five ten. She guided Munch over to a fireplace near the middle of the room. "Let's sit here," she said. "It's kind of cold."

Munch was anything but cold. She shed her brown leather jacket and set her purse at her feet.

Another girl dressed in a short teddy took a seat on the hearth.

"Dirk said you knew me."

"I was hoping to talk to you," Munch said. "If you don't mind."

"We're all good listeners," Testarosa said. She held her face one inch from Munch's, speaking loudly over the music. "That's mostly what we do here. Listen to the men's problems. You know. Maybe their wives or girlfriends don't have the time for them. We make them forget about their problems for a while. It's all about the fantasy."

Munch nodded, mesmerized by this woman, who periodically punctuated her words by pressing her large breasts together.

"I'm trying to find out what happened to Veronica Parker."

Testarosa's manner instantly changed. A scowl replaced her smile. "Some fool ripped her off, that's what happened, and then dumped her on the freeway like some piece of trash."

"You know who it was?" Munch asked.

"If I did, I'd be telling someone before this," Testarosa said. She looked at the girl in the teddy. "Ain't that right?"

The girl nodded.

"We stick together," Testarosa added. "Help each other out. If we see someone making a mistake, we try to talk to them. You know." The tall stripper looked side to side the way people do when they're about to let something confidential slip. "The only way they found her is because her leg was sticking straight up. Dude left her like that, with it all hanging out, tied up like some dog or something."

"That's some cold shit," Munch said, easily slipping into street vernacular.

"What's Veronica to you?" the dancer asked.

"I think the same guy who did her did some other broads I know. He gets off on torture. He killed this one woman, a nice older lady." Testarosa's face wasn't registering a strong interest. Munch saw her troll the room with her eyes and changed tactics. "Do you have any kids?"

This brought another suspicious scowl. "Why you want to know that?"

Munch didn't back down. "Because I've got a little girl. She's seven. The other day I found a note pinned on her jacket saying if he needed to hurt me, he could."

"Same freak?"

"That's right."

Dirk started coming toward them. Testarosa stood.

"C'mon," she said. "I think the harem room is available."

She led Munch to the back of the club where there were several theme rooms. The first room they passed had a little girl motif complete with stuffed animals and cheerleader pom-poms; the second resembled a torture chamber with manacles and whips hanging from the walls. Munch paused to stare.

"We get a lot of CEO's in here," Testarosa explained. "They feel bad cuz they got to be firing people all the time. They like us to spank them and pull on their nipples, tell 'em how bad they is."

She led Munch to a third room decorated with peacock feathers and large rattan fans. Testarosa crossed the Persian carpet to sit on a large round bed covered with satin-slipped throw cushions. She leaned back on her elbows and arched her back, which caused her large breasts to protrude even more.

The bed was the only furniture in the room. Munch slouched against the doorway, trying to look more relaxed than she felt.

"This is really something," she said, at a loss for anything else to say. "You like it here?"

"It's all right. Money's good." A pause. "Real good."

"But no actual sex."

"That's right. It's all about the fantasy."

"How long have you been, uh, performing here?"

"Eight years," she said proudly. "One more year to go and then I'm done with this."

"Is that right?"

"Yep. A lot of these girls, they don't plan for their futures. Spend all their money on costumes or partying, living in them hotel rooms. I tell them they should be buying a house, saving their money.

Me? I've been going to school, getting my MBA. Soon as I graduate, I'm joining the real world."

"Good for you," she said, meaning it. The song blasting out of the speakers in the main room changed to "Fooled Around and Fell in Love." Testarosa's head started nodding to the beat.

"What did you mean about the guy tying her up like a dog?" Munch asked.

Testarosa fixed her with a look curiously devoid of expression. "Dude put a rope around her neck. Yanked her around with it. Shot her with one of them stun gun things the cops use."

"Do you know how I can get in touch with her? I'd like to ask her some questions."

"She's still hanging out with some loser used to work here. Joey Polk, the worthless fuck. He was supposed to be looking out for the girl. Shit, she might as well have been working the corner."

"You know where I can find the fool?"

"He runs a business out of his house in West Hollywood," she said. "Takes those boudoir pictures for womens want to give them to their men. This here is their ad." She handed Munch a copy of *L.A. Weekly.* "Polk Studio he calls hisself. Cute, huh?"

Right up there with Ginger Root and Testarosa, Munch thought. They were all selling the same thing. "He doesn't use a Polaroid camera, does he?"

"I don't know, he might."

"Can I have this?" Munch asked, holding up the newspaper.

"Sure," Testarosa said. "They're free."

"So, uh," Munch leaned in close until she was eye to eye with the dancer, "what do you do when the guys come?"

"They just do it in their pants."

"Oh, yeah, of course." She kept forgetting that the guys didn't take their clothes off. She'd have to ask Garret about this. Maybe he could explain the thrill. She handed Testarosa one of her cards. "Thanks for your help. If you hear anything else about this guy, would you call me?"

Testarosa took the business card and put it in her leopard skin handbag.

"And good luck," Munch added, sticking out her hand.

"You, too, honey." Testarosa shook Munch's hand with a limp grip, then moved aside one of the cushions to reveal a small television. She turned it on and Munch saw that it was tuned to a financial channel. The dancer studied the ticker tape. The progression of numbers and letters suddenly clicked with Munch.

"One last thing," she said.

Testarosa looked up.

Munch pulled out her wallet and found the business card where she had copied the numbers and letters that were scribbled in the margin of Diane Bergman's guest list—*100,000s CARC 35¼ –23.* She showed those to Testarosa now.

"Does this mean anything to you?"

"Oh, yeah," the dancer said. "I remember this. It

was in the *Wall Street Journal* last Friday. Somebody done fucked up but good."

"Why? What does it mean?" Munch asked, noticing how Testarosa's speech patterns wove in and out of street slang. Munch could relate to being on the cusp of a new lifestyle—each foot in a different world. There were still times when she didn't know what to do with her hands when she walked.

"CARC is a Nasdaq symbol for a company called California Recycling," Testarosa explained. "I was watching the stock. The company was bidding for a government contract but didn't get it. Somebody must have thought they would because you see here," she said, touching a long lacquered nail to the first large number, "one hundred thousand shares changed hands just before the announcement."

"And the –23?" Munch asked.

"The stock went down twenty-three points. Whoever bought those hundred thousand shares lost hisself two point three million dollars." She snapped her fingers. "Just that quick. You know some heads rolled on that one."

Munch thought about the last time she'd seen Diane alive and wondered if this was the cause of the argument she hadn't wanted to talk about. "I'll bet they did at that."

She checked her watch and decided she might just have enough time to go pay Polk Studio a call.

CHAPTER 22

Polk Studio was in reality an old two-story Spanish-style house in a part of West Hollywood that had once been swank but was now in a state of decline. This sinking of status was evidenced by overgrown tropical plants and burglar bars on every window. Yet parking was still almost impossible, Munch soon found, unless you were a resident with a sticker or had staked your claim earlier in the decade.

She had called first and confirmed that Joey Polk was there. She pressed the doorbell when she reached the stoop, but hearing no ring within the house she worked the solid brass knocker bolted to the center of the large dark wood door. Looking up she noticed a string of old-fashioned glass Christmas lightbulbs attached to the roofline with rusty nails.

A woman with long black hair answered. She was about Munch's age, dressed in stretch pants and a sweatshirt, and obviously stoned. *There, but for the grace of God, go I*, Munch thought.

"Are you Veronica?" Munch asked.

The woman threw back her head and made a little derisive snort. "No, I'm Shana."

Of course you are. "Is Joey here?" Munch asked.

"Did you have an appointment?" Shana asked.

"Yeah, I called a little while ago."

Shana turned her head and yelled behind her, "Joey, you got company." Then she stepped aside and Munch walked in. The rooms visible from the entryway were furnished in a mishmash of overstuffed furniture. A meager collection of plaster-of-paris Cupids gathered dust on an end table. Shana sat down behind a desk near the foyer, managing to look instantly bored.

A man soon joined them and offered Munch a plump, sweating palm. His eyes did a walkover of her body that began and ended below her chin. She could see why Veronica Parker had fared so badly, if this sleazeball was her so-called protection. Not that Munch bought the concept that any kind of pimp ever deterred trouble. She'd had a friend named Roxanne in the bad old days who turned tricks on Main Street in Venice. Roxanne used to have her biker old man park nearby and watch. Maybe it somehow made her feel better, maybe she wanted him to appreciate all that she did. Munch never saw that he was any kind of help. How much could anybody do for a woman once she was alone with her trick, except take a cut of her pay?

"Are you Joey?" she asked the man.

"The Polk man himself," he said. Shana groaned.

"You said on the phone that you'd help hook me up with Veronica?" Munch said.

"I'll need a reason," he said, fluffing his niggardly chin hair with the back of one of his pudgy hands. She didn't miss the suggestion in his tone.

"I wanted to talk to her about some guy we both know."

"What guy is that?"

She figured she might as well put her cards on the table. "A couple of months ago she was raped and abandoned on the freeway. The same thing happened to two other women I know. One of them was killed. The other is still being stalked by the guy and has disappeared. I have reason to believe that all the victims of this guy posed for nude photos at some point."

"Are you a cop?" Joey asked.

Munch felt oddly flattered. "Do I look like a cop?" Then she realized that that statement could be construed as a dodge and quickly added, "No, I'm not a cop at all. I just want to stop this guy. He's seriously twisted. In fact, he's been calling me. For all I know, I might be next." She turned to Shana. "Or you."

Shana fixed Munch with a look that focused two feet past her shoulder. She wasn't exactly shaking in her go-go boots.

"What do you want from Ronnie?" Joey asked, still eyeing Munch with mistrust.

"I don't know. Maybe she could tell me something else to help catch this guy. Something maybe she's remembered since. I'm not looking to cause her any more grief."

He used the same intercom system as Shana. Turning his head so that his straggly goatee grazed his shoulder, he yelled, "Ronnie, shake your ass and c'mon out here a minute." Then he turned back to Munch and said, "Don't take all fucking day."

Veronica Parker emerged from a back room. She wore black shorts and a halter top. Her white legs were punctuated by several black circular bruises. Her eyes were rimmed with red and glassy enough to throw a glare across the room. "Whas up?" she asked.

"Lady here wants to ask you some questions," Joey said.

"What about?"

"Think we could sit?" Munch asked, indicating a sofa in the far corner of the room.

Veronica shrugged. "Yeah, sure." She scratched her nose. "You got anything for the head?"

"No," Munch said, leading Veronica to the farthest corner of the living room. "I need to ask you about the guy who attacked you a couple months ago."

"What guy?"

Munch wondered if there had been more than one incident. "The guy who tied you up and left you on the freeway."

"Oh, that. What about it?"

"Did you know the guy?"

"No," she said, not bothering to lower her voice, "he was just some guy. Some fuckhead jerk."

"How'd you meet him?"

She looked over at Joey for guidance. He lifted his shoulders and let them drop. "Tell her."

"He was in the parking lot outside the club, said he wanted a private dance. I told him it would cost double. He didn't have a problem with that."

"Did you go to his place?"

"No, I don't know where we went."

"How's that?"

Veronica got interested in her hands, pushing down cuticles on first one finger and then another. "You sure you don't have anything to smoke?"

"No, sorry."

She sighed and then the story came out in a rush. "It was dark. I never saw his face too clearly. He had one of them buzzer things. You know, like when someone has cancer or something and they cut a hole in your throat and you have to talk through this thing that makes you sound all weird?"

"Yeah, I know what you mean."

"So I didn't want to stare or anything. You know, like if he was handicapped or retarded or something." She lifted her hands, palms up. "I don't want to make anybody feel bad." She smiled sloppily, obviously proud of her egalitarianism.

"Then what happened?" Munch prompted.

"All of a sudden he puts something over my head, a coat or a blanket, something heavy like that. Then he ties it up tight around my throat with that thick silver tape."

"Duct tape?"

"Yeah, duck tape. He picked me up and threw me in his car. I thought there were a couple of guys at first. Then I realized he was just talking to himself."

"What kind of things was he saying?"

"Whacked-out shit, like, 'Just this once' and 'Just to see.'" Veronica brought a hand to her shoulder and squeezed. "I waited to see what would happen. He told me to close my eyes and then he unwrapped my head. He said he needed my mouth free, but he was closing my eyes for my own protection." She looked sideways at Munch. "Real nice guy, huh?"

"Did he take you somewhere?"

"Nah, we just stayed in his van."

"His van? I thought you said car."

"No, it was a van." She rubbed a bony hip and cracked a grin. "No carpet either. If you catch that fucker, tell him he owes me a hundred bucks. No, make that two hundred. I had that sticky duck tape shit in my hair for days."

Behind them, Shana laughed. Munch saw no point in saying anything about their attitude. What could she say? Gee, you're not reacting right. You should be much more traumatized. Denial had its uses.

"He shocked the other women with electricity," Munch said.

The memory seemed to sober Veronica. She stood and showed Munch what were now familiar-looking shiny burn scars on the backs of her legs. "He did me, too," she said quietly, as if ashamed of being the victim of torture. "I thought I was paralyzed at first. Took forever for the burns to heal."

Munch winced in sympathy. According to Mace St. John, a stun gun's 100,000-volt charge completely overrides the victim's central nervous system. She started to feel bad for bringing it all up again, but she knew any scrap of information would be helpful. On Monday she would relay everything she learned to Agent Hogan now that St. John was out of the picture.

"Can you remember any specific sounds or smells from inside the van?" she asked.

"Trees," Veronica said after a moment of thought. "Smelled like Christmas trees."

"You mean like pine?" Munch asked.

"Yeah," Veronica said, scratching her nose as if the scent still tickled it. "That was it."

"This freak likes to use the phone, too. Did you get any kinky calls before or after you were attacked?"

"I'm lucky if a regular phone call gets through in this place." She shot a look at Shana.

"Hey, bitch," Shana said. "I'm not your fucking answering service."

"How about photographs? Did he take your picture when you were naked or have any of you?"

"I don't know. He might have. He could have gotten some from the club. I was Miss August."

Munch reached in her purse for one of her limo cards. She handed it to Veronica. "If you think of anything else, or if the guy calls you, let me know. And if you ever want to come up for air, I can help with that, too."

"What do you mean?"

Munch pushed back her sleeve to reveal her own faded needle marks. "I've been out of the life for almost eight years. If you're interested, you got my number."

"Thanks," Veronica said. She folded the card carefully and stuck it in the back pocket of her short shorts.

Munch left Joey Polk's and got on Sunset Boulevard heading west. She checked her watch. Asia's game would be half over by now. She still had time to stop by Robin's before going back to the park. Not wanting to hassle with the gate guard, Munch used the unattended entrance to Barrington Plaza Gardens.

Her note to Robin was still stuck in the front doorjamb. She pulled it free just as she sensed a presence behind her.

"Are you a friend?" a man's voice asked.

Munch turned around. It was Frank Fahoosy. "Are you?"

"Yes," Fahoosy said. "Very good friend."

"Do you know where she is?" Munch asked.

Fahoosy was on the path, she on the short concrete stoop. If his intention was to stop her, he could easily catch her and physically overpower her before she had a chance to flee. Not that she would be taken quietly or without inflicting pain.

Fahoosy seemed unaware of her calculations. His expression was anxious, even worried. "No, I haven't heard from her since Thursday. This is not like her."

"I'm worried, too," Munch admitted. "She hasn't returned my calls."

"Nor mine," Fahoosy said. "And she missed an appointment for a job. Also not like her."

"What kind of a job?" Munch asked.

"A photo layout." Fahoosy wiped a hand across his mouth and looked to either side. She didn't feel any threat emanating from him; rather he seemed at a loss.

"Did you know she was getting meals delivered to her?"

"Yes," he said. "Meals-On-Wheels."

"I talked to one of the delivery guys and he said she called in to the office at the hospital and told them to cancel her service."

"When was this?" he asked.

"Umm. Thursday, I guess."

"This is very strange," he said. "Why call them and not let me know what was going on?"

"I wondered the same thing," Munch said.

Fahoosy seemed close to tears. "Did you talk to these Meals-On-Wheels people yourself?"

"No, just to the volunteer guy."

"Maybe he was mistaken."

Munch started to reply then stopped. The pieces of information flashed together in her brain like cards shuffling into a deck. The van with its smell of pine. Her refusal to respond to D.W.'s dating overtures. Thursday morning at the bakery. Who was that second cup of coffee for? And hadn't D.W. known all about her involvement with Robin? He had been in the room when she offered her help.

Man, how stupid could she be?

"I've got to go," she told Fahoosy. "If I find out anything about Robin, I'll let you know."

She rushed past him. He offered no resistance. She ran to her car, wondering whom she would go to with this important news. St. John was effectively out of the picture. That left Pete Owen or Emily Hogan. Munch drove to the gas station to use the phone there.

The shop offered only minimal service on Saturday and none on Sunday. The lube bay doors were closed, but several vehicles were parked in front. Among them was a Rolls-Royce getting its battery charged, and what looked like a gardener's truck with its hood up. From the smell of it, it had overheated badly. Next to the truck a Volkswagen Rabbit was jacked up and one of the front tires was off.

Pauley's detail business was also open. Saturday was a big day for him. A Mercedes and a BMW were parked under the awning, their paint jobs hazy under a layer of wax. One of the kids who worked for him was spraying Armor All on the tires. Pauley was nowhere in sight.

She went to Lou's office, sat at his desk, and looked through the phone book. Emily Hogan's card was at home. She hadn't known she was going to need it. Agent Hogan had no separate listing. Munch dialed the number for the Bureau. An operator answered and transferred her to Agent Hogan's voice mail, which gave out a pager number in case of emergency. Munch hung up, dialed the pager number, and left the gas station's number.

While she waited for the callback she went through the box of work orders until she found the invoice with D.W.'s information on it. Finding it, she returned to the desk and willed the phone to ring.

Outside the office window, the crew of gas pumpers ministered to the weekend flow of customers. One of them passed in front of the window on his way to the rest room and they waved at each other.

The phone rang, making her jump.

"Bel-Air Texaco," she answered.

"This is Agent Hogan."

"Hi, this is Munch Mancini."

"What can I do for you?"

Munch gave the agent a quick rundown of the information she had uncovered, including her suspicion that D.W. had kidnapped Robin and was holding her somewhere.

"Have you alerted Detective St. John?" Agent Hogan asked.

"No, he's out of commission, in the hospital." Before Hogan could ask, Munch gave her all the information she had on D.W. This included his address, phone number, and license plate number.

"I'll get right on this," Hogan said. "Will you be at this number?"

"No, I have to go pick up my kid at the park. Then I'll be home."

"All right. Thank you for your help."

CHAPTER 23

Munch took off for the park where she had left Asia and Garret. She drove up Sunset toward the freeway, then took a right on Church Lane, figuring she would fare better on surface streets. Before she reached the Montana Avenue underpass, a van pulled behind her and honked. She looked in her rearview mirror and saw it was Pauley. He gestured for her to pull over.

She parked underneath a large tree. He signaled for her to come over to him as he walked around to the passenger side of his van.

"Look who I found," he said.

Robin poked her head out the passenger window and said, "Hi." Then she opened her door and got out. Munch was overwhelmed with relief and rushed to her, giving her a big hug. The hug brought a wince to Robin's face.

"Where have you been?" Munch asked. "We've been worried sick."

"I'm sorry about that."

Behind Munch, the van's side door slid open. Too late she noticed the large bruises on Robin's arms. Just as the smell of pine-scented cleaner wafted out from the inside of the van, Robin's face crumpled in grief.

"I'm sorry," she said again.

Munch turned. Pauley was standing behind her. He had what looked like a twin-pronged remote control in his hand. A blue spark arced between the terminals with a wicked buzz. Pauley pressed it to the side of her neck. Every muscle in her body seemed to contract at once, pulling her into a fetal position. The pain was excruciating. Her legs folded beneath her; her head hit the curb with a dull *thunk*. Pauley pulled her into his van, stuffed a sock in her mouth, and wrapped duct tape around her face and head to hold it in place. Her limbs refused to respond. She remembered Veronica's description of feeling paralyzed.

"This isn't your show anymore," Pauley said. He turned to Robin. "Shut the door."

The side door of the van slammed shut. In the sudden darkness, Pauley used plastic tie straps to bind Munch's wrists and feet. Her eyes focused and she saw that Robin was back in the front seat. She wasn't restrained in any way. What had he done to her to produce such submission?

Munch looked at Robin, feeling betrayed, confused, scared.

"If we could just get rid of you," Robin said, reading the question in Munch's eyes, "we'd be all right."

Munch shook her head no, but Robin had already turned away.

Pauley climbed back into the driver's seat and put the van in gear. They made several turns and then climbed a hill. From the sounds of traffic, Munch knew they were back on a busy street. Probably on Sunset Boulevard. She wasn't sure. They could just as easily be on Sepulveda. He made another series of turns. She could do little to brace herself as the van swung first one way and then the other. She prayed that his erratic driving would draw the attention of some traffic cop. From her vantage point she could look up and out the windshield. A green, tree-shaped air freshener dangled from the rearview mirror. Also pine-scented, she realized. The feeling returned to her arms and legs in the form of pain. They passed beneath a canopy of mature trees. Munch knew they were headed up one of the canyons, perhaps Mandeville. Robin had described such a trip to her and St. John less than a week ago. Before this asshole had climbed inside her head and broken her. The van veered once more and the ride grew bumpy as if they were traversing an unpaved road. Then they came to a stop.

"Let's go," Pauley said, wrenching the shifter into park and killing the engine.

A moment later the doors opened and Pauley reached for Munch, pulling her out and dumping her on the ground. He cut the tie binding her ankles. She stood. They were in what would one day be the front yard of a large house. There were signs of dated, unfinished construction everywhere. Rusting rebar. Tarps for walls nailed imperfectly to water-stained framing. Slate tiles in wooden crates, stacks of timber, and bags of concrete that were partially buried beneath a season's worth of fallen leaves. It looked as if the owners had run out of money or somehow had been distracted from the project.

At Pauley's prodding, Munch stumbled toward the front door on legs that were now half asleep. He dragged her down a set of stairs into a basement room, with Robin following of her own volition. Munch concentrated on taking deep breaths in through her nose. The sock in her mouth was working its way down her throat. It took massive willpower not to gag and panic. The only way she was going to win was by keeping her head. She needed a plan.

She'd learned a lot about sexual predators in the last week. Much of the information had confirmed knowledge she had already acquired through hard experience and stored on an unconscious level. She'd learned how these animals feed. Their need for total submission. Veronica had surrendered without much of a struggle and lived to tell about it. Robin, also. Diane Bergman must have refused to give in, and she had died.

Now Munch had to decide if survival was worth it. To let this predator have his way with her. And she knew, for Asia's sake, it would have to be. As she thought, her fingers found the nubs on the plastic tie strips binding her. These were different from the Flex-Cuffs the police used. She ran her fingertips along the ridges, finding and bending back the tab that locked the strip closed.

She looked around her as she worked. The walls were plastered with pictures of Veronica and Robin, mostly of Robin. The *Penthouse* pictures were there, but there were other shots, too. Shots of Robin fully clothed and performing mundane tasks. There were even photographs of Munch and Robin together, taken at the gas station while both of them were unaware. And then there were pictures of Robin tied to the bed, writhing in terror and pain.

Munch pulled her hand free slowly, trying not to move her shoulders much in the process. Pauley glanced over just then. A look passed over his face and Munch knew that she had already crossed his line of tolerance. There were no choices left to make. She tore the tape from her face and took a deep breath of air.

He yelled and rushed her. She stood her ground, fists clenched and teeth gritted. She kicked at him, aiming for his crotch. The blow barely slowed him down. *This is not about genitalia,* she remembered. He knocked into her, but he didn't hit her with his fists. Instead, he grabbed her shoulders and forced her to her knees. Her kneecaps slammed into the

concrete floor. She only registered a moment's
pain. What she mostly felt was anger. Anger and a
need to hurt him back. Her hands flew to his face.
She went for his eyes, cursing her lack of fingernails. He pulled away from her clawing, trying to
keep her at arm's length. She got a handful of his
face. Somewhere it registered in her brain how soft
the skin near his eye was as it pulled away beneath
her grasp. She felt a wetness where the skin parted.
Felt the warm soft curl of flesh beneath her short
nails. They were quiet throughout their struggle,
saving their breath for the business of survival. Her
fists bounced off his head and face ineffectually,
like something out of a dream. Then he began hitting her, using his open palm. Holding her by her
hair. Stinging, slapping blows. He struck wherever
he could, but she kept her head down, offering him
only the back of her skull where the bone was the
thickest. The need to hurt him was stronger than
ever. Hurt him as badly as possible. She spotted a
putty knife in the corner. He swung her down onto
the floor on her back. She brought up her knees. He
used his forearm on her throat. She tried to tuck in
her chin, but he forced it back with his superior
strength. She felt the lack of breath, the panic in her
chest that was heaving for every breath already.

No, she thought, *I will not die for you.*

Then she remembered what fed him. He needed
his victims conscious. He ripped her shirt from her.
She closed her eyes and went limp. He backed off
her throat. She didn't wait, arching her body in one

tremendous buck upward. Both thumbs poised for his eyes. He reeled back. She put her head down and butted his face. He grunted. Her hand reached for the tool. As her fingers closed around the handle, she knew she had only one chance. His male muscle mass was going to win out. He pulled her down again. Her thumbs dug deep into his biceps, reaching for his bones. She would leave her mark. As many ways as possible.

Pauley forced her arms to her sides and then pinned them there with his knees. She kicked at the back of his head, but he seemed oblivious to her efforts.

Behind her she heard a whirring sound. She craned her head back, searching for the source of the noise. What she saw was Robin sitting on the floor. A camouflage-painted box was wedged between her legs. She cranked the handle on top, all the while watching Pauley as if asking for his approval. Wires trailed from the box. The ends were clipped to a lamp cord. As Robin cranked, the lamp glowed brighter. Munch smelled something cooking—some kind of meat. There was a sizzling sound and then the lamp went dark.

"Broke the connection," Pauley said. "Bring me the cooker, Robin. Let's show her how it works."

"He's really very smart," Robin said. She picked up a piece of two-by-four. A blackened tube of something hung by one of the large nails protruding from the surface of the board. Munch realized it was a charred hot dog.

"Robin, he's going to kill us," she said.

"Bring it here, Robin," Pauley repeated. "That's a good girl."

Robin walked zombie-like across the floor to them. She moved like some kind of wind-up doll, head wobbling ever so slightly, mouth agape.

"Stop him," Munch screamed.

"I can't," Robin said.

"There's two of us now," Munch said. "Together we can take him."

Robin hesitated. A look of confusion fluttered across her face.

Pauley said, "Honey, remember we talked about this. It's you and me. *We're* the team."

"I'm sorry," Robin said again. She turned the board so that the points of the two nails were facing down. She raised the contraption above Munch's exposed chest. Munch shut her eyes and twisted her face in anticipation. Then she heard a wet-sounding *thunk,* and the weight on her arms lessened. She opened her eyes. Pauley was weaving. One of his hands spread across his face. Blood leaked out from between his fingers. Robin pulled the board back and swung again. This time when she connected, something went crack in Pauley's face. Munch pushed him off her and jumped to her feet. The lamp had fallen off its table. She picked it up and swung it down on Pauley's head with all her might. He slumped unconscious to the floor.

"Let's not take any chances," Munch said with a grin to Robin. Then the two women hit him again.

He didn't even groan. Munch rolled him onto his stomach. "Hand me that tape," she said to Robin.

Robin still moved in odd, jerky motions. Fast and then slow. Munch pointed at the half-used roll of silver duct tape on the floor by the bed. Robin picked it up as if it might bite her and handed it over. Munch used it to wrap Pauley's wrists together. Then she moved down to his feet and wound three layers of the strong, thick tape around his ankles. He wasn't going anywhere.

Robin picked up the tape when Munch was done with it and tore off a twelve-inch strip. She lifted Pauley's head up off the floor by his ear. His lips parted slightly. Bright red blood dripped from his nose.

"Let's just get out of here," Munch said. "We'll call the cops."

Robin found a rag on the floor and began forcing it into Pauley's slack mouth.

"Robin," Munch said. "C'mon. Time to go."

Robin stretched the strip of tape across Pauley's face, making it impossible for him to spit out the rag. His eyes flickered open.

"My turn," Robin whispered. She walked across the room and retrieved the camouflage box she had been cranking earlier.

Munch realized where she'd seen such a device before. It had been on TV, in one of those old World War II movies. The guy who carried it was always called "Sparks." While artillery fire held the platoon at bay, Sparks would crank up his field gener-

ator, power his radio, and put in a desperate call to
command for backup. At some point, Sparks usually took a bullet in the back right through his
equipment pack.

The spinning, ringing sound of the generator
building current filled the room. The concrete
walls and floor amplified the noise. Robin's eyes
filled with a queer, even maniacal light. Munch
reached down, putting her hand over Robin's,
making her stop.

"Don't do this," she said.

Robin looked disappointed, then her shoulders
sagged and she began to cry.

"C'mon," Munch said, helping her to her feet.
"Let's go find a telephone."

Munch stared at the photographs covering the
wall and then down at Pauley again. All this time,
he had been watching her. His short, short hair and
clean-shaven face was a disguise, as was the soft
voice and concerned air he presented at the station.
She thought of the peephole in the bathroom wall
and knew it had been Pauley. He had spied on her
and every other woman who came into the station,
getting some strange vicarious thrill from catching
his victims unawares. He probably fondled himself
as he watched the women wipe, listening to conversations not intended for his ears, intruding and
perversely sharing their most private moments. It
was revolting.

"You're still inadequate," she told him, not caring if he understood. She picked up the odd con-

traption made of wood, careful to avoid the charged nails. It was tempting, all right. She stepped on the trailing wires and yanked the piece of wood upward until the solder broke. "We're better than this," she told Robin.

The two women hiked back up the stairs and out to the van. Munch found Pauley's mobile phone in the console between the seats. She called 911 and explained the situation. The operator asked for her location.

"Mandeville Canyon, I think," Munch said, looking at Robin for confirmation.

Robin nodded. "Bluebird Lane."

"Bluebird Lane," Munch repeated for the operator. "And call Detective Pete Owen of the West Los Angeles Police and Emily Hogan of the California Bureau of Investigation. They know all about this."

The operator told Munch to keep the line open until the police arrived.

"No problem," Munch said. "Tell them to hurry. You know, code three."

The patrol car arrived first. Followed soon afterward by Pete Owen in his unmarked Buick. Munch led the cops back inside the house. They made her stay behind them, descending the stairs with their flashlights and guns extended.

Pauley had rolled onto his back. The duct tape around his ankles and wrists had held. Blood spattered his shirt, but wasn't flowing actively. One of the patrol cops shined his flashlight down the length of Pauley's body.

The second uniformed cop panned his flashlight across Pauley's trophy wall, then let the beam come to rest on the bed where four leather restraints lay in wait for the next victim.

"Shit," he said.

Owen leaned down and shined his light in Pauley's face. One pupil was larger than the other. Owen removed Pauley's gag and said over his shoulder, "Head injury here, it looks like."

Pauley only blinked. A tear rolled down his cheek.

"Let's get him out of here," Owen said, straightening.

The first uniformed cop rolled Pauley back onto his stomach and replaced the duct tape with handcuffs.

Owen looked at the wall of pictures and shook his head in disgust.

"This is Veronica Parker," Munch said, pointing to a photograph of the stripper she'd met at Joey Polk's studio. "She got raped about two months ago."

Owen grunted when he saw the photo of Robin tied to the bed, her mouth twisted in pain.

"What I don't see," Munch said, "are any pictures of Diane Bergman."

"That doesn't mean much," Owen said.

"How can you say that? The pictures were a huge part of his ritual."

"The guy's a wacko. You can't expect him to follow an exact schedule."

"But he kept pictures of the others."

Owen looked at Pauley's trophy mural again. "He didn't kill the others."

"That's part of my point," Munch said. "He didn't know we'd ever see this wall. So why would he leave her out?"

"Give it a rest," Owen said, not unkindly. "We got the guy. It's over. With what we got here we can put him away for a long, long time."

Munch noticed a sheet of Peg-Board studded with key hooks mounted by the door. From the hooks dangled keys, both automotive and residential. Beneath these keys were neat labels listing addresses and license plates. She found the key to her house on the next to the bottom row. That explained why her keys had been out of order on her ring after Pauley waxed her GTO. She also found Robin's address and corresponding keys, but on none of the labels did she see a Chenault address nor mention of a Honda Prelude.

Pauley groaned as he was helped to his feet. He spit blood. "Arrest her," he said, pointing with his shoulder at Munch. "Her and that other cunt assaulted me. I probably got a concussion."

Owen held his middle finger extended in front of Pauley's face. "How many fingers do you see?" he asked. He spun Pauley around and gave him a rough shove, propelling him in the direction of the stairway. "We give medals for what they did, you little piece of shit."

Munch followed the procession of cops and prisoner out into the light. Emily Hogan had arrived. She was wrapping a blanket around Robin's shoulders and leading her to her car. Munch joined them.

"I guess this means you'd better cancel that all-points bulletin on D.W."

"Already handled."

"Can I catch a ride with you?" Munch asked.

"Yes," the agent said. "I need you to come to the office and make a statement."

"I'd be happy to, but first I need to get back to my kid and boyfriend and let them know what's going on."

"I'm sure they'll be very relieved to know it's over," Agent Hogan said.

Munch wished she felt as mollified as everyone seemed to think she should be.

CHAPTER 24

Emily Hogan took Munch to her car. The engine was still running. Munch checked her watch, knowing that she had missed all of Asia's game and how it wasn't going to be simple to explain why to her daughter without revealing some of the world's ugliness. At least Garret had been there. It had to be so much easier to raise a kid with a partner. Not to mention how much cheaper it would be to split the expenses of rent and utilities on a bigger place compared with what she spent on a smaller house alone. But wasn't there supposed to be more to a relationship than a pooling of resources?

She heard people talk about needing others. And she bought the concept up to a point. She needed customers. She needed the fellowship of A.A. meetings. But another adult human being in her life was going too far. Dependency on other people only led to trouble. Disappointment and worse.

She pulled into the ball field's parking lot where

a few scattered station wagons remained. Two figures were sitting on the bleachers. Asia and Garret. Asia raised a hand in greeting. Munch waved back.

"What happened to you?" Garret asked. "We were starting to worry. How'd you get that bump on your head?"

Munch put a hand to her forehead and fondled the goose egg that had risen there. It was tender. The skin around it felt stretched. She pulled her collar up to hide the stun gun burns. "I ran into a little problem. The good news is that Robin's attacker has been caught. He was holding her captive. My guess is since Thursday."

Garret grabbed her arm and pulled her to him. "Thank God you're all right," he said, holding her face tenderly to his chest and kissing the top of her head.

I should be feeling something, she thought. *Not just waiting for him to finish.*

"Are you still up to house hunting?" he asked. "I've been telling Asia all about the new yard. We've been trying to decide what color to paint her room."

"Yeah, listen," Munch said, looking at both of their open, hopeful expressions, "about that . . ."

"You're tired now," Garret interrupted, "it can wait."

Munch looked at him sadly. Maybe now was not the moment to tell him, but sometime soon he would have to hear her decision.

"Let's get some food and go to a movie," Garret said. "How does that sound?"

Asia slipped her hand into his. "Can we get ice cream, too?"

"Sure." He turned to Munch. "How about you, Mom? Can we bribe you with ice cream?"

She relented with a smile. "Yeah, okay, anything but hot dogs."

Munch couldn't concentrate on the movie. She kept replaying all the events of the last few days. Begging fatigue, she sent Garret home. Emily Hogan called. Munch answered all her questions and learned that Robin had been transferred to a psychiatric hospital in Brentwood.

"How could Pauley brainwash her so quickly?" Munch asked.

"It's a defense mechanism," Agent Hogan explained. "Human nature. Robin was faced with a situation where her captor controlled her life. She had to find something sympathetic to attach to in his personality in order to survive."

"Like when Patty Hearst joined the SLA?"

"That's a perfect example. We see this with battered women time after time."

"Abused kids, too, I bet," Munch said.

On Sunday, she unplugged the phones and spent the day with Asia. They went to the nursery and bought flats of flowers, sacks of fertilizer, and vegetable seeds. Together they worked the dark rich soil of the flower beds, planting the small seedlings that would bloom in the coming months. Sweet William and stock for scent. Pansies and snapdragons for color.

The year before, Derek had brought Munch rail-road ties and built a ten-by-ten-foot raised bed for vegetables. Now, Munch dumped several cubic feet of manure into the bed and then attacked the clods with hoe and shovel until sweat poured down her face. Asia sat on the edge, arranging the bright packets of seeds.

"Almost ready," Munch said, feeling the blisters rising on her palms. Typical. Everything to extreme. Any job worth doing was worth doing until you dropped.

Asia cupped her hand over her eyes and squinted at her mother. "You're not hurting your-self, are you?"

Munch drew straight furrows in the dirt with the edge of the hoe. "You know me." It struck her how comforting those words were. "You know me," she said again.

"I heard you twice the first time," Asia said.

Munch laughed and squirted Asia with the hose.

Asia screamed, reaching that decibel that little girls achieve so easily.

Munch pointed at the seeds. "Rip those babies open."

Asia started with the radishes. Under Munch's tutelage, the little girl knelt beside the newly formed rows, poking one hole at a time with her perfect little finger, then dropping the tiny black beadlike seed into the aperture, and covering it up.

They labored for hours, content to be working, to be together, smelling the earth, feeling the sun on their backs, the knees of their jeans soaked with muddy water.

Garret would see the product of their loving labor. See the empty packets of snap peas, carrots, radishes, and broccoli stuck on round wooden stakes identifying the coming crop. And he would realize that he was witnessing a work in progress.

Maybe she had a problem. She wasn't sure if she suffered from rape trauma syndrome. Hell, she barely believed in carpal tunnel syndrome. One fact was clear. A fact that she couldn't deny any longer. She wasn't in love with Garret and never would be.

Mace St. John had been moved to a private room. The doctors successfully restored blood flow to his heart. He would not be as good as new, but the damage to his heart muscle was minimal. Munch and Asia came to see him Sunday night. Caroline was there with a stack of magazines, surrounded by junk food wrappers.

"How's the patient?" Munch asked.

"Grouchy," Caroline said.

"So back to normal, huh?"

"What happened to you?" St. John asked.

Munch touched the bruise on her forehead. "You should see the other guy."

"I heard you had some excitement," he said. His eyes were sober, awash with conflict. He turned to his wife. "Honey, why don't you and Asia go grab a bite."

Caroline looked from one to the other and said, "All right. We'll be back in a little while."

After they were gone, St. John asked, "What the fuck is the matter with you?"

"What?"

"I can't turn my back for five minutes."

"Hey, it's not like I planned it."

"That's the problem."

She told him everything then, from her interviews with the strippers until the police took Pauley into custody. "A few things are bugging me, though."

"Just a few?"

"Do you know if Pauley confessed to Diane's murder?"

"No, he hasn't. But don't worry. He's not going anywhere."

Munch went home that night and searched through her tax records until she found the receipt for her donation of limo time. Diane had typed her a formal thank-you note on Bergman Cancer Center stationery. She could use the documentation, Diane said, as proof of her contribution. The members of the board were all listed along the stationery's left margin. Diane Bergman's name came first, identifying her as the founder and president. Logan Sarnoff was second, the first vice president, next in command, attorney for the estate. Then there was the treasurer, Ken Wilson, the stockbroker.

Everyone was so anxious to tie Pauley's activities to Diane's murder. What if they had all been wrong?

CHAPTER 25

MONDAY

Monday morning came with the usual head-aches. Asia woke up grumpy and had to be argued into every step of the getting-ready-for-school process. This meant a seven-minute delay in getting on the freeway, which then translated into a fifteen-minute morning go-to-work traffic snarl, and Asia almost missed the school bus.

The news of Saturday's misadventures and Pauley's subsequent arrest had already reached the gas station. Lou had had to come in Sunday and allow the cops to search Pauley's locker. Among the items recovered were telephone repairmen's handsets, a twelve-inch masonry drill bit, and three women's negligees in pastel colors. All were bagged, tagged, and taken away.

Munch used the rest room and noticed that the

tiny hole by the toilet paper dispenser had been filled in with epoxy. Things would be getting back to normal soon.

At ten o'clock Lou came out to the back room. Munch was replacing the timing belt on a Volkswagen Scirocco.

"How's it going?" he asked.

"Getting there," she said.

"You know, if you wanted to take a few days off . . ."

"And what?"

"I don't know. Relax a little."

"I relax better when I know my bills are getting paid. But thanks. I did want to run an errand later."

"Take all the time you need," he said.

She finished the Volkswagen first. Called the woman who owned it to let her know it was ready and then flipped through Lou's Rolodex until she found Ken Wilson's business card.

She dialed his number. His secretary put the call through when Munch identified herself.

"What can I do for you?" he asked.

"I wanted to talk to you about buying some stock," she said. "Can I stop by?"

"Sure."

The first level of the underground parking lot was all reserved parking and full. Munch continued down the tight circular driveway to the lower level, noting the black scrape marks on the walls from other drivers' miscalculations. She found a slot in the center row and headed for the bank of elevators. After pushing the elevator button, she studied the building roster. Smith Barney was on the fifth floor. Logan Sarnoff's firm was on the eighth. Her elevator arrived. A minute later she was at Ken Wilson's door.

The brokerage office reminded Munch of a detectives' bull pen. Essentially it was one large room divided into cubicles with desks, phones, and ticker tape monitors. A young woman sat behind the reception desk.

Ken came out from the back. He looked paler and thinner under the fluorescent lights. Munch followed him to his desk.

"Is there any stock in particular that you're interested in?" he asked.

"California Recycling," she said. "The Nasdaq symbol is CARC."

His hand went to the knot at his throat. He loosened his tie before speaking. "How many shares do you want to buy?"

"I understand that the stock took a big drop a few weeks ago, right after one hundred thousand shares changed hands. Do you know anything about that?"

Ken cleared his throat. "I read the article in the *Journal* last week."

"Can you explain it to me?"

"Earlier this month, an investor acting on an erroneous inside tip bought the large block of CARC stock. After the transaction went through, the news broke that the company had failed to land a government contract and the CEO had resigned. The value of the stock dropped when the news hit. That's not to say it won't recover. This is a good time to buy."

"But meanwhile," Munch said, "somebody's client lost two point three million dollars, plus commissions."

"Hardly the broker's fault," Wilson said. He looked as if he were going to be ill.

She met his eye and said, "Sarnoff is telling the story differently. He says that he bought the stock on his broker's recommendation. On your recommendation."

"That's bullshit. He came to me and he knows it."

"And what about Diane Bergman? What did she know?"

"I think you'd better leave now," Wilson said. He picked up his phone. She understood this gesture as some implied threat. It didn't matter. She'd gotten what she came for.

She walked out to the hall and pushed the elevator down button. The car on the left arrived first. Its doors opened with a ding. She stepped inside and pushed the button marked G2. Moments later she stepped out into the dark, quiet parking lot. She was heading for her car when she heard another ding and the doors of the second elevator opened. Instinct made her turn, but she wasn't particularly surprised to see who stepped out.

Sarnoff's face was flushed. His fists clenched, arms bent slightly at the elbow. "What kind of game are you playing?" he asked. Spittle flew as he spoke.

"No game," she said, backing away from him.

"I don't need any more shit," he said, advancing. His eyes were open wide. She could see the white all around his irises.

"Did Diane find out what you had done? Is that what happened?"

"Of course she knew," he said. "Every investment I made had her approval. But here's the thing"—his eyes were glittering, even in the dim light—"everybody approves when you're making twice the going rate. Nobody remembers that that means twice the risks."

"That must have really pissed you off," she said. Her hip bumped into the hood of the car behind her. To her right was a concrete wall. He blocked her exit to the left. "Was that why she had to die? Was she going to blame you?"

"You're crazy," he said. "And you're a liar. I'll prove it. I'll discredit you."

Munch sidestepped across the front of the car, which she now saw was a Jaguar. "You had to know your luck would run out eventually," she said to him, desperately trying to form a plan while she thought out loud. "You've been pretty lucky for a while now, haven't you? You lose a large sum of the Bergmans' money and then Diane meets her tragic fate. No one left to ask where the money went. Pretty great timing for you."

He glanced around him as he reached inside his

coat. "Shut up now," he said, licking his lips, "before you go too far. I'm warning you."

Munch ran her hands behind her, feeling the smooth finish of the car. She came to the door handle and tried it, but it was locked. "How about the photographs you let St. John find? Did you plant them or was that just luck again?"

"I have no idea what you're talking about."

She looked him in the eye. "I saw the pictures of her body. You staged it so carefully to give the suggestion of sexual assault. And those burns all over her body? How could you do that to her?"

A pained expression crossed his face. At least he had a tiny shred of conscience left.

"She was already dead by then," he said, in a strained, barely audible voice. "She didn't suffer."

"Oh," she answered, feeling no sense of relief at his admission. He was still a killer.

When he looked at her again, his eyes were much older, sadder. He pulled out his hand from inside his coat and showed Munch that he had a pistol. "We're going to take a drive," he said. "You don't have to worry. I'm not going to hurt you."

Mace St. John had told her more than once never to go anywhere with a bad guy, that it was better to scream and shout and take your chances while you were still somewhere where you could be heard. Bad guys didn't drive you somewhere so they could let you go. They drove you to deserted stretches of national forest land where nobody would see them dump your body and they *always* lied when they said they weren't going to hurt you. St. John had also told her that if she ever found herself in a one-on-one situation with a mugger or a rapist that she was better off yelling "Fire!" than "Help!"

She glanced over her shoulder and saw that a small LED light glowed on the dashboard of the Jaguar. This told her two things. One: it had an alarm. And two: the system was armed. She squinted her eyes against the pain and then threw her body against the side of the car. The alarm's motion detector did its job. The air around them filled with a shrill, pulsating siren.

Sarnoff jumped back. She darted past him. The Jaguar alarm echoed off the concrete walls. She picked up a chunk of concrete, lying there broken beside a parking bumper, and threw it with all her might at his head. He raised the arm holding the gun to protect his face. The hunk of rock bounced off his arm. His gun went flying and crashed into the passenger window of a white 380 SEL. The Mercedes's tempered glass exploded in a shower of glittering shards. The loud pop of the breaking glass was followed immediately by a high-decibel air horn that began to blast at one-second intervals.

Munch darted for the driveway. She pulled the small pocket screwdriver from her shirt pocket as she ran. If he managed to catch her, he'd learn new meanings of the word *uncooperative*. The clamor in the garage was terrible. She felt disoriented, deprived of one of her senses, and hoped it was affecting him in the same way. Her body felt weightless as her legs pumped beneath her. If he was behind her, she would never know it. It was too dark for shadows, and looking back would only slow her down.

She sprinted up the exit ramp. There was a concave mirror mounted at the curve of the driveway leading to the next tier of parking. A reflected movement caught her attention. A flash of red and chrome. She realized it was the front end of a car and it was headed their way. The cacophony of alarm horns masked its screeching tires.

A strong hand clutched her arm. She tried to spin out of the grip, but it held fast. Her legs kicked out in front of her. Her head snapped back. She turned to face Sarnoff. The screwdriver with its puny four-inch shaft led her hand. She slashed his cheek. His mouth opened to emit a cry. A cry that was lost amid the clamor of alarms. He looked down at the blood dripping from his face in amazement. Munch took the opportunity to jump back and away from him. She flattened her body against the wall just as the front end of a red Mercedes emerged from the top of the driveway. Smoke surged from the tires as the horrified valet parking attendant tried desperately to avoid hitting Sarnoff, who was standing in the middle of its path. The car slowed, fishtailed, and then rammed into Sarnoff. His body flew back, coming to rest facedown on the cold concrete.

The parking attendant threw the Mercedes into park and rushed to Sarnoff's side. The attorney was still conscious. His right leg bent outward at an obscene angle. Blood soaked his suit.

Munch walked up the parking ramp, away from the noise and the blood. Other people ran past her, too, drawn to the mayhem. She shrugged off their shouted questions and kept walking until she reached the lobby. The security guard on duty let her use the phone. She called the West Los Angeles police station. A recording told her that if this was an emergency she should hang up and call 911. She stayed on the line until an operator answered.

"I need to speak to whoever's in charge," she said.

"What is this regarding?" the man asked.

"An ongoing murder investigation," she said.

"Have you spoken to a detective yet? What is the name of the victim in the case?"

"The detective is not available," she said. "I'd like to speak to the guy in charge. The lieutenant or the captain. Somebody like that."

"Can I get your name and number?"

"I'm a good friend of Mace St. John," she said. The door of the lobby opened and the sound of the blaring alarms filtered into the room. "And this is urgent." To punctuate her words an ambulance arrived with its siren whooping. Munch held the phone out in the direction of the noise.

"Please hold."

Munch waited ten seconds and then a man's voice came on the line. "This is Lieutenant Graziano."

Munch told him her name, where she was, and what had happened. "Sarnoff made it look like Diane was attacked by Pauley, the rapist you arrested on Saturday. Sarnoff knew enough to dress Diane in a negligee and to electrocute her. He even knew about the pictures of the victims. Sounds to me like he had some insider knowledge of Robin Davies's case. My bet is his source of information was Pete Owen."

"Where's Sarnoff now?"

"They're taking him to the hospital."

"I want you to stay put," Graziano said. "I'll make sure an officer is assigned to you."

"What are you going to do about Pete Owen?"

"I'll be having a word with him myself," Graziano said. "Don't worry. We'll get to the bottom of this."

"I'm sure we all want the same thing," Munch said.

EPILOGUE

Ten days after his admittance to the hospital, St. John was released. Dr. Krueger gave him strict orders to quit smoking and cut down on stress. Caroline came to pick him up at ten in the morning. He insisted on driving home.

"I talked to the lieutenant this morning," he said when they came to a traffic light

"What did he say?"

"Oh, you know, the usual bullshit. Get well soon. Don't worry."

Caroline nodded, looked out the window.

"I'm not quitting," he told her.

"Cigars or the job?" she asked.

"I can live without the smokes."

"Glad to hear it." She didn't seem surprised or even disappointed by his announcement. "What else did you two talk about?"

"The D.A. filed murder one on Sarnoff. Owen

received a reprimand for having a big mouth. I don't think he's losing any sleep over it."

"So he wasn't involved?"

"Nah, just stupid. I have several witnesses who confirm that he was revealing details of his cases at the party he worked for the Bergman Cancer Center. Robin Davies's rape was one of these. He redeemed himself somewhat. He served a search warrant on the Bergman Cancer Center and pieced together a scenario that the D.A.'s happy with. We even located the victim's missing Honda in one of the permit-only parking structures. Her purse was under the seat with money still in the wallet."

"What do they believe happened?"

"Sarnoff and Diane Bergman went over to or met at the Bergman Cancer Center at UCLA on Saturday morning. The facility is not up and running to full capacity yet, so they would have had the place to themselves. She confronted him about the millions of dollars that the foundation trust lost because of the CARC stock fiasco. It was downstairs, in the diagnostic lab, that he killed Diane, but not by electrocuting her. The coroner reexamined the body. We had already ruled out blunt trauma. The tox report came back clean. Her hyoid arch was intact and there were no petechiae evident. Both of these would be symptoms usually associated with strangulation. "

"Petechiae. Those are the small broken veins in the eyes?"

"Exactly."

"So how was she killed?"

"Sugarman found some bruising around her lips and nose consistent with a forced closure of her mouth and nose."

"So he smothered her to death."

"Right, he probably used a plastic bag and then put her body in cold storage until he could carry out the rest of his plan. She couldn't just disappear. He needed her death confirmed or her money would be tied up for years. Owen had told Sarnoff about the rape he was investigating, how the rapist dressed his victim in a negligee and used electricity to subdue her. Owen also mentioned the victim's spread in *Penthouse* prior to her assault. All of this, it turned out, inspired Sarnoff to set up his scenario. You see, he'd been to Sam Bergman's safety deposit box to retrieve the man's burial instructions and he knew Sam kept the nude Polaroids of his wife there. It was a setup waiting to happen.

"On Saturday afternoon, Sarnoff went to Diane's house, brought in her mail, played the messages on her answering machine, even posted some letters she had ready to go on her desk and generally made it look like she had been there. Another misdirection so he could establish an alibi for Sunday. Then very late on Sunday night, he returned to the still unopened lab. Remember, this place is also a teaching facility. It even has its own morgue full of study cadavers. Good place to stash a body while you figure out a way to dispose of it."

"Wasn't he taking a chance someone might see her and recognize she wasn't one of the regulars?"

"He stuffed her in a body bag. One of his mistakes was leaving her in the clothes she died in. Cold storage retards decomposition, but a certain amount of rigor mortis sets in immediately. We found impressions on the body made from panty hose and the label of the suit jacket she was wearing at the actual time of death."

Caroline clucked her tongue in disapproval.

St. John continued. "Sarnoff rigged up some kind of apparatus with the two-twenty outlet in one of the treatment rooms. There's all kinds of equipment there including a portable X-ray machine that operates off two-twenty volts. Sarnoff dressed Diane in a negligee and zapped her corpse with enough voltage to disguise or at least make us not look for any other cause of death, then dumped her body where it would be found Monday morning."

"Will they be able to make the case stick?" she asked.

"Yeah, I think so. SID went over the Cancer Center morgue and exam room with a fine-tooth comb. We have lots of physical evidence, and thanks to Munch we've put together motive."

Caroline nodded. Juries loved motives.

St. John chuckled. "Sarnoff's also going to have a hard time explaining how his fingerprints got on the inside pages of Diane's gas bill that arrived in Saturday's mail."

"And who thought to fingerprint the mail?" she asked.

He tipped his head to one side in modest acknowledgment. "Owen's running a check now on any lawsuit Sarnoff might have argued involving electrocution. You know, like a workmen's comp claim or wrongful death. Something like that. Wouldn't hurt our case to show he had some in-depth knowledge of the subject matter."

"Speaking of priors," Caroline said. She adjusted the air-conditioning and then turned to face her husband. "I talked to Munch this morning and told her they were letting you out today."

"What did she say?" he asked.

Caroline arched her eyebrows but kept her tone deceptively light. "Oh, you know, she sent you her love."

St. John wisely made no reply other than to look straight ahead. Across the seat, their two hands found each other.

ACKNOWLEDGMENTS

First I need to thank a few special friends, beginning with the incomparable Patrick Millikin of Poisoned Pen Book Store for his guidance, friendship, and encouragement. Others who helped me early on in the process were my good friends and skilled readers Marie Reindorp, Kathleen Tumpane, and mystery buff extraordinaire Lou Boxer, M.D.

For assistance on the medical details:

Larry Shore, M.D., my brother the doctor, who walked me through the heart attack and many other crises; Dr. Joe Cohen, Chief Forensic Pathologist of Riverside County; Dr. Douglas Lyle for certain gory details.

Other choice bits of information were provided by Jack Kemp of Jack Kemp Enterprises, distributor of laryngectomy patient products; investment specialist Dave Shore; broker and friend Ken

Hansen; and Ken Jonsson for the bit about the 220v; and Steve Ricketts, my communications expert.

And on the cop stuff:

Detective Carl and D.A. Diana Carter for their continued friendship and expert feedback; Gary Bale, the sweetest cop in Orange County; generous and charming Paul Bishop, author, LAPD detective; retired LAPD detective and current private investigator Don Long, who doesn't know how to give a short answer (writers love this); Special Agent Allen Grimes, who schooled me on the nature of rapists.

Many thanks to longtime friend and estate attorney Fred McNairy, who hates the part in books and movies where they gather everybody into one room for the reading of the will. They never do that, he says.

Thank you, Gordon Crosthwait, owner of the beautiful La Condesa, for taking me into your world and showing me around. Thanks also go to Brian Reese, John Clark, Phil Palmari, John Skinner, and Dave Davies, train enthusiasts aka "foamers." So named because when you ask them about trains, they tend to foam at the mouth.

On the writing end of things:

Many thanks to my writing "families" for making the journey less lonely: the Orange County Fictionaires and my free-writing, desert Tuesday group—Doug, Diane, and Sylvia. Two of the smartest groups of people to ever assemble.

Deepest appreciation to Russ Isabella, for his honesty in the eleventh hour.

Kudos also to my tenacious, yet gracious, agent, Sandy Dijkstra, and her exceptional staff.

My phenomenal, hardworking publicists: Jackie Green and Jim Schneeweis.

My superb editors: Susanne Kirk and George Lucas.

Thanks all. Let's do it again soon.

NO MAN STANDING

BARBARA SERANELLA

**Available in Hardcover
from Scribner
May 2002**

**Turn the page for a preview of
No Man Standing. . . .**

CHAPTER 1

Los Angeles Homicide Detective Art Becker studied the trail of ants streaming into the open mouth of the dead man. After a minute he hefted his portly frame upright and waved to his new partner, Rico Chacón.

Chacón's athletic younger body moved effortlessly toward him. "We've got one more in the house," Chacón said, staring down at the first victim. Even on this overcast morning, he wore sunglasses—Carreras, the kind that adjusted to the light.

The two detectives belonged to a team of robbery/homicide investigators that worked out of the Pacific Division station on Culver and Centinela. Homicide was not unheard of in these parts. The projects up on Slauson were usually good for at least a stabbing on a Saturday night. There was a block on Short Avenue where every other graffiti-covered house was for sale, the signs riddled with bullet holes. This street was more your working-class residential—a lot of Hispanics, a few blacks, but mainly Midwest transplants.

The two victims had been tentatively identified

by the first unit on the scene as Dwayne and Lila Mae Summers. Approximate ages: midfifties. Becker made a note of the date, Thursday, January 17, 1985, on a fresh page of his notebook and next to that he wrote, *Cloudy, 50°*. In cross-examination, a criminal-defense attorney had once asked him what the weather had been like the day of the crime. It had looked bad to the jury when he had to admit he didn't remember. That was the last time he was going to get caught like that, he thought, as he continued his inspection of the corpse.

Cause of death for the guy was probably going to be related to the hole in his head. It looked like a bullet wound, but Becker knew better than to assume. He had seen enough tools, kitchen and garden implements, and scraps of hardware stuck in bodies to know how deceptive entry wounds could be. Skin stretched and hair made scalp wounds even more difficult to reckon. Size and shape of the projectile would be determined later by the coroner. However, judging from the scuff marks in the dirt, it was safe to say the vic had died on the run. Becker looked for scorch marks from muzzle flash but found none.

The two uniformed officers who had first responded to the call and now had the duty of guarding the bodies had made a game of picking an ant in line and wagering on the number of seconds it would take it to reach the guy's mouth.

"Just to the lips?" Becker asked. "Or all the way inside?"

"Inside," the taller of the two uniforms said.

Becker noticed a little piece of machinery sticking up out of the dirt. He kicked at it with his toe, and it came loose from the ground. The piece of black metal was an inch long, cast in a figure-eight pattern. Not a tool, he decided as he stooped and picked it up, but some sort of hardware. Two round half-inch stainless steel prongs, their ends grooved, connected to the figure-eight shaped flange. He turned it back and forth in his hand, and showed it to Chacón. "Know what this is?"

"No, maybe a car part."

"Let's bag it," Becker said.

Chacón put the piece in a little plastic evidence bag on which he recorded the date and location.

"Who's the mope?" Becker asked, indicating the middle-aged white man sitting within the outside layer of yellow tape. Two perimeters had been erected. Tape one protected the interior scene. The second, encompassing driveways on either side of the house and part of the street, formed a staging area where the officers, witnesses, and forensics people could operate and be separated from the public and media.

"Neighbor," the cop answered. "He's the guy who found the DBs and called it in."

"What's his name?" Chacón asked.

"Johnson. Cal Johnson."

Becker nodded toward the house. As primary officer assigned to this case, he made the call on how they would proceed. Before speaking to

Johnson, he wanted to familiarize himself with the entire crime scene. He walked around an anemic flower bed of mostly dirt and dying daisies and stepped up the single wooden stair leading to the front door. To the right of the door a rusted hibachi sat in cement. The woman's body was just inside. From the neck down, her body faced the ceiling. It took him a second to realize that he was looking at the back of her head. Her face lay buried in the blood-soaked, gray carpet. The torque that had snapped her neck had exposed white vertebrae. The fingers on both hands were bruised a deep purple and twisted at unnatural angles.

Chacón came up behind him. He was one of those tall, quiet types who observed everything but said little. Now he made a small grunt of shock.

Becker closed his eyes and took a deep breath through his mouth, giving his senses a break. He had seen death before, but this one made him check his gag reflex. Murder was one thing. People get mad, lose control, snap or whatever, and kill someone. It happened every day, every minute of the day somewhere, probably. But what kind of a human was capable of committing such extreme torture? That he would never fathom. Maybe he was old-fashioned, but the fact that the victim was a woman made this cruelty even worse. He flexed his own undamaged hands, unwillingly imagining the ache of having his fingers snapped like wishbones.

"Let's get to work," he said.

He opened his eyes and looked around the room. The table in front of the couch had been upended and several pictures torn from the wall. Rectangular patches of unfaded paint testified to their previous locations. From the doorway he could also see that drawers in the bedroom dresser had been pulled out and dumped on the floor. The two men toured the rest of the house. The first police on the scene had done this also, making sure no other victims had been overlooked. Becker and Chacón took care to travel in pathways already used by those officers. The kitchen appeared undisturbed as did the bathroom. They returned to the front room where the body was and tried to reconstruct what had happened.

It seemed that either the unknown subject(s) had found what they were looking for or something had interrupted them. A mass of aged papers was on the floor of the bedroom closet. The cardboard box that had apparently held the papers sat upright beside them. ELLEN was written in Marks-A-Lot across the front. Clearly a parent's collection of mementos. They were arranged in chronological order, starting with grammar school report cards and childish drawings rendered in happy colors—a girl and her mom and dad holding hands in the sun with flowers growing at their feet. Becker thought of the abused flower bed out front.

The artwork turned more sophisticated. Pencil sketches of horses and dogs. His own preteen girls were nuts for horses and dogs. Directly to the right of the sketches was a 1971 junior high school year-book opened to the S's. He looked for and found a Summers. Ellen Summers. If she was in ninth grade fourteen years ago, that would put her age at about twenty-eight now.

The documentation that was fanned across the floor filled in those missing years. Release forms from county jail, bail receipts, and probation reports. There was also a flyer from a club called the Spearmint Rhino. It advertised itself as an adult cabaret. The picture of the sultry blonde on all fours and clad only in a G-string filled in the sub-text. The face of the girl on the flyer matched the ninth-grade black-and-white photo of Ellen Summers given a few trips around a rough block. The flyer had crease marks in it, as if it had been folded in thirds and fitted inside an envelope.

An uneven spray of blood over the papers told him that they had been arranged here prior to at least some of the carnage.

"Time to talk to the neighbor," Becker said. The two detectives left the house and approached Cal Johnson, who was still sitting between the tapes.

"I couldn't figure it out," Johnson said. A black cap with SIR MIX CONCRETE PRODUCTS written in white letters above the brim shaded the top half of his face. The stub of an unlit cigar was wedged between his fingers.

He sat on a frayed lawn chair. It sagged under his weight. He was in his midfifties and had the milky eyes of a serious drinker. Broken capillaries flecked his nose and cheeks. His jowls wobbled as he shook his head, too overwhelmed to go on.

Becker waited patiently for the guy to continue. He'd seen this before. People needed to pick their own way to explain horror.

"I thought maybe her hair was covering her face. I even tried to push it aside so she could breathe, but her face wasn't where it was supposed to be. Then I saw all the blood." Johnson stopped to spit.

Becker nodded, feeling the bile in his own throat. And then there were the fingers; he wouldn't have missed those. Judging from the darkness of the bruising, the damage to them had happened prior to death. Becker wondered again if the killers had gotten what they wanted.

"Did you touch anything else?"

Johnson shook his head. "I just wanted out of there."

"Where did you call from?"

"My house," he said, nodding toward next door. "There's a daughter, I think."

"Yes, sir," Becker said. "I believe you're right."

"Dwayne wasn't the daddy," Johnson added, indicating the male victim. "Second marriage."

The rest of the forensics team arrived and the next four hours were spent going over the crime scene and taking statements. One woman was almost certain she had heard a car speeding away, but she could offer no description.

It was midday when Becker and Chacón drove back to the station. They ran the daughter's name through the Criminal Justice Information System and were soon rewarded with an abundance of data. They cleared their intentions with the coroner's office. Death notifications usually fell to the medical examiner or at least were done in conjunction with the ME's office. This one Becker wanted to handle personally.

The two cops drove to the daughter's current known address: The California Institution for Women at Frontera. Becker had made many visits to closest of kin in his twenty-year career. Delivered horrible news—a fifteen-year-old struck down on his bike in a straight-up hit-and-run. Spouses killed in freak accidents. An elderly relative not heard from in a while—found dead a week and God forbid if a hungry Fido had been locked alone in the house with the dearly departed. It always surprised him how calmly most people took the news. Shock, probably. They'd shift into host mode, invite him in, make coffee, ask their questions politely and he'd always put on his best I-give-a-shit face. There was the one time a guy acted differently. His father had been killed in a home invasion robbery. The guy ranted and railed, got hysterical. Later it turned out the son had contracted the hit. Becker never forgot that.

Two things were on his mind as he headed east to San Bernardino county. He wondered how Ellen Summers was going to take the news and if his stomach would settle in time to enjoy Flo's daily special at the restaurant on the grounds of the nearby Chino Airport.

CHAPTER 2

Munch saw the cops approaching, but she wasn't quick enough.

"Nicky, Sam," she yelled to the two dogs frolicking in the surf. Nicky, the Border collie mix, could always be depended on to heed her summons, but Sam, the Lab/husky, had developed her usual case of deafness. Munch faced the cops and grinned. "I know, I know," she said, trying to ward off their lecture. "No dogs on the beach. We were just leaving."

They weren't even real cops, but city-employed Beach Patrol with the authority to write tickets. The first officer, a somewhat pudgy unsmiling white guy in a blue windbreaker, hung back. His partner, a blonde woman with her hair tied into a ponytail, pulled out her citation book. A gust of cold wind blew sand over them.

The dogs' choke chains and leashes hung heavily in Munch's hand. She rattled them at the dogs and made a last attempt to mollify the pseudo cops.

"Nobody else was down here, and they love the water so much . . ." She left it up to them to fill in the rest and to maybe have a heart.

Nicky came bounding up to them. Her mouth hung open in a dog smile. She accepted the chain that Munch dropped around her neck.

"C'mon, Sam," Munch yelled again.

The cop opened her ticket book and poised her pen to write. "I'm issuing you a citation for failure to observe the posted signs and violation of Health and Safety Code—"

"Spare me," Munch said, cutting her off. No point in being friendly now, the bitch was obviously going to write her a ticket. There was no law saying Munch had to listen to this junior cop's justifications. Instead, she clamped her thin lips tightly together and searched her mind for the words that would wound the deepest.

Keeping Santa Monica safe, are we? she wanted to ask. *Solving major crimes? Was this how cops grew up to be bigger assholes, starting out by harassing taxpaying citizens for letting their dogs play? Are you proud of yourself, you glorified meter maid, with your walkie-talkie and your little rule book?* She realized her inner tirade had taken on a sexist slant. Gender wasn't the issue. This junior cop was being a jerk regardless of her personal plumbing.

Munch wanted to point out that even the cop's own partner was keeping his distance, standing twenty yards away and not looking at them.

"Your name?" the blonde cop asked.

The rookie was not going to ask to see any ID and why should she? It wasn't like Munch was driving, and it wasn't like the old days in Venice. In Venice Beach the real cops, the kind that carried guns and drove black-and-whites, would pull over and harass her for just standing on the street corner. They would ask her not just for her ID, but also to roll up her sleeves. The act of unbuttoning her shirt cuffs and pushing them up past her elbows always made her feel like a rape victim who removed her own clothes. *If I go along, if I make this easier, will you please not hurt me as much?* There was always a good chance that they wouldn't bust her, although they would have that right. Especially when she exposed her recent needlemarks, still red and freshly scabbed. Internal possession of a controlled substance, they called it. A felony. But the whole exercise was not about what she was guilty of. It was more of a power thing, daring you to commit the worst offense: Contempt of Cop.

And yet . . .

Those were the kind of cops she loved. Getting busted had rescued her from her life on the street. Going to jail had interrupted the savage spiral of her existence and had given her a chance to come out from under the fog of addiction.

"Your name, Ma'am?" The cop asked again, her tone peevish now. They hated it when you made them wait.

"Miranda," Munch said, hearing her own voice tight with anger for being busted for something as stupid as walking two dogs on a deserted beach in the middle of winter. "Miranda Mancini." Even as she said the words, she couldn't believe it. Why was she giving this broad her real name? Times sure had changed.

While the cop wrote, Munch remembered another ticket she'd gotten with her old running partner, Ellen. The two of them had been stopped for jaywalking of all things. This was ten years ago. They'd been in downtown Los Angeles and dressed in their full biker regalia. Munch in grungy jeans so thick with grease that they looked like leather. Ellen in tight bell-bottoms and one of her big floozy wigs. The cop riding shotgun had said, "Don't get much cooler than you two." And despite herself Munch had felt a thrill of pride, even though she didn't miss the sarcastic tone of his voice.

Ellen. Or as she was referred to in Munch's private lexicon, *Fucking Ellen.*

She was thinking about her friend a lot lately. Ellen was getting out of prison soon. Again. Munch had recently resumed a relationship with Ellen's mom, Lila Mae. Now that Munch was a mom herself her sympathies for Lila Mae had undergone a huge overhaul.

When Munch got sober eight years ago, she soon realized that there were many persons she had hurt besides herself. Her influence on Ellen and, by extension, Ellen's long-suffering family was a prime example. It was curious, this role reversal of her and Ellen. Ellen had always been the more controlled of the two, keeping her shit a little better together, usually with the aid of some man. Munch had taken her craziness to the brink of destruction. Ellen had the fatal flaw of continuously rallying from her various misadventures, never quite being beaten. She landed on her feet, usually with someone else's money or husband, but on her feet just the same.

Crashing and burning, hitting bottom had ultimately saved Munch. As with most of her fellow members in A.A. and Narcotics Anonymous, she had to find her way to salvation through a journey to the very depth of hell. It was only then, with no other options left, that she was ready to try something as radical as complete sobriety.

Munch tried to explain all this to Lila Mae, that she would do her best for Ellen, but that they could only hope that Ellen had suffered enough. Lila Mae had thought that odd, to wish enough suffering on anybody. Munch had shrugged and said that was only one of a long line of paradoxes in this life. Lila Mae had said, I expect so.

Munch slipped the chain over Sam's head and casually positioned the wet canine, dripping with seawater, between herself and the cop. Sam shook herself, spraying cold water on both of them.

"Sorry," Munch said. Sure.

The cop looked annoyed, which helped ease Munch's irritation. The real irony was that the dogs belonged to LAPD Homicide Detective Mace St.

John, the man who had also had a huge hand in Munch's current state of salvation. She was watching Sam and Nicky while Mace and his wife Caroline were up in Big Bear on their second, or maybe it was their third, honeymoon. Munch tried not to keep count.

The detective was also still recovering from a heart attack. St. John would have a fit if he learned she was letting his precious dogs run around without their leashes. He was protective of those he loved, to the point of paranoia. Mace St. John was the kind of guy who looked at the beach and saw only riptides.

Munch recited the rest of her information in response to Officer Ponytail's questions. She fudged a little on the height and weight, building herself up to five foot two and one hundred and five pounds.

"Occupation?"

Now she's really going to think I'm lying, Munch thought. "Auto mechanic," she said.

To the cop's credit, she didn't blink. Munch was glad. She was in no mood for the inevitable questions that followed and the too-long answer to *How'd you get into that?*

The cop handed her the ticket to sign. Munch took her time, reading every word of the small print. The cop shifted feet and Munch smiled inwardly. Finally, she signed her name on the bottom line, keeping her lips pressed together to express her annoyance.

The cop ripped the ticket loose and handed it over.

Munch didn't say thank you. Some small part in her brain congratulated her for being in touch with her feelings.

The Beach Patrol waited while she stuck the ticket in her pocket and walked the dogs through the tunnel running under the Pacific Coast Highway. She toweled the dogs dry as best she could, then had them jump into the back seat of her GTO. The bumper sticker on the rear window proclaimed: *Reality is for people who can't handle drugs.*

"I hope you're happy," she said to the panting dogs. So much for their little excursion to relieve the drudgery of moving.